# Readers love the Home for Hope series by SHELL TAYLOR

## *Redeeming Hope*

"I really enjoyed this story. It was so deep and pulled me in. I couldn't put it down."

—Molly Lolly

"A first for me by this author and I think she did a great job with the character development."

—Scattered Thoughts and Rogue Words

## *Resurrecting Hope*

"…this was one of the most uplifting and sweet reads that I've read in quite a while. I highly recommend!"

—Joyfully Jay

"I highly recommend this series to fans of angsty reads with real characters and strong emotions."

—The Blogger Girls

By SHELL TAYLOR

HOME FOR HOPE
Redeeming Hope
Resurrecting Hope
Reclaiming Hope

Published by DREAMSPINNER PRESS
www.dreamspinnerpress.com

# RECLAIMING HOPE

## SHELL TAYLOR

Published by

DREAMSPINNER PRESS

5032 Capital Circle SW, Suite 2, PMB# 279, Tallahassee, FL 32305-7886 USA
www.dreamspinnerpress.com

Reclaiming Hope
© 2016 Shell Taylor.

Cover Art
© 2016 L.C. Chase.
http://www.lcchase.com
Cover content is for illustrative purposes only and any person depicted on the cover is a model.

ISBN: 978-1-63477-787-2
Digital ISBN: 978-1-63477-788-9
Library of Congress Control Number: 2016913578
Published October 2016
v. 1.0

Printed in the United States of America
∞
This paper meets the requirements of
ANSI/NISO Z39.48-1992 (Permanence of Paper).

For everyone who believed in me and, more importantly, believed in Kollin. I hope I've done him justice.

# ACKNOWLEDGMENTS

HOME FOR Hope wouldn't be real without the first people who told me that Kollin's story needed to be told. Without that first push, Adam's and Eli's stories would have remained locked in my head, and I never would've found myself on this incredibly fulfilling journey. Thank you to everyone who has supported me along the way, whether by a gentle suggestion that other people would like my writing, by prereading, by buying my books, by reviewing, or by just knowing it would happen.

Special thanks to the wonderful staff at Dreamspinner Press for giving me this opportunity. The entire team has been wonderful to work with, and I'm blessed to have learned so much through partnering with you.

Massive thanks to Adéle, Beth, Jayme, Shelli, and Sue for their incredibly valuable feedback on Reclaiming Hope. And for the many times you talked me down and assured me I wasn't totally botching this one.

# CHAPTER 1

KOLLIN HAVERTY glanced away from his computer screen to ogle the other patrons of the bookstore. Next to his table, a young couple talked animatedly about their summer plans as they browsed the sci-fi section. The guy had sandy blond hair and a dimple that popped up on his right cheek every time he smiled. Kollin allowed his gaze to linger on the guy's handsome face a moment longer and then returned his attention to his studies. If he didn't stop getting distracted, he was about three random hot guys away from flunking his psych final.

The chair across from him scraped against the wooden floor, and Kollin gritted his teeth, both irritated at the interruption—there were plenty of other open seats nearby—and relieved for another distraction.

"Seat taken?" a rough voice asked.

Kollin looked up. The owner of the voice looked familiar, but Kollin couldn't place where he'd ever seen him. They'd probably shared a class together at some point, but then again, Kollin didn't think he'd forget that guy if they'd spent three months in the same room. While the stranger's face wasn't particularly distinctive, his hair was shaved close on the sides but left long on top, with platinum blond streaks. Several hoops hung from his ears, and Kollin noted not only a nose ring but also a hoop adorning his bottom lip.

Kollin waved toward the chair as he continued to stare. "All yours."

"Thanks." The stranger looked nervous, but he shoved his hands in his pockets and sat down.

Kollin offered a smile and returned his attention to his notes.

He hadn't even finished reading a sentence when the guy spoke again. "You come here often?"

Kollin held back a laugh. He recognized a pickup line when he heard one, but he wasn't expecting to get cruised at Barnes & Noble while wearing ratty sweats. The guy was cute enough, though. He had a little more facial hair than Kollin preferred—there was just something he loved about a smooth face on a man—but he definitely had potential.

Kollin abandoned his notes and sat back in his seat to give the guy his full attention. "Not really. My little sister was having a meltdown at home, so I came here to get some cramming in before my last final tomorrow."

"You have a little sister?" He sounded surprised. Too surprised for a random guy chatting up a stranger in the local bookstore.

"Uh… yeah. She's twelve." Kollin fiddled with his pen. "I'm sorry. Do I know you?"

A ghost of a smile spread over the stranger's face, and his features softened as he shook his head and looked down at his hands. "No, no. I'm sorry. I can tell I'm bothering you. I'll let you get back to your studying."

The guy was gone before Kollin even realized he'd left his chair.


"COME ON, Koll," Lizzie whined. "They let you do whatever you want. Please, please, please, convince Adam to give me my phone back."

"They don't 'let me do whatever I want.' I just know how to work them. And that does not include whining about punishments. You really think I could've gotten out of a punishment if I were failing school? As strict as Eli is about earning good grades?"

Lizzie stomped her foot. "Math is stupid. That's why they invented calculators. It's not like I'll need to solve algebra equations to actually do anything."

Kollin looked around the multipurpose room at The Center for HOPE, the LGBT safe haven that his adoptive father, Adam Lancaster, founded and ran. Most of the tables were full of students preparing for the upcoming end-of-year exams. Not his sister. Not the girl who was one bad grade away from failing math. Lizzie's scowl showed the righteous indignation that every twelve-year-old seemed to master. Why shouldn't she be able to pout, bat her eyelashes, and get her phone back?

When she moved in almost three years earlier, Kollin had quite possibly been more excited than anyone. Lizzie joining them was concrete evidence that Adam and his other adoptive dad, Eli, wanted a family. Kollin had never shaken the feeling that he might be more of an obligation than a son after Adam and Eli took him in when his birth parents abused him and kicked him out. Logical or not, Lizzie coming to live with them served as Kollin's lightbulb moment. He finally understood that Adam and Eli truly wanted him in their lives for good.

Lizzie proved to be a challenge, though. Her parents died in a tragic accident when she was only four, and after a short stint with a worthless aunt and uncle, she entered the foster system. Old enough to remember her parents and how much they loved her but too young to understand why she had to live with strangers, Lizzie struggled to keep her temper in check. As a result, time and time again, she was passed over for adoption.

She was just as difficult for Adam and Eli when she first moved in, but Kollin spent as much time with her as he could. Slowly, he gained her trust and convinced her that she'd found a home where she didn't need to fear rejection. Kollin's constant support and assurances eased her worries about being different because of her skin color, her struggles at school, and her sassy attitude. With Lizzie's trust placed firmly in Kollin, he was able to bridge the gap between Lizzie and his dads. By the time the adoption finally went through, Lizzie had become a mischievous, stubborn bundle of energy, and none of them could imagine their lives without Elizabeth Constance Jones Langley.

Kollin would do anything for his sister, and she damn well knew it.

"I'll talk to Eli. See what I can do. Maybe if I promise to supervise you doing your homework, he'll give in a few days early."

"But Adam's the one who took it away from me."

Kollin rolled his eyes. "Trust me. Eli's your best bet at getting that phone back early. Just make sure they see you studying, and try to look like you actually care about math. Okay? And stop bugging the shit out of them about it. That's annoying as hell."

Lizzie grinned and grabbed Kollin around the neck. "Thank you, thank you, thank you. I'll clean your room for a week."

Kollin laughed. "No you won't, but thanks for pretending."

"If you get my phone back, I'll at least clean it once."

"Whatever, Squirt. Get outta here so I can finish this presentation for Adam."

"But I don't have anything to do," Lizzie complained.

"Uh… you could do your homework. Maybe even in Dad's office, to show you're making an effort."

Lizzie huffed and crossed her arms over her chest. "Can't. He's in there with some guy I've never seen before."

"Oh?" Kollin glanced at the door. "Someone who might need the inn?"

Home for Hope, the inn Eli helped Adam buy and renovate into a safe house for LGBT youth, was completely full, and some of the rooms even housed multiple occupants. Adam had plans to build an extension so an additional twenty beds could help keep as many youth off the street. Kollin would spend the summer helping Adam oversee the addition and gaining invaluable experience, not only in his business minor but also his human services studies.

Lizzie shrugged. "Dunno. He didn't look too bad off. Kinda cute actually. Dad hugged him when he walked in, so I guess they know each other."

Kollin frowned. He volunteered at HOPE as often as possible, but that didn't amount to much with a full college course load. He'd missed being there so much that he moved back home his sophomore year and drove the fifteen-minute commute to NC State's campus. Even so, he missed out on a lot going on around the center. That guy could be anybody.

"Ooh. Here he comes," Lizzie whispered and not so subtly nodded her head toward the doorway.

Sure enough, Adam had his arm around someone Kollin shouldn't have known but immediately recognized.

"I saw that guy at the bookstore a couple days ago. He talked with me for a few minutes," he whispered.

"Looks like you're about to see him again," Lizzie whispered back and then put on her sweetest smile. "Hi, Daddy."

"Still not getting your phone back." Adam put his arm around Lizzie's shoulder and kissed the top of her head. "And hi, baby."

Lizzie rolled her eyes and straightened her soft, brown curls back into place. "I wasn't even gonna ask this time."

"Yeah, okay." Adam rolled his eyes to mimic her and then turned his attention toward Kollin. "Look who the cat dragged in."

For some reason, Kollin's heart fluttered. Waves of nervousness raced through his body as he tried to figure out why Adam thought he should know the stranger. He'd never told either of his parents about meeting the guy at the bookstore, and even if he had, Adam couldn't have known he was the same person.

The man studied the ground, seemingly reluctant to look at Kollin, but Kollin knew he couldn't identify him even if they were staring directly at one another.

Fortunately Adam saved him from further embarrassment. "I didn't recognize Riley until he threatened to own me in Ping-Pong."

Kollin sucked in a huge gulp of air. The nervous flutters, which had been nothing more than a curious enigma, ceased, and he suddenly felt as if a boulder had settled in the pit of his stomach.

He hadn't spoken to Riley Meadows in over four years. When Kollin's parents kicked him out, Riley had been the one who kept Kollin sane. He tethered him to reality when all he'd wanted was to escape inside himself. They'd kept in touch when Riley first went to college and somehow became even closer—until Riley seemingly dropped off the face of the earth. Phone calls, e-mails, texts... all unanswered. Kollin eventually took the hint and gave up.

Now Riley was back?

"Hey, Kollin." Riley shoved his hands in his pockets and peeked up at Kollin.

"Hey, Ri," Kollin said, feeling dumb that he'd had an entire conversation with him a few days ago but had no clue. Riley looked completely different. He had clearly taken huge steps in his transition when he went rogue, but Riley's new look wasn't limited only to the steps he'd taken toward gender transformation.

Riley's formerly brown, shaggy hair was cut shorter around the back and sides. He'd left the top longer and added the blond streaks that had grabbed Kollin's attention in the bookstore. The piercings in his nose and lip were new, and Kollin could only remember Riley wearing modest studs in each ear. Riley's jaw had squared some, and he'd slimmed down but bulked up in muscle. He didn't look remotely close to the same person, but when Kollin looked carefully, he could still see Riley. His eyes hadn't changed, and he still rubbed the tips of his fingers together when he was nervous. A trio of freckles graced the side of his neck, and Kollin recognized a faint scar on Riley's forearm that he knew came from the time Riley thought he could jump out of a tree when he was a kid.

Kollin should have recognized his best friend. "I, uh... didn't know you were back in town."

Riley shrugged. "It was a last minute thing. Sorta."

"Oh." Cleared that right up.

After a moment of awkward silence, Adam spoke up. "Riley, this is Elijah's and my daughter, Lizzie. Liz, Riley used to be a regular at HOPE, before he went away to college."

"Nice to meet you." Lizzie offered Riley a small smile and then turned to Kollin and screwed up her face, clearly expecting him to take over.

A fat lot of help she was.

Kollin scrambled for something to say. *Why did you abandon me? Did I really piss you off so badly that I deserved so many years of silence? Why didn't you tell me who you were the other day?* Everything that popped into his head seemed accusatory and inappropriate for the moment. He felt so flummoxed he couldn't even come up with a sarcastic icebreaker.

"So—"

"I—"

Kollin stopped talking so Riley could finish his sentence, but Riley must have had the same intention, and once again, the four of them stood in uncomfortable silence. Adam furrowed his brow at Kollin, but Kollin gave a tiny shake of his head. He'd figure out the mess with Riley on his own.

Adam took the hint and clapped his hands together once. "This has been fun, but I need to get back to my office and finish some work so we can get home on time. I'll let you guys catch up."

Seeing her opportunity, Lizzie grabbed Adam's arm. "Can I come with you? I want to start studying for my next math test so I can get back the thing that I'm not supposed to talk about anymore."

"Subtle, but come on." Adam offered Riley and Kollin a wave on his way out.

Kollin slid his foot across the carpet and pushed out a chair on the opposite side of the table. He didn't take his eyes off his old friend as Riley sat, still silent, and fiddled with his thumbs on top of the table. Strangely enough, Riley's nervousness settled Kollin's erratic emotions.

"So," Kollin said. "'You come here often' was the best you could come up with?"

Riley spat out a laugh and looked up at Kollin through long eyelashes. "Sorry about that. I didn't know what to do when you didn't recognize me."

"I think, 'Hey, Kollin, it's me, Riley,' would've worked well." Kollin tried to keep the bitterness out of his voice, but Riley cringed, and he knew he'd failed.

Good. Riley deserved to know he'd hurt him.

"It's been so long... I wasn't sure how that would go."

"Yeah. About that. I'm assuming by the way you look that you haven't been held captive in some dark basement without access to a phone or e-mail. Even a carrier pigeon would've sufficed. So...." Kollin looked hopefully at Riley and wished he would offer an explanation good enough to ease some of the resentment currently churning around in his heart. Naturally empathetic and forgiving, Kollin rarely held a grudge. But he needed some sort of explanation for being dumped.

In fact, Riley looked so pitiful sitting across from him, wringing his hands as he searched for the right words, that Kollin knew Riley could offer some lame, half-assed excuse, and he would put the entire mess behind him. But he needed *something* to explain why he'd lost his best friend.

Riley finally looked up and met Kollin's eyes. "Long version might take a while, but the short of it is... I needed to get my shit together without dragging you down. I was slowly falling apart back then, and you had enough to worry about."

Anger flooded Kollin. "Come on, Ri. That's bullshit, and you know it. It sucked when Adam bailed, but in what world is being abandoned by you somehow better than being your friend when you needed one? I would've been there for you."

Riley shrugged. "Maybe so. But it's too late now, and there's nothing I can say to make it better, except I'm sorry. I know now it was a shitty thing to do."

Riley had always been difficult to read. Kollin used to think that's why he had so much trouble making friends. Not many people were willing to make the extra effort it took to get to know him. It was a shame, really, because he was one of the kindest and funniest people Kollin had ever met. But Riley seemed to have perfected hiding his feelings over the years.

Riley's tone and words sounded dismissive, but his slumped shoulders and constant fidgeting conveyed remorse. Kollin wanted to push Riley about why he'd left him hanging in the wind, but there had to be a better place for that conversation than the multipurpose room at HOPE.

Instead he asked, "So now that you're presumably not falling apart, what exactly are you doing here?"

"I, um… had to talk with Dr. Maggie. I'd like to start the preparations for metoidioplasty. I need a second recommendation first."

"Metoidio-what?"

Riley shifted in his seat and looked down at his hands. "You know. Bottom surgery."

"Oh…." Kollin blinked. He shouldn't have been that surprised. Riley always said he wanted both top and bottom surgery as soon as he could get it, but Kollin had trouble reconciling the man in front of him with the same Riley who had very obviously had female sex parts down below.

Kollin recovered quickly enough and genuinely smiled. "That's fantastic, man. I'm really happy for you."

Relief flooded Riley's eyes, and he smiled. "Thanks, Koll."

Kollin kicked at Riley's shoe. "Well, now that my life isn't in the shitter and yours seems to be going well, think you can handle being friends again?"

Riley's cheeks tinged pink, and Kollin almost laughed. He'd never seen Riley so bashful. "Yeah. I think I can handle that."

"Want to grab dinner tonight, then? My treat."

"Yeah?" Riley stared at Kollin, his eyes wide. "Just like that, huh? You haven't changed much."

Kollin shrugged. Technically all hadn't been forgiven, but he didn't want to ruin their already rocky reunion. "No point in holding a grudge. Chili's at seven?"

Riley nodded and stood. "Sounds good. I better get out of here, then." He took a couple of steps and turned back to Kollin. "For what it's worth… I really am sorry for going radio silent on you like that. I've regretted it every single day."

*Awesome. That wasn't super cryptic at all.* Kollin offered Riley his most reassuring smile—one he'd learned from Adam. "Don't even worry about it."

# CHAPTER 2

"AND THERE hasn't been anyone since Liam." Kollin set down his fork, and their server appeared out of nowhere to sweep away his salad plate.

"How long ago did you two split?" Riley asked. Kollin had lived such a normal, happy life since they'd last talked. No part of Riley's story even remotely resembled Kollin's, and Riley had no desire to share his disastrous past after listening to that fairy tale. Fortunately he'd become adept at deflecting over the years. Turned out most people loved talking about themselves, and a few well-timed questions worked wonders for avoiding topics he didn't want to touch.

Kollin scrunched up his face as he considered Riley's question. "Before Christmas, so about six months, I guess."

"Sounds like you got everything you used to talk about."

Kollin quirked up his eyebrow. "A series of failed relationships?"

"No." Riley laughed and then mumbled through his grin, "Jackass. Supportive family and a colorful dating scene. A few meaningless hook-ups. College education. Lots of friends."

Kollin shrugged and played with his discarded straw wrapper. "I just got lucky with Adam and Eli. You know that. A few boyfriends and a handful of guys who never made it past the second date hardly count as successful, but I guess I'm doing better than the last time we talked. I remember whining to you about that idiot Jase."

Riley shook his head. "You didn't whine. I never knew what to tell you, though. It's not like I had any experience." *I didn't even want to look in the mirror at myself, much less let someone else see me naked.* Riley shoved the self-deprecating thought to the back of his mind.

"Well, what the hell have you been up to? My past is easy with school and more school, but you...." Kollin waved his hand up and down at Riley. "You've clearly had a more eventful four years than I have. You look great, by the way. Totally hot. I definitely would've said yes to the date I thought you were going to ask me on at the bookstore."

Riley's cheeks warmed at Kollin's offhand compliment. It wasn't the time to turn into a Blushing Betty. He'd been crazily, over-the-top, and also very much secretly in love with Kollin back when they were in high school. Riley had felt the same familiar twinge in his heart when he first saw Kollin again, but he chalked it up to nothing more than a flicker of remembering one's first love. No use giving himself away, after all those years, because of some casual praise.

Kollin laughed, and his dismayed eyes met Riley's. "Oh God. I just thought. How embarrassing would it have been if I'd actually asked you out?"

The warm feeling in Riley's stomach disappeared, replaced by the sudden urge to vomit. Kollin's disgust sounded more along the lines of what he was used to—men embarrassed to be with him. Riley had become used to the derision, but hearing it come from Kollin amplified the rejection tenfold.

Clearly unaware of how deeply his comment pained Riley, Kollin sounded just as happy-go-lucky as ever when he pressed Riley again. "Seriously, Ri. Come on. Tell me what you've been up to. I'm dying to know."

Riley stared at his water glass and wiped away a drop of condensation. Determined not to cause a scene in the middle of their dinner, he cleared his throat. "Well, I guess the most obvious things are I got on T—testosterone—and I had top surgery done."

"I'm so happy for you, Ri." Kollin had already told him once, but Riley's insides still turned gooey—even with Kollin's sting of dismissal still fresh. Kollin couldn't totally understand Riley's feelings. No one could. Explaining how it felt to be trans was impossible, but Riley had always found Kollin's unconditional acceptance overwhelming.

"Thanks."

The server arrived with their meals, and once he was gone again, Kollin pointed his fork at Riley. "Now, start at the brutal beginning, from the moment you stopped talking to me, and tell me everything."

Kollin's tone was light and his smirk playful, and another twinge of regret jolted through Riley. He'd missed their banter and was glad to see Kollin really hadn't changed much. His hair still had streaks of color in it, purple and somewhat faded—he'd probably be dying it soon—and though still long, it was different. It was wilder all over and longer in the back. Some strands curled around his ears while others stuck out willy-nilly on the sides.

His sea green eyes still sparkled with never-ending mischief, but they reflected more of the world's weight in them. They were less trusting and more scrutinizing than before. The hair on his face was so short, Riley couldn't tell if the scruff was intentional or a product of laziness. Judging from his lithe body, he'd stayed in shape over the years, but whether from gym workouts, basketball, or simply good genes, Riley didn't know. The last of Kollin's baby fat had disappeared, making his cheeks hollow out a bit whenever he clenched his jaw.

He was gorgeous.

"Ri?"

"Uh… right. Sorry. Just trying to figure out where to start." *Sounds better than "Your stubble-covered jaw distracted me."* Riley pushed his food around and gathered his thoughts. "I started spiraling down after Christmas that year. Actually it started before then, and I think you could kind of tell. You started asking me questions I didn't want to answer. I didn't want to put something else on your plate, so I bailed. If I'm being honest, I wasn't ready to deal with everything I felt at the time either, and I knew you'd push me into talking about it."

"Shit, man. I'm sorry."

"No. Don't be. This whole thing would've been easier if I'd let you in. You were a good friend, and you didn't deserve my treating you like that." Kollin nodded once and sat back in his seat. His jaw twitched, possibly from anger, but this time instead of finding it sexy, Riley felt guilty. Something else to deal with later. "Anyway I stopped going to class. I'd made some friends, but none of them really knew me. I felt like such a fraud, and I knew—or thought I knew—if they found out the truth about me, they wouldn't want anything to do with me. Even though Mom and Dad cut me off financially, room and board were already paid for, so I stayed on campus. I, at least, had enough sense to look for a job, since I knew I'd be homeless after May.

"I lucked out and found a part-time job at a construction company that April. Turns out all that work we did at H4H really paid off. They started me out just working small stuff, but within a couple of months, they took me on full-time."

Kollin sat forward, a big smile on his face. "Wait till Adam and Eli find out. They'll love that."

Riley laughed. "Adam looked proud as a peacock when I told him. That's for sure."

"Oh geez." Kollin rolled his eyes. "He's liable to make us all build the new addition to H4H, instead of hiring now."

Riley's grin faltered, but he recovered quickly and moved the conversation away from the new addition to H4H. "What can I say? That job saved me from crawling back here for a place to live."

"Ri…." Kollin reached across the table to grab his hand. "No one would've thought badly of you if you had. You know that. Hell. I'd've ended up there if it weren't for Eli."

"I know, but I already felt like such a failure. I mean, I couldn't even be born in the right body, you know? That's how I saw it. I felt as if I'd screwed up my very first act on Earth." Riley shook his head and looked at his plate. "I thought going off to college would magically change everything, and it just… didn't."

"No shit, Sherlock. Life's rarely that easy."

Riley sneered at Kollin, but Kollin's brash truthfulness felt like a soothing balm. The last thing he wanted was for Kollin to tiptoe around him, using platitudes he didn't need to hear. "I found a shitty apartment. I mean it. The place was a dump. Remember room eighteen at the inn? It was worse."

"No fucking way. Nothing livable is comparable to that."

"Minus the shit everywhere, then. But it was cheap, and I wanted to pour every bit of money I had into savings. I lived off ramen and sandwiches. Found a therapist who helped me get onto T. It took a while to get the dosage right, but within a few months, you could really tell that I'd put on some muscle weight and had started growing a patchy beard. I kept to myself, mostly, at work, so at first no one noticed. But then the foreman pulled me aside one day."

"Oh shit," Kollin interrupted.

"That's what I thought, but I was lucky as hell. He has a trans sister, and he was cool about it. Helped me cover everything up with the other workers, so that, when they did start noticing, he blew off their comments or changed the subject. I told them I'd just joined a gym and gotten lazy with my shaving. After a while, he even found me a better place to stay that was still in my PB-and-J budget. I worked hard and learned a new skill every chance I got, until I had enough saved for top surgery. That was about a year ago." Riley omitted the shadier details of his past and swallowed down the guilt that bubbled in his stomach for telling half-truths. "Now here I am, hoping to get cleared to start the last phase—or the last physical piece, anyway."

Kollin's eyes, which had been bright, clouded over for a moment, and then his face broke into a wide smile. "I know I'm a broken record, but that's amazing. You're really like a new person. It's somehow both so strange and so natural."

Riley laughed and smoothed his hand down his chest. "I know what you mean. I've lived it every day, and sometimes I still wonder how the hell this is my life."

"You deserve the good things. Not to be dramatic or anything, but you helped save me back in the day. Adam and Eli were great and all, but you kept me sane. I'm sorry if I let my own drama overshadow your issues. I think I'm just now realizing how insensitive that was of me."

Riley shrugged. The last thing he wanted was for Kollin to feel guilty. "We were kids. That's how we were supposed to be. Besides, like I said, I wasn't ready."

"Speak for yourself. I'm still a kid. There is no part of me that feels like an adult." Kollin scratched the back of his head. "I know I have all these responsibilities now, but they don't really feel real. Adam says it'll always be like that."

"Sounds like something Adam would say."

Kollin pushed his mostly empty plate away. "Now you gotta tell me the good stuff. When you weren't sitting in your shitty apartment and out building stuff, what were you doing?"

Riley's face fell. Kollin's dating past, though limited, was normal, if a bit angsty. Natural teenage-drama bullshit. Riley hadn't fared as well and wasn't so sure he wanted to admit as much to Kollin. He currently felt as if he were wrapped in a quilt of Kollin's acceptance, and he wasn't quite ready to lose that warmth. Once Kollin found out everything he'd done, he would surely lose that hint of pride he saw behind Kollin's eyes every time he looked at him.

No. That was definitely not the time to get into Tony—or any of the other one-night stands—or the terrible addiction Tony brought into his life. "I think that's a story for another night. I need to get back to my hotel. It's been a long day, and I have an extra-early appointment with Dr. Maggie, since she's squeezing me in."

"Oh yeah. Of course." Kollin raised his hand for the check. "I didn't even think of that. How long are you in town for, anyway?"

Riley looked down at his hands, unwilling to meet Kollin's eyes. "Going back tomorrow, if I can. Greg, my boss, told me to take whatever time I needed, but I need to save personal days, and I need money. Hotels are expensive, and I've already been here for a few days."

Kollin huffed. "You're a fool for paying for a hotel. You could've stayed with us. You know Eli and Adam would love to have you just as much as I would."

"Yeah. Adam said as much earlier, but like I said, I wasn't sure. Didn't want to impose."

"I get it, but next time. Okay?" Kollin signed the receipt and stood as he pocketed his wallet. "You can't go running off on me just when I get you back."

Riley smiled, and his insides snuggled down deeper in that warm blanket. "You got it."

KOLLIN TRIED to wipe the frown off his face as he slid his key into the front-door lock. Suspicion over Riley's story niggled at the back of his mind. They hadn't talked in so long that Kollin didn't know if he could really trust his hunches anymore. Deflection had always been part of Riley's personality, but Kollin didn't like having it turned on him. He was exhausted by the constant teeth pulling he'd performed that night to get the smallest bit of information from Riley.

Kollin shoved the door open and hung his keys on a hook in the foyer. "I'm home," he called out.

"In here," Eli shouted. Kollin followed the sounds of the TV into the living room, where Eli reclined in his La-Z-Boy. "How was dinner?"

Kollin fell onto the couch. "Good. It was nice catching up."

"Good. He say why he shut you out for so long?"

Kollin didn't miss the hint of resentment in Eli's tone. He knew Eli was still pissed at Riley. After all, Eli had dealt with Kollin's feelings of abandonment, not once, but three times, between his birth parents, Adam, and then Riley. But Eli would never say a word against Kollin's birth parents in front of him, and he'd use his last breath to defend Adam, so that left Riley to shoulder all of Eli's blame. It wasn't fair, but Kollin didn't know how to fix it either.

He prepared himself to go to bat for Riley and took a deep breath. "The quick and dirty version is he was struggling and couldn't deal. Didn't want to disappoint us. Sound familiar?"

Eli rolled his eyes. "At least Adam only left for a few days. Four years is some shit."

Kollin grinned at the predictable response. If he ever found a partner who loved him even half as much as Eli adored Adam, he suspected he'd have more love than most.

Kollin shrugged. "Just sayin'. He had his reasons, and it's not my place to judge."

"You and Adam are *way* too nice."

Kollin sighed. "Thanks, *Dad*. Way to be proud of me for exercising forgiveness toward one of my closest friends. I don't remember you holding a grudge against Adam."

Eli sat up in his recliner, clearly agitated. "That was completely different."

"How so?" Kollin asked, and irritation underlined his words.

"We were practically married, for one. And again, a few days versus years, for another. And because I said so," Eli said. His voice trailed off as he sat back in his seat again. "Anyway we're talking about Riley, not Adam. What's he up to?"

Further argument would prove pointless, so Kollin dropped the matter and filled Eli in on what little he'd learned about Riley's life. Eli nodded and mmhmm'd in all the right places as he listened.

When Kollin finished, Eli cocked his head. "Sounds like his little sabbatical started out rough, but he's doing okay now. Steady job, looks like a man, preparing for whatever comes next.... Why are you so worried about him?"

"Is it that obvious?" Kollin asked and looked back at Eli with a grin. "You're not usually this perceptive."

Eli smirked, but Kollin could see a teasing glimmer in his eyes, beneath the affronted look. "I've learned a thing or two over the years. But yeah. It's pretty damn noticeable. You keep biting your lip, and your foot hasn't stopped bouncing since you sat."

Kollin sighed and deliberately stopped bouncing his foot. "I dunno. I just got the impression he was trying too hard to show me how perfect his life is."

"But that kind of makes sense. Right? He bailed on you for years. He's not going to waltz back in town and dump all of his problems on you."

Kollin shook his head. "That's not really what it felt like, though. I mean, yeah. He said he left because he didn't want to burden me with his issues, but I don't know. I'm probably just being paranoid, but I swear he's hiding something."

"Maybe Dr. Maggie can help him."

"I guess." Kollin crossed his arms and frowned. "I hope he keeps in touch from now on."

"Only way to find out is to wait and see."

Kollin rolled his eyes. "Your wisdom is overwhelming sometimes."

Eli sat forward and ruffled Kollin's hair. "You know I mostly like Riley. Always did. I know how much he hurt you back then, so he's not getting a free pass from me just yet. *But*—" Eli paused. "—if he… if his friendship—is that important to you, you best be prepared to fight like hell for him. Neither of you has an easy road ahead if he's struggling with something he's trying to hide from you."

Kollin closed his eyes and let Eli's words sink in. A not-so-small part of him screamed that the shit was about to hit the fan, but he had no idea what he could do about it until Riley opened up more. "Guess nothing in life is ever easy."

"Nope," Eli agreed. "Nothing worth a damn is, anyway."

# CHAPTER 3

"IT'S OPEN."

Riley twisted the knob to the foreman's trailer and clomped inside. His appointment that morning with Maggie had sucked the life right out of him, and the long bus ride back to Boone hadn't helped one bit. "Hey, boss."

"Riley. Didn't expect to see you today." Greg leaned back in his rickety chair and waved toward an even more rickety chair in the corner.

"Figured I might as well check in. Nothing to do at home."

Greg grunted. "So… what'd they say?"

Riley leaned forward and rested his elbows on his knees. He hadn't told Kollin the other reason he'd been in town. The possibility of Drummond Construction making a bid on the Home for Hope extension project seemed too good to be true, especially after Kollin had welcomed him back into his life so easily. Moving back to Cary for even a short stint would not only give him a chance to reconnect with Kollin but also put him closer to Dr. Maggie and make it easier to continue therapy.

Telling Kollin would've made the entire thing too real, and Riley couldn't bear the thought of breaking it to Kollin if they didn't pull the deal.

"Adam wants to add twenty more rooms to Home for Hope. He's open to suggestions on the cheapest way to go about that—whether it's duplicating the same setup they have or creating more of a dorm-like feel with one large bathroom to serve a set number of rooms. Whatever they go with, they want quality work, and they want to make sure the crew they hire isn't going to harass the youth there, so they aren't necessarily going with the lowest bidder."

Greg grunted again. "The materials?"

Riley grinned. "Langley Lumber will be donating most of them, of course."

"It's a big job either way. Be nice to have."

Riley nodded. Greg's words gave away nothing, but he recognized the intense stare. He wanted that job. "I can talk to Adam again. See how serious he is about hiring us, if that's what you want."

Greg scratched his chin and studied Riley. "Sure wouldn't mind it. I'm stretched a bit thin with Krazinski out. Think you could step up to acting junior foreman?"

Riley's mouth dropped. "Are you shitting me?"

Greg cracked a rare smile. "I am not. You've earned it. Just temporary for now, but it's good experience, and you're already familiar with the building and the area."

"Well, yeah. I'd love to. Thank you, sir." Riley stretched his hand across the desk to shake Greg's. "Are you sure the other guys aren't going to be pissed, though?"

"Not up to them, but I doubt it either way. Only a couple of those guys have been here longer than you, and none of them have the leadership you do. Bigwigs won't argue it either, especially if you help us get the bid. It'll be the perfect way to get our name around when the new branch opens in Durham."

"Thanks, Greg. I won't let you down."

"I know. Now get out of here. You look like shit. Take care of yourself, you hear me? Stay out of trouble."

Riley grimaced but nodded. No way would he fall back into bad habits with everything he had riding on the line. "No repeats. I swear."

Two hours later Riley collapsed into bed. He'd polished off a hearty dinner of Dinty Moore Beef Stew in record time and then eyed the top drawer of his dresser, where his last bit of weed lay, sealed tightly inside a baggie and stuffed into a Mason jar. Smoking was the only bad habit he'd kept since the grand fuckup a year before. Too worried he'd lose his job if he got caught, he rarely indulged in that anymore either. Riley kept the small stash for the occasional long weekend and cherished the short time he spent high—the only time he ever felt like he could take a deep breath and actually relax. He desperately wanted that feeling right then, but he wouldn't dare risk even a quick puff with a possible promotion coming up.

Instead he grabbed his phone and thumbed through his short list of contacts until he landed on Kollin's name. He pushed Send, and a smile formed before Kollin even answered.

"You actually called."

Riley laughed. "I told you I'd keep in touch."

"Yeah. Well, can't blame me for being suspicious. You still in town?"

"Nah. I came home. Had some stuff to take care of."

"Oh yeah?" Riley could hear Kollin's interest pique. "Got a hot man there waiting on you?"

Riley guffawed. "Hardly. You're cute if you think someone would actually want to be with me."

"Why wouldn't they?" The lightness of Kollin's voice had fallen away, and Riley instantly regretted his self-denigrating comment.

"I was mostly teasing because… you know. I'm only half male."

"Bullshit. You aren't. Parts don't matter."

Riley sighed. "To some people they do, Koll. You can't deny that. Even you. I mean, as soon as you realized who I was, you lost any interest you had in dating me."

The line went silent, and Riley had never wanted to suck words back into his mouth more than he did in that moment.

"Ri… I—"

"Forget it. That was uncalled for."

Kollin waited a moment before he spoke again. "But I don't think you understood what I meant. I was—"

"Kollin," Riley pleaded. The last thing he wanted to hear right then was some lame excuse. It was supposed to be a happy moment. "Seriously. Can we please not have this conversation right now?"

There was another bout of silence, and Kollin sighed. "Sure. Whatever you want. But you know you can talk to me about anything. Right?"

Riley closed his eyes. If only that were true. He'd accepted a long time ago that he couldn't talk to anyone about everything on his mind. "Yeah, man. 'Course I know that. Really, it was just a stupid comment. The last guy I dated was a douche about my lack of parts, and I guess I've got some lingering bitterness going on. Anyway that's not why I called. I have some potentially exciting news."

"Okay." Kollin sounded hesitant to drop the subject, but Riley knew he wouldn't push just yet. He needed to watch what he said going forward. Too many slips like that and Kollin would have him spilling his guts in no time. "What's going on?"

"Well, I wasn't 100 percent honest with you about why I was in town."

"Really, Ri? *Really*?"

Riley laughed. "I know, but I needed to talk to my boss first, so I just kept my mouth shut. There's a possibility I'll be back in town for a job."

"Seriously?" Kollin squealed, and Riley cringed. "Oh my God. That's so exciting. What job?"

"If things go as planned, Home for Hope."

"What? How? Why didn't anyone tell me?"

"Well." Riley drew the word out and tried to inflect a hopeful cheeriness into his voice. "I'm telling you now. My company is looking to open a branch in Durham. I happened to see HOPE on a list of upcoming jobs and told my foreman I knew you guys. He asked if I could check it out. That's what I was talking to Adam about yesterday."

"Adam knows and didn't tell?" Kollin shouted.

Riley pulled the phone away from his ear and only held the mouthpiece to his lips. "I asked him not to so it could come from me. Plus I didn't want to be part of it if you didn't want me around."

Kollin huffed. "So that stuff about seeing Maggie…?"

"That's true too. I was kind of hoping she'd just give me the referral on the spot, but I should've known better. She said she'd set me up with someone good here if I don't end up back there, but I already have a therapist here who can do that. I just hate going to someone new."

"Wait a second." Kollin sounded frustrated. "Back up. Dr. Maggie didn't give you the rec?"

Riley groaned. That. That right there was why Riley pulled away from Kollin. Whether Riley let dumb shit slip out of his mouth or Kollin picked up on every tiny little thing Riley didn't want him to, Kollin always ferreted out everything Riley wanted to keep in.

"Ri?"

"She just wants to be sure I'm ready," Riley said, trying to keep any sort of inflection out of his voice.

"Oh man. That sucks." Kollin sounded at a loss for words. Riley knew the feeling well.

"Doesn't matter. I'll either be in town soon, so I can keep seeing her until she thinks I'm ready, or I'll find someone here."

"The hell it doesn't matter." Kollin's indignant reaction made the corner of Riley's mouth turn up. "Why didn't she sign for you? That's bullshit."

And with that simple question, where the answer was anything but, exhaustion swept through Riley again. "Can we not get into this tonight, Koll? I don't have the energy."

Kollin's anger was replaced by soft concern. "Of course. I'm sorry. It's none of my business, anyway."

Probably not, but Riley actually found the worry welcome after going so long with no one caring.

"Don't even fret about it," he reassured Kollin. "But hey, if you can sway Adam toward Drummond's, it'd be awesome to be in town again. And my boss wants me to act as junior foreman if we get this job, which would be an incredible opportunity. Adam sounded like he'd consider us if we put in a bid, but it's all kind of last minute too. So who knows what'll happen."

"Seriously?" Kollin's voice had gotten deeper over the years, but his second squeal proved that it still rose to unnaturally high levels when he became excited.

Riley grinned. "Seriously."

"I'll talk to them tomorrow," Kollin promised.

Riley closed his eyes. He didn't love extorting his friendship with Kollin to tip the scales in his favor, but even with his mixed feelings about returning to Cary, he couldn't help but ask. Before Riley saw HOPE's name listed on that sheet, returning to Cary for even a weekend had been a subject he wouldn't even let the deepest parts of his mind entertain. Dealing with all of the crap he'd left behind there seemed insurmountable, but after spending a few days there, he could see how he might have been a touch dramatic. Maybe he'd worried for nothing.

KOLLIN DRUMMED his fingers on his knee while Adam and Eli studied the information Riley had e-mailed him on Drummond Construction. He'd already looked it over himself and been impressed, but he knew shit about construction companies, so that didn't say much. The only things he cared about were that Riley's boss seemed like a stellar guy and Drummond's getting the bid meant that Riley would be back in town.

Adam sat back and shrugged his shoulders. "I don't know much about construction, but it seems as good a company as any we already have around here. Elijah?"

"They do good work, from everything I've heard, but I agree with Adam. There are several solid construction companies already in town who would probably give us a lower bid, since they don't have to travel."

"Yeah, but this would bring Riley back," Kollin interjected.

Adam ran his fingers through his hair and tugged on the ends. "I love Riley as much as you do, but I've got to think about the youth here. We don't have an endless supply of money to build this expansion."

Kollin refrained from huffing and pointedly eyeing Eli. Everyone in Adam's tiny office knew they *did* have an unlimited supply of money—or as good as, anyway. Instead he bounced his foot up and down and struggled to think of the words he needed to make Adam change his mind. But Eli spoke before he found them. "I know this is important to you. Maybe Adam and I can play with the budget. But they have to at least offer a competitive bid."

Adam's mouth dropped open, and he smacked Eli's arm. "Elijah."

Eli made a face back at him. "Adam."

"You're such a pushover. Can't I ever be the one who gives in?"

Unperturbed, Eli snatched the papers off Adam's desk and sat back in his chair to look over them again. "You had your chance to tell him yes. Not my fault you didn't take it."

Adam huffed. "So sorry I'm trying to teach our son a business lesson. I would've thought that would be right up your alley."

"Ah, ah, ah." Eli wagged his finger at Adam. "One of the most important lessons you taught me was family before business."

"You're impossible." Adam crossed his arms.

Kollin scratched his head.

"Does this mean Drummond's will get the contract?"

"No—" Eli said.

"Maybe—" Adam said at the same time.

"Who's the pushover now?" Eli asked, his lips twitching.

"You just said—" Adam was nearly screaming until he looked at Eli's smirking face. "You're such an asshole. Why do you insist on getting me riled up like that?"

Eli laughed and nudged Adam's shoulder. "Because it's so easy, and I love seeing that vein in your forehead—yep, that one right there—pop out."

"You two are so dysfunctional." Kollin was used to their shenanigans, but he was starting to lose his patience. "Seriously? Does that mean they have the job?"

Eli sighed and rubbed his forehead. He looked at Adam and raised his eyebrows, and the two stared at each other for several moments, apparently having a silent battle. "Seriously. After talking to Riley when he was in, we'd already decided that as long as their bid is reasonable and their references check out, they've got it."

Adam nodded. "What I said earlier is still true. I'd love to help Riley out, and I can't think of a more perfect way than this. Riley mentioned Drummond's is itching to get this contract so they can get their name out, but if he's wrong and the numbers don't match and the company isn't a good fit, there's nothing I can do. Ri's foreman sounds like a great guy, and I'd love to have him out here. If he's unavailable, someone's going to have to vet whoever they send. These workers will be around my kids for months. I won't have a bunch of homophobic assholes throwing slurs or even murmuring them under their breaths."

Eyes wide, Kollin held in his urge to squeal like a little girl. Instead he jumped up and hugged both of his parents. "Thank youuuuu."

"Like we wouldn't do everything we could to help Ri out," Adam said as he returned the hug. "Do you not know us at all?"

"I know," Kollin agreed and glanced at Eli. "Four years is a long time, though."

"He tell you anything yet?" Eli asked.

Kollin shook his head and looked at Adam. "He say anything to you?"

Adam winced and shifted in his seat.

"He did," Kollin said, his eyes growing big with accusation. "What happened to him? Is he okay?"

"Koll, you know I can't—"

"Bullshit." Kollin smacked his hand down on the desk. "You can tell me. This isn't some random kid. Riley was my best friend."

"Kollin." Eli's tone was sharp, and Kollin knew he was treading a thin line.

He crossed his arms over his chest and squared his jaw. "I'm sorry I cursed at you, but the sentiment remains. Maybe I can help him."

Adam closed his eyes and took a deep breath. Kollin knew then that he wouldn't be getting any answers. Adam was searching for the right words to let him down gently.

"He specifically asked me not to tell you anything he told me. I'm sorry."

Kollin deflated. "Can you at least tell me if he's okay?"

Adam winced again, and fear raced through Kollin. "Being near the center and people who accept him will be good for him."

No. That meant no. Something terrible had happened to Riley, and Kollin had no idea what.

# CHAPTER 4

RILEY RAN his forefinger over one of the jagged, bright red scars on his chest as he looked in the mirror. Some days—most days—he hated these scars. They remained an angry reminder of the flawed body he'd been born in. On those days he covered up quickly, unable to look at himself for longer than strictly necessary. That day, thankfully, his scars reminded Riley of everything he'd survived. Maybe he hadn't been given the right body, but someone or something thought Riley would be strong enough to endure the constant battle he had with himself.

Since reconnecting with Kollin a month earlier, days like that came more frequently. Kollin had a way of making him look inside his soul to see the good parts—his wit, his intelligence, his determination. As welcoming as it felt to be relieved of his own demons, Riley knew that relying on Kollin for his happiness was entering dangerous territory.

Riley's phone rang and pulled him out of his reverie. He grabbed a T-shirt, jerked it over his head, and picked up the old flip phone.

"Ready, kid?" Greg asked before Riley even had a chance to say hello.

"Yep. Be there in a minute."

Greg clicked off without another word, so Riley shoved his feet into his construction boots and picked up the two duffel bags he'd packed. Drummond Construction was set to begin the addition to the inn the following morning. Riley's landlord, who happened to be Greg's mom, refused Riley's offer to pay his meager rent during the three-months-plus they were going to be in Cary. So Riley had shoved everything he wasn't taking with him into a corner, in case she needed to use the space. Rather than return home on the weekends, like most of the crew, Riley planned stay with Adam, Elijah, and Kollin. The thought left him both excited and terrified.

Riley left a hastily scribbled thank-you note for Greg's mom, clomped out the door, and threw his bags into the bed of the truck.

"Took you long enough," Greg complained as Riley climbed in the cab.

"Lost track of time," Riley replied. He was used to Greg's rough exterior and didn't let his bluntness or his brash personality bother him. He was a fair foreman, and though he might not be overtly kind, he treated all of his employees with respect. "Your wife sad you'll be away during the week?"

Greg's mustache twitched, and he peered at Riley from the corner of his eye. "You know how Sue is. She's glad to have the TV to herself."

"I bet she's begging you to come home by Tuesday."

Greg grunted. "Marvel show is on Tuesday nights."

"Wednesday, then."

"That's when the guy who never wears a shirt is on TV." Greg pulled into the street. "I'm tellin' ya, kid. She's happier without me home."

Riley rolled his eyes. "Whatever you say, boss."

They drove in silence for a while. Riley expected and welcomed it, so he was surprised when Greg cleared his throat. "You know I don't make a habit of getting involved with my crew's personal lives...."

He trailed off and shifted in his seat. Riley encouraged him to continue. "But...."

"I gather the people we're working for... you were close to them once. Maybe are again?"

Riley nodded. "Yeah. Adam was the first person I ever trusted. I never knew Elijah too well, but their son was my best friend at one time."

Greg's mustache twitched again. "You know I have no problems with you or who you date, but I know you've kept the rest of the crew in the dark. You're in charge of them now, and that requires a certain level of trust."

The air in the cab felt thick, as Riley realized where Greg was heading. He gripped the door handle.

"I'm not saying you should or shouldn't tell them. It's none of their concern, but you might want to have a conversation with your friends about how they treat you in front of the boys. I won't stand to hear them say anything derogatory on site. They know what and where we're building, but I can't stop everything. I'm their boss, not their conscience."

Riley remained silent for a while, thankful Greg wasn't the type to ramble. "You think I should tell them?"

Greg shifted in his seat again. "Didn't say that either."

"So you think I shouldn't tell them?"

Greg sighed. "Look, kid. I think you have a bright future ahead of you. Maybe you got into some trouble in the past, but I know how much my sister struggled and how much she continues to struggle. I'd hate to see you go back to that type of life because of some assholes."

Riley cocked his head and studied Greg. He hadn't answered his question at all.

"Sooo… don't tell them?"

The ends of Greg's mustache pointed down as he frowned. "Don't believe I'd do it just yet, but if you do, you have my support."

Riley sighed. Less than two hours earlier he'd looked at his scars in the mirror and found strength in them. At that moment he felt the imaginary pain of the scars digging into his skin, into his soul, reminding him he couldn't be honest about his true self without risking the very thing that had helped him come so far.

"LOOK AT you, big boss man."

Riley looked up from the plans laid out before him to watch Kollin strut across the site. Even wearing the obnoxious hard hat, complete with tufts of green hair poking out, he looked ridiculously cute.

Riley shoved that thought right out of his mind. He didn't have the parts Kollin wanted in a partner, and their friendship was too important to risk fucking up because of some lingering schoolyard crush.

"What're you doing here? And how'd you con your way into a hard hat?"

Kollin jerked his head toward where Elijah and Greg stood talking. "Eli wanted to stop by and intimidate your boss, and I asked if I could tag along. Greg gave me this," he said, knocking on his hat. "Do I look official?"

Riley looked at Kollin's oversized tank top, skinny jeans, sockless feet, and slip-on shoes. "Sure, buddy. Just like a regular," he said, his tone dripping with sarcasm. "What's Elijah want to scare Greg for?"

Kollin rolled his eyes. "He'd micromanage the entire world, if he could. Don't tell anyone he's just a big teddy bear at heart."

"I definitely won't, since I'm not so sure that's actually the case."

"What're you talking about? You had him wrapped around your finger back in the day. He was terrified to show up on a Thursday without a sundae for you."

Riley shook his head. "First off, that was a long time ago. And while Elijah may care a great deal for the youth at the center, I'm no longer one of them. And I'm quite certain Elijah is a teddy bear in three instances and three instances only—where you're concerned, where Adam is concerned, and where Lizzie is concerned. With everyone else, he's more like a grizzly bear."

Kollin pshawed Riley with his hand. "Whatever. I wanted to stop by too, so I could find out what you're up to tonight. Are you free?"

"So far I've been working until I can't hold my eyes open anymore and then passing out as soon as I get back to the hotel."

Kollin leaned against the makeshift table where Riley had just been studying his diagrams. "How about you meet me for dinner, instead? You've been here three whole days, and I haven't seen you at all."

Riley scrubbed his face with the heel of his hand. "Yeah. Sorry about that. I've been busy as hell trying to prove Greg made the right decision promoting me. Besides, since I'm living in your basement on the weekends, I figured you guys would want a break during the week."

"No way. I'm stoked. And Lizzie is a little too excited." Kollin leaned in and covered half his mouth with the back of his hand to mock whisper. "I think she has a crush on you."

"Dude," Riley hissed. "She's twelve."

Kollin shrugged. "She's also boy crazy. You be sure to let her down easy, or I'll hunt you down myself."

"Please." Riley huffed. "You think you can take me?"

His words were flippant, but Kollin raked his eyes up and down Riley's body, presumably taking in his size. Riley was proud that he'd bulked up and defined his muscles. His physical job sure didn't hurt in that area, but after his addiction problem, Riley had started lifting weights, as well. The exercise released pent-up anxiety and helped him avoid the things he needed to stay away from. Under Kollin's careful scrutiny, Riley felt the familiar urge to shrink into himself. He prayed Kollin couldn't see any of the many imperfections still marring his physique.

Kollin gazed at Riley again. Riley couldn't quite read the expression on his face, but then Kollin smiled softly. "Guess not anymore."

Riley ignored the churn in his stomach and moved on. "Anyway I could probably get outta here by seven. That okay?"

"Sure. I'll text you later to see what you feel like eating." Kollin pushed himself off the table and offered his hand to Riley.

The blood drained out of Riley's face, and he glanced around the open space to see who was watching. They normally parted ways with a quick, very platonic hug, but Greg's words had been rolling around in his head all week. Would hugging Kollin, an obviously gay male, indict Riley?

Seeming to realize that Riley wasn't going to reciprocate his gesture, Kollin slowly lowered his hand. "We not allowed to be friends at your work or something?"

Riley hated how small and hurt Kollin's voice sounded. He knew how often people shied away from Kollin, simply because he was overtly flamboyant. No one wanted to be guilty of gay-by-association. Riley never understood how people could be such assholes, but now he was the one causing that look on his best friend's face.

"It's not like that. I just—"

"It's okay." Kollin looked around at the other men on site. "I get it. I better get going and let you get back at it, though."

"Kollin…." But Riley didn't know what to say next, so he just sighed.

Kollin shoved his hands deep in his pockets and backed away. "See you tonight, Ri."

"Fuck," Riley muttered. For the five seconds before he ruined everything, Riley had really been looking forward to dinner with Kollin. But now he'd spend the entire dinner feeling guilt-ridden and uncomfortable because of his own stupid insecurities.

"Yo, Riley," one of his guys shouted. "Need you a minute."

Riley took a deep breath, grabbed his plans, and buried his shame for later. He had a job to do, and he couldn't afford to fuck it up.

# CHAPTER 5

KOLLIN PULLED into the gravel parking lot of The Homeplace several minutes before seven. The building was an old farmhouse the family had converted into a restaurant. It was only open a few nights a week, and it served homemade Southern food. It stayed packed with a clientele ranging from older folks who wanted to eat the food they were raised on, to college students who wanted something that reminded them of home, to everyone in between.

He gave his name to the hostess and took a seat in the waiting area, which looked like the inside of a seventeenth-century one-room church, complete with pews. No longer as excited about his dinner with Riley, Kollin propped his elbows on his knees and rested his head in his hands. The likelihood of anyone on-site taking notice of their awkward good-bye was slim to none, but Kollin still felt humiliated. Logically he knew Riley had every right to shy away from any form of physical contact at work. Eli rarely showed any affection to Adam while at Langley Lumber. But he and Riley weren't together, and his rejection felt like a slap in the face.

The couple who walked in ahead of Kollin approached the hostess. Kollin checked his phone and found no messages, but it was only a couple of minutes after seven. He shoved his phone back in his pocket and bounced his heel while he waited. At ten minutes after seven, Kollin wondered if Riley had decided to bail on their plans. Surely Riley would at least send a text if he couldn't make it. Besides, if anyone had the right to not show up, it was Kollin, not Riley.

Moments later Riley's frazzled face appeared in the doorway, but relief relaxed his features when he laid eyes on Kollin. As if waiting for Riley to appear, the hostess arrived to lead them to their seats and saved them from what was sure to be an awkward greeting.

Their waitress appeared immediately and flashed Riley a big smile. "You boys want a pitcher of tea or lemonade?"

"Can we have both, please?" Kollin asked, knowing Riley liked Arnold Palmers as much as he did.

"Sure can." She looked over Riley again, and her eyes lingered on his face. "We have fried chicken, country ham, and roast beef tonight. What can I get you two?"

Kollin looked at Riley, who shrugged. "I want ham and roast beef. You wanna splurge and get all three, Ri?"

Their waitress laid her hand on Riley's forearm. "You won't regret it, sugar. It's the best fried chicken in town."

"Might as well." Riley offered her a small smile but quickly returned his gaze to the table where he diligently worked to shred the corner of his napkin.

"I'll bring it right out with your drinks." With a final persisting look at Riley, she sauntered off. Despite his mixed feelings toward Riley at the moment, Kollin grinned. Riley seemed completely unaware that their waitress was into him.

"Look, Kollin. About earlier—"

"We should probably wait to get into that," Kollin interrupted. "You know she'll be back in two seconds."

The Homeplace didn't cook any of their food made-to-order. Instead every table was served family-style and received the same sides, allowing the customer to choose only which meat came with the meal. The result was delicious, home-cooked food, on the table within minutes of the patrons being seated.

Sure enough their small table soon nearly overflowed with food. The smell made Kollin's stomach growl, and he immediately grabbed the pitchers and filled his and Riley's glasses with a mixture of sweet tea and lemonade.

The waitress stood next to Riley, her hand on the back of his chair. "My kind of table. I love a good Arnold Palmer."

Kollin flashed her a quick smile and returned to his task, while Riley continued in his oblivion.

"Well, if you need me, just give me a wave."

"Thank you," Riley replied politely, and she finally left.

Riley spooned some green beans onto his plate, offered the bowl to Kollin when he was finished, and moved on to the apples. Once their plates were full, Kollin nudged Riley's foot. "I don't think the waitress could've been any more obvious, and you still didn't notice she was checking you out."

Riley's eyes widened. "What?"

"Our waitress. She was trying like hell to get your attention. Touching your arm, standing at your chair, calling you sugar."

Riley shook his head. "That's a Southern country girl right there. They all do that."

Kollin shrugged. "If you say so, but I think she's interested. She sure didn't look at me like that. Might want to let her down easy."

Riley cocked his head, and his features turned hard. "That I'm not a guy?"

"What?" Kollin said, jerking his head back. "No. That you're gay."

Riley's body slumped. "Oh."

The anger that seeped out of Riley's eyes flooded straight into Kollin. "You really believe that's how I think?"

"I don't know. Maybe you meant it as a joke."

Kollin set down his fork. How the hell did they get to this point? Didn't Riley know him better than that? "I'd never joke about that. And I don't know what I've done to make you think I would."

"Come on, Koll." Riley sighed and ran his tongue over his lip ring. "You haven't done anything. I'm a fucking mess. Okay? That's why I shoved you out of my life. You deserve better than a friend like me. You deserve someone who can fucking hug you good-bye in front of people."

"No. *You* come on." Kollin took a deep breath. Between getting blown off and then being accused of being a thoughtless dickwad, Kollin was starting to think he'd be completely justified in dumping a pitcher of tea on Riley's head and walking out on him. But blowing up at Riley would solve nothing and only make everything worse. Adam had already told him Riley was in a fragile state, and Kollin promised himself he'd do everything he could to help. If that meant sucking up his hurt feelings sometimes, then that's what he'd have to do. Riley was worth it.

He leaned forward and kept his voice low so the tables on either side of them couldn't overhear. "I love you, Ri, and I want to support you however I can. But I guess we both agree I can't do that at my own expense. If you don't want the people you work with to know we're friends, then I need to know that ahead of time. I can't stop being me. I won't. I understand if you need to keep quiet about who you are, but you need to let me in on who you're supposed to be, when and where. If that's a straight man on the job, I'm not going to look down on you for doing whatever it takes to get through the day."

Riley shifted in his seat. "You make it sound so cowardly."

Kollin raised his hands in supplication. "I think I was trying to do the opposite, actually."

Riley stabbed a piece of roast beef with his fork and swirled it around in his mashed potatoes. "I've just never had a reason to share anything personal about myself with my coworkers. Coming out as gay is terrifying. Coming out as trans is a mixture of terrifying and humiliating. The thought of coming out as both is nearly debilitating."

Tears welled behind Kollin's eyes. Riley's words cut him to his core, and he wished he could make his friend's road easier. But Kollin couldn't force Riley to come out, and he definitely couldn't force the men and women Riley worked with to accept him. He sighed. "Well, now that I know where you stand with them, I'll stay away from the site unless Adam or Eli needs me there."

Riley closed his eyes for several moments, and then his gaze met Kollin's. "You know you're my best friend. Right? Even still. I'm sorry I acted like an asshole earlier. I just want to do really well on this job, and I need my team to respect me."

Kollin squinted his eyes at Riley but allowed a small smile to play on his lips to indicate he was teasing. Mostly. "You know that makes you sound like a bigger asshole. Right? I'm not respectable?"

Riley huffed.

Kollin shook his head. "Dude. We're good. Okay? Just stop pouting or your face will freeze like that, and you won't be able to snag any boys at the club Saturday."

Riley's fork clattered against his plate, and he hastily picked it up again. "Do what, now?"

Kollin sat back and grinned. "I thought we could go to Raleigh this weekend. Go out dancing."

"Uhh...."

"Come on, Ri. Remember back in the day? We used to talk about when we'd be old enough to go out together. Well... now we can."

Riley shook his head. "I dunno. I'm not a very good dancer, and it's not like I can hook up with anyone."

"Why the hell not? You've done it before. And you clearly have the looks to grab people's attention." Kollin gestured toward their waitress, who just happened to be looking in their direction.

Riley scrunched up his face and tossed a few pinto beans into a hole he'd carved in his mashed potatoes. "It's just different. You said yourself you were interested in me until you found out who I was. Nobody wants someone like me for more than a night, and honestly, I'm over the one-night stands."

Kollin ground his teeth together and took a deep breath. "I said that because you're you, and we're friends, not because of what parts you do or don't have. You just refused to let me explain that."

Riley stabbed one of his apples as he avoided Kollin's gaze. "Doesn't change the fact that you only like cock."

Kollin blinked, taken aback by Riley's harsh tone and stung by his words. He opened his mouth, ready to defend himself. Whatever had put Riley in a foul mood, Kollin didn't deserve to take the brunt of his misplaced anger. But though he searched for the words to tell Riley how wrong he was, he couldn't find them.

Kollin did like cock. He'd only been with a few men, but he enjoyed the physical aspect of his relationships immensely, and a big part of that was loving the way another man's cock felt rubbing against him or moving inside of him. All that time, Kollin had been so focused on building up Riley and convincing him that he was no different than any other guy, he'd forgotten Riley *was* different. Maybe it didn't make him any less of a man, but the difference couldn't be ignored. Shouldn't be ignored. Riley deserved more than that.

"Never mind," Riley said softly. "I shouldn't have said anything. It's just been a long and weird week. Greg told me to make sure I don't let my secret out while we're here, and now I'm hyperaware of every little thing I do. It's so draining."

"Ri...."

"Can we get her to pack up this food? I'd really like to go back to the hotel and go to sleep."

Kollin studied Riley's face while he signaled their waitress. Panic had settled over his features. He refused to look at Kollin, and every movement he made was exaggerated.

For the second time, and against his better judgment, Kollin dropped it. What else was he to do? What if Riley were right? He'd never considered having a sexual relationship with any trans man. Maybe there *was* more to his dismissal of Riley as a potential date than he thought.

Kollin forced a smile on his face. "If that's what you want. Sure."

They didn't say anything else as their waitress brought over two take-home boxes. Kollin paid the check for both of them, and Riley offered a quiet thanks. Uncertain of how Riley would welcome any form of physical contact, Kollin kept both hands deep in his pockets as he jerked his head toward the far side of the lot. "I'm over here. Guess I'll see you Friday evening?"

"I'll be there. Thanks again for dinner."

Kollin nodded once and turned toward his car, more confused by Riley's hot-and-cold actions than ever.

RILEY TURNED on the shower in the hotel bathroom. He didn't particularly feel like showering, but he didn't want to sit in the room with Greg either. While the water heated up, Riley slowly pulled off his clothes. He avoided the mirror and stepped into the shower. Instead of standing under the spray, he immediately sank to the floor and curled into a ball. The water was hot—too hot, really. But Riley welcomed the bite. He lay on the shower floor, pushed everything out of his mind, and watched the water swirl down the drain.

A knock on the door eventually pulled him out of his nothingness, and he heard Greg's gruff voice call his name. "You okay?"

Riley closed his eyes for a moment and forced himself off the bottom of the tub. *How long have I been in here?* He cleared his throat and called out, "Yeah. Just working out the kinks from the day."

No way would Greg buy his bullshit. Riley could hear the hollowness in his tone. Nevertheless, he exited the shower quickly, not even bothering to soap himself up after all that time, and pulled on his sleep clothes. A quick glance in the mirror confirmed he'd been crying. His eyes were puffy, red, and impossible to hide at that point.

With as little fanfare as possible, Riley darted out of the bathroom and crawled under the covers. One of the best perks of hotel life was leaving the air conditioning on frigid temperatures, and the room currently felt cold enough to host the Winter Olympics. His sheets were cold, and Riley shivered beneath them so hard that Greg asked if he should turn down the AC.

"No. I'll warm up in a minute."

Greg grunted and returned to his TV show. Riley assumed he'd gotten off scot-free, until the next commercial hit, and Greg cleared his throat. "Sure you're okay?"

The concern beneath Greg's abruptness made tears prickle at the back of Riley's eyes. Rather than brush him off, Riley found himself opening up. "I screwed up a lot today with my friend." He sniffed and held in his urge to cry. "First I made him think I didn't want to be seen in public with him, and then I all but accused him of being a transphobe, which is the furthest thing possible from the truth."

"He the fruity-lookin' one?"

Riley slapped his palms over his face. "Oh my fuck, Greg. It's *not* okay to say that."

Greg shrugged. "Call 'em like I see 'em." He didn't sound sorry, but they'd had enough conversations for Riley to know Greg truly meant no harm when he said stupid shit like that.

"Just don't say that to his face, please," Riley said through his hands.

"You know I wouldn't." Riley thought Greg sounded almost hurt, but he ignored it.

"What am I gonna do if the crew finds out about me?" Riley asked, still speaking through his hands. "Kollin's my best friend. I don't want to hurt him."

"Guess you're gonna own that shit. What else is there to do?"

Riley jerked his head toward Greg. "But you acted like I needed to keep it a secret."

"What do I know?" Greg crossed his arms over his chest.

"Well, I *thought* you knew a lot."

Greg grunted again, and Riley resisted the urge to pull his hair out. They sat in silence for several minutes, and then Greg cleared his throat. "My sister…. She had some horrible shit done to her, man. I don't want to see that happen to you, is all. Don't suppose you should be hurting your friends to protect yourself from something that might never happen, though."

"How bad would the crew be if they found out?"

Greg shook his head. "I don't know them half as well as you do. More 'n likely some won't care, some will be pissed, and some will be supportive."

Tired of Greg's nonhelpfulness, Riley snapped, "Thanks for that wonderful insight into something that could ruin my life."

Greg whipped his head around to look at Riley. "Get a little big in the britches when you're stressed out, do you?" he asked. "Look, kid. If he's as good a friend as you say, he'll understand."

Riley flipped over in bed and buried his head under the pillow. He appreciated Greg's willingness to help, but he wasn't in the mood for his almost-but-not-really advice. Kollin had already said he would understand if Riley downplayed their friendship. But could Riley live with himself if he did that to Kollin?

# CHAPTER 6

THE TAPPING of Kollin's pencil eraser against his notebook grew louder with each passing second. When Adam could no longer take it, he leaned over his desk, grabbed Kollin's wrist, and forced a smile onto his face. "Something on your mind?"

Kollin's eyes widened for all of two seconds, and then he let the innocent façade fall away.

"Do you think I'm a hypocrite?"

Taken aback, Adam turned his chair away from his computer to face Kollin. "No. Of course not. What in the world gave you that impression?"

Kollin bounced his heel against the floor. "I've never considered dating a trans man."

Adam frowned. Fear and confusion laced Kollin's confession. What in the hell happened?

"You can't help who you're attracted to, Koll. Just like you can't force yourself to like women, you can't force yourself to have feelings for someone who's trans. That doesn't make you a bad person. You still treat everyone with respect. That's what's important."

Kollin huffed and shook his head. "How can I tell Riley that he'll find someone when I don't know a single gay man who'd want to date a trans guy?"

*Ah, Riley.* He should've known. Adam sat back in his chair. "The world's a whole lot bigger than your circle, man. Someone who's bi or pansexual could be interested in Ri. And I'm sure there are gay men who would date him, not to mention everyone out there who doesn't want to label themselves. You trying to hook him up or something?"

Kollin ignored his question and asked another instead. "Did you ever do it with a girl?"

"Uhh… that came out of left field."

Kollin leaned closer to Adam. "Just answer the question, please."

Hearing the frustration in Kollin's voice, Adam held up a hand. "No, I didn't. I always knew I was gay, and even though I hid it from some of my foster families, I never stayed anywhere long enough to feel the need to pretend like I had a girlfriend. Plus I was still pretty young by the time Matthew and Amelia took me in, and I didn't have to hide, living with them. I felt no reason to test the waters." Adam waited for Kollin to say something else. When he remained silent, Adam sat next to him on the old, ratty couch in his office. Elijah hated that piece of shit couch, but Adam refused to let him replace it. The thing was an eyesore, for sure, and hardly even comfortable anymore, but Adam had saved too many lives on it to give it up. "What's going on, man?"

Kollin hunched his shoulders, shame written in his downcast eyes. "A couple days before Riley showed up at the center, I saw him at a bookstore. He asked to sit with me while I was studying. I didn't recognize him at all. I thought he was trying to flirt with me, and I'd even made up my mind that I'd go out with him if he asked me. As soon as I learned who he was, that day he came in here, I lost interest."

Adam hesitated, still not certain what Kollin specifically struggled with. "I'm a bit confused here. Do you *want* to date Riley? Or do you just think you *should* want to date him?"

"I don't know," Kollin said, his voice miserable. "It's not like he even wants to go out with me, but I feel like a huge hypocrite for constantly telling him he's no different than any other guy when I didn't give him a second thought. Ri's a great catch. Anyone would be lucky to be with him, and it never even crossed my mind."

"You probably lost interest because he's one of your best friends. What if the guy at the bookstore had asked you out and then told you he was trans? Would you have turned him down?"

Kollin groaned and leaned against the back of the couch. "Maybe? I don't know. I'm a horrible person."

"Stop. You are not, and you're worrying about this for nothing. You said yourself that you don't even think Riley is into you. Why are you beating yourself up over a hypothetical situation?" Adam paused to give Kollin a moment. "I know you want to do whatever you can to make Riley happy, but you can't take that responsibility upon yourself. That's his job. As his friend, it's your job to support him." Adam nudged Kollin's shoulder with his own. "You're not a hypocrite. Far from it."

"I guess," Kollin mumbled.

Adam groaned internally. This was one of those times he wished Kollin weren't so empathetic. More often than Adam liked, Kollin needlessly took on other people's burdens without recognizing how detrimental it was to his own emotional health. "I don't know why you're having these doubts, but I know you. Just be careful with Riley. Okay? He's in a delicate place right now and probably will be for a while. But it's *his* journey."

Kollin nodded, indicating he'd heard, but he didn't say anything else, so Adam returned to his desk chair. Kollin might've heard his words, but that didn't necessarily mean he'd listen. Kollin and Riley were both adults, so there was only so much Adam could do. Time to take his own advice and butt out.

KOLLIN PEEKED out of his bedroom window, but the driveway remained empty. His stomach churned as he checked the clock again. *Twenty minutes late.*

He flopped back on his bed and tried not to stare at the clock. Kollin had spent the past couple days thinking over everything he and Adam had talked about. He still wasn't sure how he would feel about dating any random trans man, but he had finally accepted that he wasn't a hypocrite. He had lost interest in Riley because Riley had always been nothing more than a friend to him. Maybe when they first met, it was because Riley looked more like a girl than a guy, but that wasn't the case anymore. But the new perspective had given Kollin a lot to consider.

He loved Riley. Plain and simple. Riley had always been the one person Kollin felt most comfortable being around. He was smart, athletic, kind, thoughtful, and had just enough sarcasm to be funny instead of mean.

Best of all he got Kollin. Really got him. On a level that so few people did. His friendship was invaluable to Kollin. And *now*... now Riley was cute. Like hella cute—especially on the rare occasions when he shaved. Though Riley's scruffy look was starting to grow on him.

Asking Riley out would be awkward as hell. And their first date would probably be sixteen kinds of weird, but it could also be the start of something amazing. Did he want to miss out on what could easily turn into the most fulfilling relationship he'd ever have, just because he loved the feeling of a hard dick? There was no doubt that he loved Riley more, and his attraction to men had never been limited to just a sexual organ. He'd been with guys with small dicks. It wouldn't be much different.

Kollin rolled off his bed and peeked out the window again. Still no truck. He crossed the room, turned on his iPod, and then turned it off again immediately. If Riley didn't hurry the fuck up and get over there, Kollin was bound to lose his nerve. Damned if he'd let that happen. Kollin grabbed his phone to call Riley, but the distinct grumble of a diesel truck kept him from dialing. Kollin rushed downstairs and flung the door open for Riley before he even reached the stoop.

"You made it," he said and then immediately felt dumb for stating the obvious.

"That I did." Riley jerked his thumb over his shoulder at where Greg was pulling out of the driveway. "Last chance to change your mind. Once he's left the gates, he's not coming back for me."

"Don't be ridiculous. You're ours for the whole weekend." Kollin grabbed Riley's wrist and tugged him inside, toward the basement stairs. Excitement replaced his nervous energy. He couldn't wait to show Riley that they'd changed the downstairs room for him.

"Wow. This is amazing," Riley said when they reached the last step. He threw his duffel bag onto the bed. "You shouldn't have gone to all this trouble. I could've slept on the couch. I can't thank you guys enough."

Kollin grinned. He knew Riley would have slept on the couch. Kollin had slept on it several times, and it was nearly as comfortable as his bed. But they all wanted Riley to feel at home, so Eli had bought a twin-sized bed and set it up in the far corner.

"Good thing there's no need to, then," Kollin said. "It'll be fun having you right downstairs."

Riley looked around the room. Aside from the huge TV on the wall being curved instead of flat, the room hadn't changed much since the last time Riley had been there. Kollin hoped the familiarity helped Riley feel at home. The pool table sat in the same spot, but the kitchenette in the other corner held real food in the fridge instead of just junk food and beer. With the complete bathroom off to the left, Riley could spend his entire weekend down there in complete privacy and not come upstairs for anything.

Not that Kollin had any intentions of letting Riley do that.

"So I was thinking again about going out tomorrow night."

"Kollin, I told you—"

"Just listen." Kollin sat on Riley's bed and gathered up his courage. *Shitty shitballs.* His apprehension returned. Too late now. "I thought we could go out dancing *together.*"

Riley stared at him, his face unchanging.

"Well?" Kollin asked.

"You told me to listen. I haven't heard anything different from what you proposed the other night."

"Don't be difficult, Ri. *Together.* Like on a date."

Riley's face clouded over in something Kollin couldn't quite identify—hurt, maybe, or possibly anger—before Ri covered it up. "You don't have to do this just because we've been friends forever. Besides, you're gay."

Kollin took a deep breath and stood up. Slowly, and very deliberately, he reached out and grabbed the tips of Riley's fingers with his own. He felt like the biggest idiot in the world. It was Riley, for Pete's sake. What was he doing?

Riley's hand felt strange in his own. They'd held hands before, but this touch carried unknown possibility and excitement. Riley's eyes were wide, and Kollin smiled. "And you're a man."

"Kollin…." Riley sounded desperate. Kollin didn't know exactly what Riley wanted to say, but he understood the conflicted and confused look behind his eyes.

"I know you're not interested in me that way, and that's fine. I wasn't either before the idea popped in my mind." Kollin took a deep breath. "But I've thought a lot about this, and before I knew who you were that day in the bookstore, I was looking forward to getting to know you. I may not be your dream guy, but you have to know there are gay men who are interested in more than just a one-night stand with you." When Riley didn't say anything, Kollin wiggled Riley's hand. "Come on. It's just one date. It might be awkward as hell, but what first date isn't?"

Riley shook his head. "I can't be some experiment to see if you like freaks. Not with you. I can't lose you when you decide I'm too gross."

Kollin swallowed hard. What the hell happened to Riley to give him such a low opinion of himself? "Lucky for you that I don't put out on the first date, then."

Riley pulled away and took a step back. "I'm serious. I can't."

Properly admonished, Kollin took a step forward. "I'm sorry. I didn't mean to make a joke out of it, but I'm serious too. I'd never intentionally hurt you, and all I'm asking for is a chance to see what happens. We don't have to do anything physical, and if it's clear we can't see each other that way, then we go back to being friends. Imagine how perfect it would be if it worked out. We already know everything about each other, so we get to skip that terrifying get-to-know-you mess."

Riley looked down at the floor and put his hands on his hips. Kollin held his breath, stayed in place, and patiently waited for an answer while he tried his best not to flip the fuck out. Finally Riley met his eyes. "Kollin...."

"Ri.... Come on. It's me. We're good together. You know this. Just one date?"

God. He sounded so pathetic. Was he really begging his best friend to go out with him? Did he not know how to take a hint? Or in their case, a very clear 'no'?

"I'm sorry." Kollin started to backpedal. "I shouldn't have—"

"Yes."

Riley's voice was so small that Kollin nearly missed it. "Come again?" He grinned.

Riley met his eyes. "Yes." He squeezed his eyes shut. "I can't believe I'm saying this, but yes."

"Yes," Kollin exclaimed. "But wait.... Are you sure? I feel like I pressured you into saying yes. Don't do it because you feel bad for me or some shit. Or maybe I should just shut up and take advantage of your pity."

Riley laughed. "I didn't know you were so bad at this. I got the impression you had some experience asking people out."

Kollin did his best to look affronted, but then he sobered. "None of them were as important as you. So, seriously... are you sure? Because I want you to be sure."

Riley shook his head. "No. I'm not sure, but yes, I still want to go."

Kollin danced a little two-step jig and Riley laughed again.

"But can you please not tell Adam or Elijah yet?" Riley asked. "That's just too much parental pressure right now."

The flash of relief and joy faded as quickly as it appeared. "Umm... about that."

"You've already talked to them about this?" Riley looked appalled, and his voice rose in his panic. "What is with you guys? Can't you be like a normal family and keep secrets from one another?"

"I didn't tell them I was going to ask you." Kollin fell back on the bed again. He liked being able to talk to his dads about everything, even if it was only because he considered them friends before they adopted him. "But I may've had a chat with Adam about some stuff to do with you before I decided it would be the most amazing plan ever. You know he won't tell anyone, though."

"Oh no," Riley nearly shouted. "Only *Elijah*, who already hates me right now for abandoning his favorite son."

"Well, now, that's not really fair. I'm his only son. Besides, he doesn't hate you. He's just a little protective."

Riley scoffed. "I don't think little means what you think it does."

"Oh, loosen up. It'll all be fine." Kollin grinned. "Look how well this is turning out. We haven't even been on our first date, and we're already fighting like an old married couple. This'll be epic."

"More like a disaster." Riley closed his eyes and took a deep breath and then looked directly at Kollin. "I mean it, Koll. I can't lose you as a friend. I need you."

The weight of everything Riley said settled in Kollin's chest. He didn't have the right words to convince Riley that he'd never let that happen, so he stood up and crossed the room. Slowly Kollin wrapped his arms around Riley's shoulders and pulled him into a hug. He didn't make it sexual, but he pressed their bodies together and held on, hoping Riley understood. It took a while, but eventually Riley slipped his arms under Kollin's and wrapped them over his shoulders.

They stood like that for a while, and the enormity of Kollin's actions settled in. Riley was right, what they were about to do was risky. Riley had never once expressed an interest in dating Kollin, and Kollin wasn't even sure he'd be able to have a satisfying physical relationship with Ri.

But what if…. Kollin couldn't live with not finding out.

# CHAPTER 7

RILEY PEEKED at the clock from beneath his pillow. The outfit he planned to wear later lay draped over the arm of the couch, and he'd already showered and trimmed his scruff. He didn't need to start getting ready for another thirty minutes, so he burrowed back under the pillow and returned to not freaking the hell out.

Too bad he was nothing but a miserable failure in that effort.

After Kollin convinced him that going on a date would be a good idea, they'd spent the remainder of the evening lounging in front of the TV and somehow managed to avoid awkward conversations.

Riley fell asleep feeling optimistic, as if it made sense for their friendship to oh-so easily transform into the very thing he always wanted. Riley could no longer deny what part of him had always known. Lingering schoolyard crush be damned—Riley wanted Kollin more than ever. And he wanted him because of who Kollin had become, not because he was holding on to some idealistic version of his best friend.

Reality set in when he woke that morning, though. It would be his one and only chance with Kollin, and Riley couldn't fuck it up. Nothing would be the same after their date—either because they took tentative steps toward a new kind of relationship together, or because the evening ended in disaster and their friendship became too awkward to continue. Riley didn't know, but he felt 87 percent certain the anticipation of not knowing would kill him before he had to walk upstairs to meet Kollin.

Riley briefly considered squeezing in another workout to calm his nerves. Elijah's home equipment was better than any real gym he'd been to, but that meant taking another shower. That meant soaping up his body, soaping up his nonmale body parts, and that didn't sound like the smartest plan, given the gargantuan boulder of anxiety already sitting on his chest.

He settled, again, for ruminating on every possible scenario that could happen on their date, and he only momentarily allowed himself to dwell on the possibility of the evening actually going well and turning into a long, successful, happy relationship. Too apprehensive to consider that possibility for more than a few seconds, he moved on to one of the more likely scenarios—that the entire thing would end with Kollin running away and screaming in terror while Riley curled into a ball and slowly cried himself into dehydration and eventual death.

God. He was such a moron.

When he could no longer stand his thoughts, Riley dressed slowly and spent ten minutes to do what normally took five. He took a deep breath as he stared at himself and did his best to focus on Dr. Maggie's voice. *Don't look at the bits of baby fat still hugging your waist. Don't pay attention to the imaginary burn from your scars. Don't focus on the empty feeling between your legs.*

Riley studied his square jaw, covered in bristly hairs, and then gently ran his hand up his shirt to scratch the hair on his chest. He studied his shoulders and arms, and though they weren't as muscular as he preferred, they looked masculine.

He closed his eyes and pictured Kollin that day back in the bookstore. Riley remembered the brief flicker of interest he'd seen in Kollin's eyes. He was distracted but amused at Riley's attention. Riley's feelings for Kollin crashed right back at that moment, as if he'd never even gone a day without seeing Kollin. He'd been an idiot to try to deny it. Just being around Kollin made him feel like a different person, like a whole person.

"Holy shit," Riley whispered. "Don't fuck this up, Ri."

He forced himself away from the mirror and somehow made it up the stairs. He followed the voices that filtered out of the kitchen and found Kollin and Adam snacking on carrot sticks.

*Oh holy God.* Kollin looked downright sexy in his black skinny jeans and oversized, dark gray, sleeveless tee. They couldn't possibly look any different from one another, since Riley had chosen a more conservative outfit in an attempt to tone down his normally abrasive appearance. He'd even added a loose tie over his snugly fit button-up shirt. A slow smile formed on Kollin's lips as his eyes swept up and down Riley, and Riley knew he'd done at least one thing right. He grinned back at Kollin.

"You look nice, Ri. Almost dapper, if I may say," Adam said and chomped off a bite of carrot. "Where you guys going tonight?"

Kollin dusted off his hands and pushed away from the counter. "Figured we'd see what's going on at Legends and then go from there."

"Well, have fun," Adam said. "And you know the rules. If you need a ride home, call Elijah."

"Har, har. We'll be sure not to disturb you from your wild and exciting night of dozing in front of the TV," Kollin quipped.

When Kollin moved next to him and smiled, Riley became acutely aware that he hadn't said anything since he entered the kitchen. "Thanks, Adam," Riley said, feeling dumb for taking so long to acknowledge the compliment. At least his voice didn't squeak when he spoke.

Riley looked at Kollin, who was still grinning at him with twinkling eyes. He wanted to tell Kollin how good he looked. He wanted to take his hand, lead him to the door, and open it for him. He wanted to promise Adam that he'd get Kollin home safely. Instead he allowed his nerves to win out and waited silently while Kollin told Adam bye.

When Kollin jerked his head toward the foyer, Riley offered Adam a small wave and followed Kollin out. They walked in silence to the car, and Kollin rushed forward to open Riley's car door as well. Feeling like an idiot, Riley cleared his throat. "Actually, I meant to ask if you wanted me to drive. I don't have a car, so I'd have to drive yours, but… I dunno. If we're doing this thing, I'd like to try to be a gentleman."

Kollin nudged his arm. "Maybe I was trying to be a gentleman. I did ask you out, you know? This is supposed to be my treat."

Riley felt his face flush. "Oh, yeah. I didn't think of that."

"Hey." Kollin grazed the back of Riley's elbow. "I'm teasing, okay? I'm a little nervous. I don't want to say the wrong thing."

Riley eyed Kollin.

*He* was nervous?

*Kollin* was nervous?

"This is a mistake," Riley blurted out and turned back toward the house. The entire evening would be a cataclysm of epic proportions if at least one of them didn't have their shit together. And Riley couldn't handle that loss.

Kollin grabbed Riley's arm. His eyes were wide and confused, and Riley thought he recognized a hint of hurt in there too. "Because I don't want to offend you?" he asked, his tone incredulous.

"Yes," Riley nearly shouted. "You've never worried about that shit before. I told you I can't lose our friendship. We haven't even gotten in the car, and it's already weird."

"Oh, for fuck's sake. This problem is not unique to trans couples." Kollin pulled Riley back toward the car. "Get in the damn car. I asked you out, so I'll drive. If we decide there's a next time, you can drive. If we get there, and ten minutes in, we realize it's a mistake, we can call the date off and just hang out as friends. But I'm not letting you bail on me before we even leave the driveway because we can't decide who drives."

The door to Kollin's car stood open, so Riley sat obediently. He crossed his arms over his chest and waited until Kollin pulled into the road. "You don't have to be so bossy about it."

"Yes I do," Kollin snapped. "Or you'd already be back in the basement, hiding under the damn covers."

Riley rolled his eyes. He hated that Kollin was right. With a heavy and intentional sigh, Riley said, "And?"

Kollin laughed. "Aaaand… we're going to have fun tonight. So stop being a dick."

Riley cut his eyes at Kollin. "Remember when you were worried about saying the wrong thing?"

"Fine, then. Stop being an asshole." Kollin sounded frustrated. "We both have one of those. Right?"

Riley groaned. Why the hell was he trying to start a fight with Kollin? It was too late to apologize without making the entire situation even more uncomfortable. Riley settled for a lame half-truth, half joke. "If it's any comfort, this is still the best date I've ever been on."

Kollin shook his head. "Something tells me you're actually serious. I don't know whether I should feel sorry for you or be glad it's me."

Riley clamped his mouth shut. He didn't want to be a pity case. Kollin genuinely seemed excited for their night out, or at least he had earlier, but Riley didn't expect the feeling to last. Kollin had no idea how huge their date was to him, and so far, all Riley had done was treat Kollin like shit while Kollin patiently endured his mood swings.

He struggled to find something truthful to say that wouldn't make him sound pathetic, and eventually he offered a quiet, "*I'm* glad it's you."

Kollin made no indication that he'd heard Riley other than a small shake of his head as he stared at the road before him. Vowing not to let his anxieties fuck everything up, Riley settled back in his seat and watched the city fly by from the passenger window.

KOLLIN COULDN'T look at Riley, or the expression on his face would surely start another argument. Riley's past remained an enormous question mark that hung between them, silently burning away his patience every time Riley let slip one of his many insecurities. He tried not to be annoyed by Riley's insistence on his privacy, but then shit happened.

If Kollin knew what demons Riley fought, maybe Kollin could manage not to fuck things up by saying dumb shit. Instead he had to guess what was okay to say, what he could joke about, and what was completely off limits. Then he had to hope and pray he'd correctly read the expression on Ri's face or the tone of his voice. The constant battle exhausted him, and Kollin didn't know how much longer he'd be able to keep his frustration in.

Just as quickly as the anger swept through him, guilt for not being a better friend shoved in and battled for dominance. Riley needed Kollin to be the one in control, to be strong. He needed patience and understanding from Kollin, not anger and snarky comments. If he couldn't rein in his emotions, he'd only end up pushing Riley further away.

Kollin turned up the radio and used the distraction as an excuse not to talk. He hoped he'd be able to stamp out his anger by the time they reached the club.

When they arrived at Legends, Kollin parked across the street and waited for Riley to meet him in front of the car, rather than rushing to open his door. Determined to have a good time, Kollin shook off the last dregs of frustration and grabbed Riley's hand as they awkwardly shuffled toward the door. "I didn't tell you back at the house how good you look tonight."

Riley smiled and shook his head. "I can't believe we're doing this. Doesn't it feel weird to you?"

Kollin shrugged. "A little, maybe. Doesn't mean it's a bad thing, though."

Riley got to the door first, pulled it open, and gestured with their joined hands for Kollin to enter. The bar wasn't too crowded, so they decided to have a few drinks. Riley ordered a gin and tonic and thankfully managed to keep the surprise off his face when Kollin whipped out a fake ID and ordered a raspberry sweet-tea vodka. Riley shoved some cash at the bartender before Kollin could, and they left the bar to find a table.

"I've never been to a club like this before while actually *on* a date," Riley said as he took a sip of his drink. "I've always thought of clubs as places to hook up."

"That's tragic. You know how much I love to dance." Kollin swirled his drink around with the little red straw the bartender had plunked in it. "It's fun with friends sometimes, and dancing with strangers is always a bit exciting. But coming here with a date, with someone I care about, and getting out on the floor… it's almost like foreplay."

"Oh?" Riley's voice squeaked. He took another sip of his drink and studied the room, avoiding Kollin's gaze.

Kollin waited until Riley looked back at him. He didn't want to freak Riley out, but he wanted to make sure Riley knew he was interested. Maybe a little innuendo would help loosen him up. "Best way to be intimate with someone without taking your clothes off."

Riley choked on his drink and ended up spitting a little bit of it back into his glass.

*Or… maybe it would terrify him.* Kollin grabbed Riley's hand. "I know you think I've gone into this willy-nilly or out of pity or some shit like that."

Riley nodded.

"I promise it's not that." Kollin pulled his hand away. "Once the idea of asking you out popped into my head, I couldn't get it out. I don't know what changed exactly, but it felt like before, something was blocking the possibility of us dating from entering my head. We've been friends for so long, it just never occurred to me. But once the barrier was gone, I saw how perfect we could be. So tonight is me being 100 percent selfish."

Riley traced a scratch on the tabletop as he contemplated his response. "I don't understand why you think anything romantic between us would be perfect when we've never been anything more than friends."

"Are you kidding me?" Kollin glanced around the room, which had filled up while they talked. "We already know we're meant to be a huge part of each other's lives. I knew from the moment we met that you're my soul mate. Maybe at first I thought we would only ever be friends, but I can't explain why I definitely wanted you to ask me out in that bookstore or the butterflies I got in my stomach when I saw you walk into the center again for the first time after all those years. Besides, one look around the room and I can see two guys checking you out. You're incredibly cute and sexy. Why wouldn't I want to try for more?"

Riley remained silent as he stared into his drink.

Feeling as if he'd made Riley uncomfortable, Kollin spoke again. "I mean, I guess I'm getting way ahead of myself here. I kind of bullied you into this date because I wanted to see what could happen between us. I wanted to at least try, but if you already know there's no way you could be into me...." Kollin trailed off. Every time that thought crossed his mind over the past few days, he'd flat-out ignored it. The entire point of their date was to see what could exist between them, and he hoped Riley would be open to the possibility. But Riley's face looked as if he'd rather be anywhere else than with Kollin.

When Riley spoke again, Kollin couldn't make out the words. The music had just grown louder, making their serious and private conversation nearly impossible. Kollin gestured to his ear and moved to Riley's side of the table. He angled Ri's chair so close that their knees bumped, and Kollin waved for Riley to continue.

"I was just saying I'm willing to give it a chance." He offered Kollin a rare, genuine smile, and his voice sounded a bit less burdened. "After all, I'd have to be some kind of imbecile to not be interested in you."

Kollin grinned, and a flash of hope streaked through him. He leaned in closer to Riley and bumped their foreheads together. "There's the 'I guess you'll do' spirit I was looking for." Kollin winked. "Let's get another drink and hit the floor."

He didn't wait for an answer. He just grabbed Riley's hand again, pulled him toward the bar, ordered two shots of tequila, clinked their glasses together, and chugged his down. When they reached the adjoining room, guys dancing together and by themselves filled the dance floor, but they still had plenty of room to move without bumping into anyone.

Knowing Riley's hesitancy, Kollin gave him plenty of space but stayed close enough so other guys knew they were together. Then he lost himself to the music. After a few songs, Riley loosened up and eventually hooked his fingers in Kollin's belt loops and pulled their bodies flush. Kollin grinned and threw his arms loosely around Riley's shoulders. He followed Riley's lead as they danced and stopped himself more than once from leaning in to kiss the soft skin of Riley's neck. Instead he ran his hands over Ri's shoulders and down his chest. He even dared to squeeze his ass once.

When the music changed again, Kollin twirled around in Riley's arms and pressed his back against Riley's chest. He grabbed Riley's hands and guided them across his stomach as they danced.

Whether because of liquid courage or a jolt of actual confidence, Riley became more assertive, and their dancing turned more sexual. Riley's lips grazed Kollin's shoulder. His breath was warm on the back of Kollin's neck. Kollin tilted his head to the side to give Riley more access. A shiver of lust ran through him when Riley accepted his invitation and dropped a wet kiss on his bare shoulder.

The song ended, and the music slowed down. Rather than head back to the table, as Kollin fully expected Riley to do, Riley spun Kollin around and tugged him close to slide his arms around Kollin's waist. At a meager five foot eight on a good day, Kollin wasn't accustomed to being taller than his dates. He shivered when Riley pressed his cheek against Kollin's neck, sweat be damned, and decided he preferred the more equal footing. Though Kollin had been grinding against Riley just a few minutes earlier, with their bodies melded together from head to toe, their new embrace felt far more intimate.

Kollin's heart rate sped up as he realized just how much he stood to lose if either of them fucked up. For just a moment, he wished he'd heeded Riley's fear, listened to his words of caution. They were on a reckless path. They should've had dinner and watched a movie like normal—as nothing more than friends.

But then Riley sighed and burrowed deeper into his arms. Maybe it wasn't such a bad idea, after all.

# CHAPTER 8

"WAS I right or was I right?"

Without opening his eyes, Riley smiled. Sitting in the passenger seat as Kollin drove home from Legends, firmly holding Kollin's hand against his leg, and tired in the most pleasant way possible, he couldn't recall why he thought going out with Kollin would be a bad idea. Once he loosened up and got used to the idea of being on a date with Kollin, he'd had, literally, the best night of his life. Kollin's appreciative looks and lingering touches made Riley feel sexy and confident. After stumbling over a few awkward conversations, they'd spent most of the night laughing and dancing. For a few hours, Riley pushed all of his baggage to the back of his mind and enjoyed the moment.

Kollin wiggled his hand. "Hey, Sleeping Beauty. I really want an answer. I love hearing those three little words."

Riley sighed loudly. "Fiiiine. I admit it…. I'm an amazing dancer."

Kollin laughed. "You're an asshole. You know that? Besides, that was four words."

A grin played at Riley's lips, and he studied Kollin's smiling profile. He was so handsome. "You were right," he said softly. "Happy?"

Kollin raised their joined hands and kissed Riley's knuckles. Riley's insides did a little somersault. "Very." They reached the entrance to Knollwood Community, the gated neighborhood where Kollin lived with Adam and Elijah, and Kollin shook his hand free to swipe his card and then grabbed Riley's hand again. "Was I right enough that you'll go out with me again?"

*Flip-flop.* There went his stomach again.

"I thought I was supposed to ask you this time."

Kollin shrugged. "You snooze, you lose."

Riley's heart raced. "I think I've hit my quota for dealing with large groups for a while. Maybe we could hang out in my room tomorrow. It's not really going out, but we could watch a movie. Maybe make popcorn and get candy. Would that be okay?"

Kollin pulled into his driveway and parked the car. "I'm game as long as we get Cherry Coke and Junior Mints."

Riley grinned and looked out the window at the dark house. Their night was about to officially end, and the nerves he felt before they left the house resurfaced.

Kollin let go of his hand and opened his car door. "Come on." Without waiting, he got out and leaned against the hood of his car. He didn't look back at Riley expectantly. Instead he shoved his hands in his pockets and allowed Riley to take his time.

Riley took a deep breath to steady his nerves and slowly opened the door and got out of the car.

He'd kissed plenty of guys. It should be no big deal.

Riley rounded the front of the car, and Kollin held out his hand. He clasped it tightly and allowed Kollin to pull them together. Sitting on the hood of the car, Kollin only came up to Riley's shoulders, and he gently rested his head there as he circled his arms around Riley's waist.

"I had a fuckload of fun tonight, Ri. I'm not ready to go in."

Riley laughed. "Poetic as always."

Kollin shrugged and looked up to offer a dopey grin. "It's true." He nestled back into Riley's chest, and Riley could smell a faint hint of Kollin's shampoo mixed with the saltiness of their sweat from hours of dancing. Riley set his chin on top of Kollin's wild locks, and they stood like that for a while as Riley's nerves settled down.

When he finally worked up the courage, Riley pulled back again. "I hear you don't put out on the first date, but could I at least get a kiss?"

Kollin scrunched up his face as if pondering Riley's proposition, but Riley could see the playfulness in his eyes even in the dim outdoor lighting. "I suppose, but if you get too frisky, I have two dads inside, chomping at the bit to defend my virtue."

Riley laughed and brushed aside a few strands of hair from Kollin's eyes. He trailed his finger over Kollin's ear, as if tucking a hair behind it, and then fondled the curls gathered beneath it. "Before we do this, I want to thank you for tonight. No matter what happens next, this was the best date I've ever had. I think you've realized I haven't been completely honest with you about everything that went on the past four years, but to go on a regular date and feel normal the entire time is rare for me. Add to it the fact that it was with you—someone I already love and admire— well, the feeling is indescribable."

Kollin's smile was soft, almost bashful, and Riley wondered if he'd gone and ruined the entire night with his word vomit. But then Kollin tugged him closer so Riley stumbled into the space between Kollin's legs. "Now who's the poetic one?"

Riley laughed, but Kollin didn't make another move, and Riley understood Kollin was waiting for him. Riley leaned down and ever so gently brushed his lips against Kollin's and then pulled away to check Kollin's reaction. Kollin only offered a small smile, but he left his fingers hooked firmly in the waist of Riley's shorts. Riley gathered his courage, settled his hands on either side of Kollin's neck, and leaned down again.

He pressed his lips more firmly against Kollin's top lip. A jolt of need rushed through Riley's body and begged him to take more. He slid his hands down Kollin's back and dipped his fingertips beneath Kollin's waistband. Tilting his head to the other side, Riley kissed Kollin's bottom lip. He felt Kollin's hands leave his waist to trail up his back, and the next time their mouths met, Riley snuck his tongue out to sweep against Kollin's lip.

Urgency built deep inside Riley as they kissed. He pulled Kollin off the car and pressed their bodies together, but Kollin still wasn't close enough. One of them moaned—Riley was pretty sure it was Kollin—and Riley craved more. He swiveled his hips in a desperate attempt to relieve the pressure building in his groin. When Kollin slipped his hand down to Riley's ass and pulled them together, Riley felt Kollin's hard cock pressed against him.

Kollin gripped Riley's bottom lip between his teeth and pulled, and it was Riley's turn to moan. He jutted his hips forward and rubbed his crotch against Kollin's shaft. *Oh God.* It was everything he'd been missing before. Everything felt so good, so right. Warm and solid against Riley, Kollin felt to him like the missing piece of a puzzle he'd been frantically trying to solve.

Riley broke away from Kollin's mouth and trailed his lips across Kollin's jaw to sink his teeth into the warm flesh just below his ear. Kollin groaned again and slipped his hands beneath Riley's shirt to settle on his waist, but the touch startled Riley. He broke out of his lust-filled haze and suddenly became aware that he was practically dry-humping Kollin.

In Kollin's driveway.

With Adam and Elijah and Lizzie right inside their home.

Mortification flooded every bone in his body. Riley pulled away abruptly and took a few steps back. He leaned over, placed his hands on his knees, and sucked in oxygen in a feeble attempt to regain his composure.

Kollin's soft laughter floated through the night, and Riley's heart might as well have dropped out of his chest. Kollin was laughing at him already? Tears sprang behind his eyes, and a fresh wave of disgust swept through him.

"Damn," Kollin said, his breaths coming almost as quickly as Riley's. "If I'd known it was going to be that good, I would've kissed you a long time ago."

Riley snapped his head up. "What?"

Kollin sat back on the hood of the car, not at all discreetly shifting his package. "Don't tell me you didn't enjoy that." Kollin rubbed the back of his neck as he studied the ground and avoided Riley's eyes. "I mean, usually I can tell when a guy is into me. Either he pops a boner or he doesn't. I used to think it must suck for straight guys to not be able to know if their partner is turned on, but clearly there are other ways to tell. That was fucking hot."

Riley stared at Kollin, who was still shifting himself in his pants, and tried to decipher everything he'd just said. In the end all he could focus on was the last bit.

"You thought that was hot?"

Kollin met Riley's eyes and gestured toward his bulge. "Do you need further proof?" He studied Riley for a moment, and his face fell. "I'm sorry. Did I misread? I thought… I mean, I thought you pulled away because we were getting carried away. I didn't realize you weren't enjoying it. Shit, Ri. I'm sorry."

Kollin stood up and took a step toward Riley, his arms outstretched, and Riley shook himself out of his shock. "No. God, no. Don't be sorry. I thought you were grossed out by me rubbing all over you like that. I've never lost control like that before. I don't know what came over me."

The slow, confident smile returned, and Kollin took another step forward and grabbed Riley's hands. He lifted them, placed their palms together, and gently intertwined their fingers.

"I'm not gonna lie, I was really nervous about doing that. Still am a little bit. But so far, so good. At no point during that kiss was I thinking anything other than, 'Holy fuck, I'm kissing my best friend, and it feels amazing, and I want more,' and 'Oh my God. Don't stop doing that.'"

Riley's face flushed. He dipped his head against Kollin's chest to hide his face. "There's my poet."

"And you didn't even know it."

Riley groaned. "You're ridiculous."

"Only according to 95 percent of the population. I'm perfectly normal to the rest of us."

Riley looked up at Kollin. "I liked the kiss too. Sorry I spazzed at the end."

Typically, as if he didn't have a care in the world, Kollin shrugged. "Probably best we stopped. We agreed to take it slow, and I was two seconds from begging you to let me take your shirt off—protective dads or not."

Riley's heart skipped a beat as he imagined Kollin's hands on his bare chest. But Kollin had never seen his scars, and that thought made him want to vomit, so he gratefully accepted the excuse. "Yes. Slow is good. Clothes stay on until further notice."

# CHAPTER 9

KOLLIN REACHED around Riley, who was lying against him in Riley's small bed, to grab a few kernels of popcorn from the bowl in Riley's lap. "So when can I tell Adam and Eli about us?"

Riley shot up and hacked on whatever candy he'd just shoved in his mouth. Kollin slapped his back a few times and tried to hide his amusement by handing Riley a glass of Cherry Coke.

"You okay?" Kollin asked, and he grinned.

"Yeah," Riley muttered. He took a long swig and settled back against Kollin's chest. "What exactly do you want to tell them?"

"I dunno." Kollin watched as President Whitmore delivered his famous speech. *Independence Day* was one of Adam's all-time favorite movies and solely because of that part. Having seen it so many times and listened to the glee in Adam's voice as he recited the speech along with Bill Pullman, Kollin had grown to love the film as much as Adam. Neither he nor Riley had paid very much attention to the movie thus far, but Kollin still got goosebumps during the speech. "Maybe we just tell them we're dating."

"We?" Riley asked, his voice high.

"Fine. Me. Whatever. I'm just not used to keeping secrets from them. It'd be one thing if I weren't living in their house… if both of us weren't living here." Kollin laid his cheek on the top of Riley's head. "I mean, they don't give a shit what we do, but I don't want to feel like I'm sneaking around."

"That's what we're doing, then? Dating?"

"What the hell else would you call it? We went on a date yesterday, and now we're on our second one."

Riley harrumphed, and Kollin laughed.

"Maybe we shouldn't make a big deal out of what we call it, just yet."

"Then why tell them at all, if it's not a big deal?" Riley asked.

Gently Kollin pushed Riley up and moved around the bed so they were facing one another. "I didn't say *this*"—he gestured between the two of them—"isn't a big deal. I said what we call it isn't a big deal. If you really don't want me to, I won't say anything, but I'm not sure why you're hesitant. You know they're not like most parents."

Riley worried his lip and tugged his ring in and out of his mouth with his teeth. Guilt overcame Kollin for pushing Riley, and he was about to take the suggestion back when Riley sighed loudly. "Fine. But you have to at least wait until tomorrow, when I'm not camped out in the basement, and you make sure to let them know this was your idea. I'm not some creeper trying to seduce you deeper into the queer lifestyle."

Kollin snorted. "I'm not sure there are levels of queerness, but whatever you say."

Riley blushed and looked down, and the awkwardness in the room multiplied ten times over. They'd spent most of the movie cuddling and talking, but aside from Riley lounging a little more on top of Kollin than normal, their second "date" was pretty damn close to hanging out as friends.

With so much uncertainty between them, Kollin didn't think that was necessarily a bad thing. Riley clearly struggled with body dysphoria, and Kollin had no interest in inadvertently pushing the wrong button. They needed to talk about everything, at some point, but with their friendship being so established, starting that conversation felt more awkward than it would if they'd just met.

Kollin already cared deeply for Riley—the idea of hurting him in any way was unbearable—but he didn't know how to bring some of his concerns up *without* hurting Riley, which was one of the main reasons he wanted to tell Adam they'd started dating. After so many years of therapy, Kollin had grown accustomed to talking out his feelings as a way of understanding them, but he didn't want to see a therapist just so he could have a boyfriend. Besides, Riley was likely to turn tail and run if Kollin said he needed a therapist because they were dating.

But... Riley looked pretty damn adorable at that moment, and Kollin remembered how fitting Riley felt in his arms the night before. He placed his hands on Riley's knees to garner Ri's attention and then leaned forward to kiss him softly. The sounds of American aircraft attacking alien ships floated around them as Riley responded, tentatively at first, and then with more confidence. Kollin kept it light to honor the pact they made the night before to take it slowly, but when he tugged on Riley's lip ring with his teeth, Ri grabbed him around the waist and jerked backward and tumbled them onto the bed.

Kollin laughed as they untangled their legs, but neither broke their kiss. Riley clutched at the back of Kollin's shirt until it shifted up enough for Riley to press his hands to Kollin's bare skin. Riley's palms were rough, and his touch tickled until he gripped Kollin more firmly. He squeezed Kollin's sides and then let out a groan that sounded more frustrated than turned-on.

Kollin tore his mouth away from Riley's. "What? What's wrong?"

Riley shook his head, and instead of answering in words, he flipped Kollin off him and rolled on top. With Riley sitting astride Kollin and both of them in t-shirts and basketball shorts, there was no way Riley couldn't feel Kollin's erection. Kollin grinned up at Riley and jutted his hips.

Riley laughed, leaned in for another kiss, and manhandled Kollin to hold his arms against the bed. He licked and bit at Kollin's neck while squirming around on top of him, which Kollin could only assume was a successful effort to drive him insane. When Riley finally stopped kissing Kollin long enough to bury his face in Kollin's chest, Kollin groaned. He wanted more.

"Ri. Please. Can I touch your skin?"

Riley didn't raise his head from Kollin's chest, but after a moment, he nodded quickly. Kollin wiggled his hands free from Riley's grasp to slide them under his shirt. There was a patch of coarse hair at the base of his back, and Kollin lingered there briefly and then skimmed his fingers up.

Riley's back was solid, and when Riley swiveled his crotch against Kollin's, Kollin felt those strong muscles flexing beneath his hands. Precome leaked from Kollin's dick, and it flitted across his mind to slow down before they went too far. But then Riley's hand slid under Kollin's shirt. With his palm spread, Riley ran his hand up Kollin's side and over his ribs, and with his thumb, he kneaded right over Kollin's nipple.

Kollin was pretty young when he discovered his nipple had a direct connection to his penis. Apparently Riley would discover it on their second date. Kollin bucked his hips, which made Riley groan. Then he swept his thumb back over Kollin's nipple, and Kollin bucked again.

"Oh shit," Kollin panted.

With a grunt Riley tugged Kollin's shirt up and latched his mouth onto Kollin's nipple while he teased the other one. Slowing down became the last thing on his mind. Kollin squeezed his hand between them and shoved it into his shorts. Riley rode Kollin's hand with the same amount of fervor as he had Kollin's shaft while Kollin gripped himself.

The sounds that came out of Riley were nearly obscene, and between his own rough tugging and the pull of Riley's teeth against his nipple, Kollin grew closer and closer to orgasm, until his entire body froze. In several quick spurts, Kollin came all over his hand and briefs and created an entirely too-sticky mess in his pants.

Clearly not done, Riley continued to whimper and rub himself against Kollin. As he came down from his haze of lustful euphoria, Kollin floundered about what to do next. Touching Riley beneath his shorts was not an option, but he wanted to make Riley feel as good as he did. Having no experience with a vagina, Kollin fell back on the minimal knowledge he'd gained from watching porn.

Kollin gripped the back of Riley's neck and pulled him away from his now too sensitive nipples and into another deep kiss. Sticky hand be damned. Kollin tentatively touched Riley over his shorts. His concern for overstepping his boundaries and upsetting Riley outweighed his nerves, but to his relief, Riley didn't push him away. Instead he moved Kollin's hand farther up and showed him how to rub—sometimes up and down and sometimes swiveling his fingers around in circles. Riley's gyrations became more unpredictable, he seemed to pull away and then come back for more.

When Riley buried his head back into the crook of Kollin's neck and let out a long, low whimper, Kollin felt his dick start to twitch with renewed interest.

"Holy fuck, that's so fucking hot, Ri." Kollin planted a sloppy kiss beneath Riley's ear and wrapped his free arm around Riley's waist to keep him from squirming away. Soon Riley's whimpers grew louder until he nearly shouted. His body seemed to curl into himself as he strained out a final moan. And then he immediately pulled Kollin's hand away and collapsed on his chest.

They lay like that for a few moments, panting against one another, until Kollin found the energy to loosely throw his arms around Riley's back.

So much for taking it slow.

Kollin couldn't bring himself to regret it, though. They'd kept their clothes on, and they'd gotten one big question out of the way. There was no doubt that they were sexually attracted to one another.

"So…," Kollin said with a slight chuckle. "That just happened."

Riley turned his face so it was completely on Kollin's chest, and he nodded.

"You okay?" Kollin asked him and trailed his hand lightly up Riley's back.

Riley nodded again. "Are you?" he asked, his voice muffled. "Was that okay?"

Kollin laughed. "Are you kidding? That was hot as hell. I can't remember the last time I jizzed in my shorts. You're like… I dunno, man. Snails and chocolate and pineapple all rolled into one."

Riley finally looked at Kollin, his face scrunched up. "I'm like a snail?"

"Yeah. They're supposed to be an aphrodisiac. Ya know… to get you in the mood."

Riley shook his head. His smile was lopsided, and there was a twinkle in his eyes that Kollin didn't get to see often enough. "I know what an aphrodisiac is, but I think you're thinking of oysters."

"Oh." Kollin threw his head back against the pillow and laughed. "I was close. One disgusting, slimy food is the same as the next. Right?"

"If you say so."

Riley rested his head against Kollin's chest again, and they lay in silence for a few more minutes, until Kollin gently squeezed his sides. "What about you? Was it okay for you?"

Riley didn't answer right away, but he tightened his grip around Kollin, so Kollin waited. When Riley's eyes met his again, they were pooled in tears.

"Hey." Kollin cupped Riley's face in his hand. "What's wrong? What'd I do?"

Riley looked down. "It's so dumb. I've never…. I mean, no one's ever…. Guys don't usually want to…." Instead of finishing his thought,

Riley burrowed back into Kollin's chest. And as Kollin figured out what Riley was trying to tell him, anger raged inside him.

"No one's ever done that for you before?"

Riley shook his head. "I told you, most guys want a dick. If they can't get one, a quick lay will suffice, and those don't generally come with reciprocation."

"Fuck, Ri." Kollin tightened his arms around Riley. "I wish you'd told me. I would've…." What? What would he have done differently? Kollin didn't know.

"It's okay. I wouldn't have wanted anything different anyway." He tilted his head to the side to rest his cheek on Kollin's chest. "I don't want pity or to be treated like a head case."

Kollin nudged Riley's side with the inside of his elbow. "Hey. Shush. I was a head case at one point. Stop talking about my kind."

Kollin's sarcasm seemed to work. Riley grinned and lightly kissed Kollin's chest over his shirt. "So you have sensitive nipples, huh?"

Heat flared up into Kollin's face, and he was searching for the least embarrassing response when the basement door flew open. Feet pounded down the steps, and Elijah's voice filtered down with it. "I said to knock first, Lizzie."

Riley scrambled to get off of Kollin, but it was too late.

"You guys want some—oh." Lizzie gaped at the two of them on the bed while Riley flopped onto the space next to Kollin. Then she did an immediate one eighty and ran back up the steps. "Daaaaad!"

Kollin laughed but stopped when he saw Riley's face.

"Oh shit, shit, shit, shit, shit. Kollin." Riley flapped his hands in the air and pointed up the stairs. "Go. Go. Go fix it."

Kollin grabbed Riley's hands and kissed each of them, then placed them in his lap. "Calm down. It's going to be fine. We're both clothed, and there's no way she knew what we just did. I am, however, going to wash my hands before I go up there and smooth everything over. You good?"

"Right. Yes. Okay. I'm good. I'm never leaving this basement again, but I'm good. Just send boxes of ramen down once a week or so."

Laughter bubbled out of Kollin. He kissed the top of Riley's forehead and shoved off the bed to clean himself up. He could hear Eli's and Lizzie's muffled voices from upstairs, but he knew no one would come down the stairs again until they had the all-clear to invade Riley's space. He wished he could comfort Riley more, but the only way to make him feel better was to let his parents in on their relationship. Then Riley could see with his own two eyes that Adam and Eli were happy as long as Kollin was.

Kollin dried his hands. "I'll let you know when we're done talking. You can decide then if you want to join us or not."

Riley nodded and shrank back against his headboard. Kollin sighed. As bad as he felt for Riley, he couldn't help grinning at the tremor of excitement coursing through him. Riley needed time to work through his issues, but they'd just passed a huge test in their relationship.

# CHAPTER 10

KOLLIN OPENED the basement door and walked into the kitchen. He lightly bopped Lizzie on the back of her head and grabbed an apple from the fruit bowl as he leaned against the kitchen island. "Ever heard of knocking?"

Screwing on her best pout face, Lizzie rubbed the spot Kollin just smacked. "Ever heard of locking a door? Or, I don't know, not making out with your supposed best friend in your parents' basement?"

Kollin laughed. "What're you talking about? Riley *is* my best friend."

Lizzie huffed. *"Dad."*

Eli put his arm around Lizzie and pulled her in front of him. "Your sister seems to think she caught you two in a precarious position." He raised his eyebrow at Kollin. "You're an adult, so what you do is your business, but you need to remember there's a twelve-year-old girl in the house."

"Oh please. It wasn't anything worse than that time we caught you and Adam on the couch supposedly 'keeping each other warm.'" Kollin rolled his eyes as he used his fingers to make quotes. "We were watching a movie together, and he was on top of me. We were also fully clothed and *not* under a blanket. If she told you it was anything more than that, she's lying."

"Liz," Eli said, exasperation heavy in his tone.

"It's not fair," Lizzie huffed. "Why does Kollin get to have a live-in boyfriend, and I can't even go on a date?"

"It's very fair," Eli said, tugging on one of her braids. "As I just said, Kollin is an adult, and you are twelve. Besides, I'd hardly call Riley a live-in boyfriend. You just got confused. Right, Koll?"

Kollin took a large bite of his apple. He twisted his face up and grunted. "Eh."

Eli's eyes narrowed. "Why don't you go to your room, Liz."

She stomped off with as much righteous anger as she could muster and mumbled about the injustices of living in a man's world. Kollin held in his laughter and faced Eli.

"She's going to be the death of me. I have gray hairs now. Did you know that? Fucking *gray* hairs."

"I bet Adam digs the salt-and-pepper look. Sounds like something he'd like. All professor-y and shit."

Eli stared at him. "'Old man' sounds like something Adam would like?"

Kollin shrugged. "I dunno. I was just trying to make you feel better."

"Don't think I don't know some of these are because of you," Elijah said, pointing to his head. "Now what's going on with you and Riley? What the hell does 'eh' mean?"

"Don't flip out." Kollin hoisted himself onto the counter. "It's new. Really new. We had our first date last night, and it went well." Kollin grinned. "We just had our second date, and it also went well."

Eli's mouth dropped open, and he pointed accusingly at Kollin. "Oh my God. You *were* messing around with him down there."

"I swear she didn't see anything. We fooled around earlier"—Kollin hurried forward when Eli moved to interrupt him—"*with our clothes on*, but we really were just lying there when she came down."

"*Kollin.*"

"I know, and I'm sorry. I swear it won't happen again. Locked doors all the way from now on." Kollin offered his most sincere smile.

"Why're we locking doors?" Adam asked as he breezed into the kitchen. With a loud *thwap*, he smacked Eli's ass and then opened the refrigerator door.

"Apparently your son and Riley are dating, and our daughter caught them making out downstairs in Riley's room." Eli's tone was bland. He didn't look amused.

Adam stood from where he'd been hunched over searching for something in the fridge. His eyes were bright when he turned around. "So you decided to go for it?"

"Wait." Eli held up his hand. "What? You knew about this?"

"Not really." Adam grinned at Kollin. "He mentioned the other day he might ask Riley out."

Eli looked from Adam to Kollin with his mouth hanging open. "Why am I always the last one to find out about every damn thing?"

Kollin grinned. "You were the first to find out we made out."

Eli narrowed his eyes. "Actually your sister was."

"Again, technically she only saw us lying on the bed together. You were the first one who knew for sure."

"Whoa, whoa, whoa," Adam interrupted. "Can someone please catch me up with what's going on?"

Kollin gave Adam and Elijah the CliffsNotes version of everything that had gone on between him and Riley over the past few days. When he finished, Adam was unsurprisingly supportive but cautious. "I think it's great. But you'll both need to be careful. Riley has a lot going on, even if he weren't still midtransition. He might not be ready for something serious. And just because you like doing over-the-clothes stuff with him, doesn't mean it'll transfer when you two get more serious. Communication is key if you guys want this thing to work out."

Eli, though, crossed his arms and studied Kollin, his expression serious. "You really think you could love him?"

Kollin sobered. "Yes, sir. I do."

Eli nodded. "You're going to have to fight for him. He's terrified. I can see it in his eyes. He's ready to rabbit, the first chance he gets. But I know Riley has a good heart, and I hope you two work it out." He crossed the kitchen to Kollin, wrapped one arm around Kollin's neck in an awkward hug, and kissed the top of his head. "But for tonight, don't listen to Adam and don't overanalyze everything and go see what kind of pizza he wants."

"Hey." Adam whacked the side of Eli's arm, but a slow smile spread across Kollin's face. Sometimes he wished everyone could see how amazing Eli was, but at that moment, he felt awfully special knowing Eli reserved those rare glimpses of his foolishly romantic heart only for them.

With a quiet "Yes, sir," Kollin slid off the counter and returned downstairs.

# CHAPTER 11

"YOU SURE this is a good idea?" Eli asked as he set two bags of groceries on the counter. "Don't you like Riley?"

"Duh. That's why I want to do something nice for him." Kollin pulled all of the food out of the bags and placed it on the counter.

"Yeah, but have you tasted your cooking?"

Kollin made a face at Eli. "You're so funny."

"What time is he getting here?"

"Said he'd get off work around six." Kollin washed his hands. "So soon, I guess. I need to get started."

"Want some help?"

Kollin glanced at Eli from the corner of his eye. In general Eli was a terrible cook, but he could grill a mean hamburger, which was what Kollin planned to make. But he wanted to fix the whole meal by himself. "Maybe you could hang out with me. Just in case?"

"Sure." Eli sat on one of the bar stools at the island and propped his chin on his hand. "And not that I'm telling you what to do, but it's going to take longer to cook the potatoes than the hamburgers, so I'd start on those first."

"Thanks." Kollin flashed Eli a grateful smile and got to work peeling and chopping potatoes. Eli messed around on his phone, probably reading the news or some boring shit like that. He'd never met anyone as business-minded as Eli. He actually enjoyed watching C-SPAN and never seemed to mind when he had to work from home. Originally Kollin thought Eli just accepted that was the price he had to pay for being so involved in HOPE, but Kollin eventually realized Eli worked from home even when he wasn't overly busy at the center. He seemed to enjoy it.

Kollin spread the chunks of potatoes onto a baking sheet, covered them with olive oil, and then mixed in salt, pepper, parsley, and Cajun seasoning. He slid them in the oven and got to work on making the hamburger patties.

"Any tips on these?"

Eli looked up. "Cook them on a medium-low heat so you don't burn the outside."

"Got it." Kollin grabbed a chunk of meat and formed a patty. He cast another sideways glance at Eli. "You mind if I ask you something?"

"'Course not."

"You gotta promise not to freak out, though."

Eli closed his eyes and put his forehead on his fingertips. "Oh, geez."

"That's not a very good start." Kollin finished one patty and started on another.

"Go ahead."

"I want to preface this by saying we've only been dating a week, so this is a long ways off. Ri doesn't seem thrilled with the idea of me even seeing him with his shirt off right now. But...." Kollin paused and tried to decide the best way to phrase his problem. "I don't know what to do," he finished lamely.

Eli frowned as he thought, and Kollin placed the patty on the plate and grabbed a handful of meat for another. "I guess I'd wait until he's comfortable with having his shirt off."

Kollin sighed. "Uh... yeah. I got that part. I meant later on, when we're doing more stuff. Like... down below."

"Oh...." Eli's eyes widened. "Ohhhh."

"Yeah. I've just never been with anyone who didn't have a dick," Kollin blurted out and felt his cheeks warm.

"Oh," Eli said again. He looked a little pale. Kollin normally asked Adam about stuff like that, but Adam had never been with a woman. No matter how uncomfortable it made both of them, Eli was his only hope at getting advice.

Kollin finished his last patty, which turned out about half the size of the others.

Eli remained silent until Kollin finally sighed. "Never mind. I'll figure it out somehow."

"No, no," Eli said. "I want to help. It's just... weird. I'm trying to figure out how to phrase things. You're still fifteen to me sometimes, and that's way too young for some of these words."

Kollin nodded and waited, the hamburger patties forgotten.

"Okay, look. I've been with plenty of women, but it's not going to be the same as being with Riley. The best thing you can do is talk to him and see what he likes."

Kollin shook his head. "I just don't know if we're to that point yet, though."

"If you're not to the point of being able to talk about it yet, maybe you shouldn't be doing it."

Kollin fixed a hard stare toward Eli. "'Cuz you talked about all of your fears with everyone you fooled around with?"

"No. But that doesn't mean I shouldn't have." Eli snapped out his words and then cleared his throat. "I think we both know that no one I dated before Adam meant much of anything to me. Casual sex and what you're thinking about doing with Riley are completely different. I also never dated a trans person during midtransition. Now turn your grill on."

Kollin huffed but obeyed.

"Wait a few minutes for it to get hot before you put the meat on it." Eli sighed, long and loudly.

"Thanks," Kollin mumbled and set down the meat he'd been about to put on the grill.

"So, what? Are you looking for specific instructions or something?"

Kollin winced. "I dunno. Maybe."

"That's tough, Koll. Everyone's different. They like different things. Haven't you learned that from the guys you've been with?"

"Well, yeah. But at least I had years of practice on *myself* before I touched another guy. Now I'm going in blind to something that may or may not gross me out."

Eli buried his head in his hands against the counter. If Kollin hadn't been so desperate for some kind of advice, he'd have enjoyed making Eli uncomfortable. "You think they're gross?"

"Well, kinda," Kollin whimpered. "Isn't that the whole point of being gay?"

Eli smacked the counter with his palm. His voice sounded unnaturally high when he spoke. "How do I know? I'm not gay."

"I know. That's why I'm asking you for help," Kollin all but shouted and then lowered his voice. "What if we make it that far, and I'm too grossed out to do anything? There's all kinds of… folds and… holes… and things. And it's all shiny sometimes. What the hell is that about? Dick, balls, ass. How simple is that?"

"Oh God. Adam," Eli screeched his name, "please tell me you're home."

"Eli, I'm serious," Kollin said, trying and failing to keep the pleading tone out of his voice.

"I am too," Eli said, his tone as desperate as Kollin's.

"Fine." Kollin turned back to the grill and threw the hamburger patties on it with more force than necessary.

He was cutting a tomato when Eli spoke again, his voice soft and back under control. "Some women like a firmer touch, some softer. Some like to be penetrated, some like their clit rubbed, and some like both. Some can only get off on oral while others hate the thought of it. All of that, plus the fact that Riley is *not* a woman, means I can't give you an easy answer." Eli paused. "You need to talk to him, Koll."

Kollin spun around, brandishing the knife in the air. "But he's already so self-conscious about his body. If he finds out I'm nervous too, he's going to bail. I really like him, and I don't want something this stupid to keep us from being together. I'm trying to somehow confidently lead us through all of this but still let him set the pace. I know I'm going to screw it up, though, because he's still keeping all these secrets from me. I don't even know what the hell to do with that. We never had secrets before."

Eli came around the counter to stand next to Kollin. "Slow down. Okay? First of all, sexual attraction isn't stupid. It's not the only thing to consider in a relationship, but without it, you won't stand much chance of success. The other day it sounded like you were pretty confident about chemistry between you two. Why are you worried now?"

Kollin turned back to the tomato to avoid looking at Eli. "Riley kinda showed me what to do then. It was a little embarrassing."

"So then why do you think he won't want to tell you what he likes?"

"He seems really self-conscious until we get in the middle of something. It's like... once he reaches a point, he forgets to freak out about everything. He forgets that he's different and lets go. It's not exactly convenient to stop and hash things out once he finally reaches that point, though. And before that, everything is taboo."

"Flip your patties," Eli said and pointed toward the grill. "And get the cheese ready."

"Yes, sir."

"You're not going to like what I have to say next."

Kollin sighed. "Great."

"Adam's right. You need to be careful. Riley needs to deal with his shit before you two get serious. Starting a new relationship when you're already dealing with emotional baggage is so difficult. If Adam weren't such a saint, we never would've made it."

"So I should tell him we can't date until he's got his shit sorted out?" Kollin rolled his eyes. "That sounds super supportive."

Eli ignored his sarcasm. "Not necessarily. But the good thing about your relationship with Riley is you two were friends first. And not just fast friends. You were best friends with a soul-deep connection. What if you weren't dating Riley, and he came to you with this stuff? What if he told you he's worried his insecurities will keep him from finding happiness with a new guy he's dating? What would you tell him to do?"

Kollin's shoulders drooped. "I'd tell him to talk to Dr. Maggie about it and talk to the new guy about it."

To his credit Eli didn't look even a little bit smug. "Exactly. I'm not saying *not* to date Riley, but it wouldn't hurt to take a step back from being the guy he's dating and slide in as his best friend. You've got this kind of romantic dinner tonight, so you should probably wait until you two are doing something that's clearly a friend thing. Maybe something you used to do before, and then ask him how his sessions are going."

"But he's never seemed to want to talk about them before."

Eli chuffed. "Koll. Come on. When have you ever let that stop you? All it takes is for you to be dating someone for you to suddenly respect people's boundaries?"

Kollin laughed. "Shut up. I respect boundaries."

"You're nosy as hell, and you know it." Eli grinned. "But we love you, so we put up with it."

"Put up with *me*, you mean."

Eli shrugged. "Same difference."

"Gee, thanks." Kollin laid cheese on top of the burgers. "Why couldn't you have just given me some kind of secret move? You've been living with Adam too long."

"I'll take that as a compliment. You good here?" Eli gestured toward the food on the counter.

"Yeah. These are almost done, and then I can cut everything up for the wraps."

"All right, then. I'm going to go pick up Adam and Lizzie from the center. We'll be out of your hair the rest of the night." Eli wrapped his arm around Kollin, pulled him closer, and dropped a kiss on top of his head.

"Thanks for talking to me." Kollin grinned. "Even if you weren't all that helpful."

# CHAPTER 12

OVER THE following three weeks, Kollin made little to no progress with Riley. In fact, frustratingly enough, Kollin thought they'd taken a couple of steps back. Riley was standoffish the night Kollin cooked for him, and when pressed, he claimed he was exhausted from the long workweek. Riley genuinely seemed to want to spend time with Kollin whenever they spoke on the phone, but then he'd keep his distance when they were together and only offer the barest hint of a kiss when they parted ways. Kollin tried not to read much into Riley's behavior, but with each passing day, his anger and frustration grew.

Was Riley playing him? Kollin told himself over and over again that Riley's insecurities lay at the core of his distant attitude, but the more time passed, the more Kollin wondered if something else was going on. On top of being emotionally frustrated, Kollin itched to take the next step physically. Hell. He'd be happy just to take the first step again. Maybe he needed to suck it up and take Eli's advice to talk to Riley.

Kollin looked up from his notes—notes he was supposed to be studying for his quiz the following day—and saw Riley walk into the multipurpose room. "There you are," Kollin said and waved him over.

"Sorry I'm late," Riley said as he pulled out a chair. "Dr. Maggie ran over, since she didn't have an appointment after me."

"It's okay. I'm just keeping an eye on everyone in here while I study. I can't believe we have a quiz on the first week back." Having started fall classes, Kollin spent most of his afternoons at the center. Most of the youth there respected the rules, so Kollin used the time to study while he supervised. "Sure you don't mind hanging out here a while?"

"Of course not." Riley grinned. "It's almost like old times."

Kollin couldn't help but smile back. That was exactly what he hoped for. "Yeah. How'd your session go?"

"Okay. Same as usual, I guess."

Kollin wasn't surprised. That was Riley's stock answer. And Kollin always left it at that. But no more. He was getting some answers, and what better setting than where they'd first forged their friendship?

He fiddled with his pencil. "She say if she's getting any closer to signing off for you to move forward with your transition?"

Riley avoided Kollin's gaze. "No. She still wants to have more sessions with me."

"That sucks, man. I know how much you want this surgery." Riley remained silent, so Kollin pushed some more. "Why doesn't she want to sign off? I thought she just needed a few regular sessions on the books to prove she'd done her due diligence."

"I don't know, Koll." Riley sounded frustrated and finally looked at him. "Do we have to talk about this right now?"

Kollin shrugged. "We never talk about it, and, you know, it's kind of a big deal. I just want to make sure you don't need anything from me."

"What exactly would I need from you?"

"Whatever…. A shoulder to cry on, an ear to listen, a punching bag when you're tired of waiting."

Riley spat out a laugh. "I'd never hit you."

Kollin reached out and covered Riley's hand. "I'm serious, Ri. What's going on?"

Riley looked away. "It's complicated."

Kollin held back his urge to growl. Could Riley be *any* more evasive? But instead of lashing out, he squeezed Riley's hand. "I'm pretty smart, you know. Come on. You know you can tell me anything."

"It's not that." Riley slid his hand out from beneath Kollin's but leaned closer to him and lowered his voice. "I barely understand how I feel about my own body most days, you know? I thought I'd come to terms with the dysmorphia, but some days I can't stand to look in the mirror, even with my clothes on. When I picture myself in my head, I'm taller, broader, not so curvy in the hips. Sometimes I can even almost feel something between my legs. It's the strangest fucking thing."

Kollin frowned. "Your hips aren't curvy."

"Not the point, Koll."

"Well, they're not."

Riley fixed a hard stare at Kollin.

"Fine. Then why won't Dr. Maggie sign? Won't transitioning help with all of those issues?"

Riley shook his head. "It's not that simple, apparently. Dr. Maggie thinks I need to be in a better place emotionally before having an additional surgery. She says it's a big step and doesn't want me to rely on the surgery to fix all my problems." Riley sat back in his seat and crossed his arms over his chest. "I sort of get it, but it sucks. I'm getting the surgery no matter what, so I don't see why I can't just get it over with. I just want to stand when I take a piss."

Ri had been on T for several years already. Kollin knew that meant his clitoris should have grown to look like a small penis and that most trans men referred to it as their dick. The metoidioplasty surgery he wanted would allow it to hang free so he could piss into a urinal—not that Riley had shared any of that information with him. As with so many other things, the topic seemed to be off the table.

Kollin ground his teeth together. Riley was finally telling him *something,* though. If he proceeded cautiously enough, maybe he'd get more out of him.

"So what do you do now?"

Riley fidgeted in his seat. "She mentioned something about visiting my parents, but I don't know."

Anger flared in Kollin's belly, but it wasn't directed at Riley. "Your parents? They all but kicked you out. Why the hell should you visit them?"

"She didn't say I had to." Riley squirmed in his seat again and looked more uncomfortable by the minute. "She just said it was something to think about, since so much was left unresolved with them."

"Unresolved?" Kollin spluttered. "They cut you off and didn't contact you again. What's unresolved about that?"

Riley finally spared Kollin a baleful glance. "It's not like I gave them the opportunity to get in touch. I didn't talk to you for four years either."

"So wait, Ri. I'm confused here." Kollin leaned forward. "Did your parents try to contact you and you ignored them, or did they cut you off completely… like you told me?"

"I don't know. Okay?" Clearly pushed to his limit, Riley shouted. Several people looked in their direction. He lowered his voice when he spoke again. "It was too hard to ignore you when there were constant reminders in my inbox every day, so I stopped checking my e-mails and got rid of my phone. But it's not like my parents couldn't have contacted me through the school if they needed to."

Kollin sat back in his seat, bewildered. Technically Riley hadn't lied to him, but he'd definitely led Kollin to believe something completely different from what had actually happened. Was that what Riley had been hiding from him? Guilt was written all over Riley's downcast face, and if he'd been resisting Dr. Maggie's suggestion to take the next step, maybe that's why he was struggling so much. He'd played a much bigger part in his estrangement with his parents than Kollin realized, and lying about it couldn't have been easy.

Excitement at finally getting to the root of Riley's issues overshadowed his resentment at being lied to, and Kollin reached out to grab Riley's hand again. "Maybe you should think about it. I mean, if there's a chance it helps and you can get your surgery sooner, wouldn't it be worth it?"

"Or maybe my parents really do still hate me, and the whole thing sets me back. And then it would be even longer before we could—"

"Before we could what?"

Riley looked down at the ground. "You know… be together."

Kollin felt a sudden urge to hug Riley. He would do whatever it took—confront Riley's parents himself, if he had to—to wipe the look of total defeat and embarrassment off Riley's face.

"You know you don't have to worry about me and all that. Right? I know what I'm getting into."

Riley rolled his eyes.

"I'm serious," Kollin insisted. "I may not be used to everything you have down there, but I'm okay with that if you are. You might have to show me what to do sometimes, but you didn't have a problem with that a few weeks ago."

Riley groaned. "Don't remind me. I'm still embarrassed about that."

"Why the hell are you embarrassed?" Kollin lowered his voice. "Do you not remember how turned on I was?"

Riley's cheeks tinged pink. "I was so loud."

"Yeah, and it was hot as fuck.

Riley shook his head. "Don't do that."

"Don't do what?"

"Pretend like it wasn't weird."

"It *wasn't* weird," Kollin insisted. "And I don't remember saying anything to give you that impression."

Riley sighed. "Yeah, but you don't like vaginas."

Kollin looked around the room to make sure no one was paying attention to them. There were a few kids playing a game on the PlayStation and some lounging on the couch. Everyone was engrossed in their own lives, probably not even aware Kollin and Riley were in the corner. "I don't know if here is the best place to talk about this, but since we can't seem to talk about it when we're anywhere else…." Kollin paused. "Look, I'm going to be honest, because Eli thinks I should be. It might be a little different for me if and when we progress to something like that, but I don't think there's any way I'll know until we get there. And I'm not bullshitting you even a little bit when I say, emphatically, that I was more turned on than I've ever been when we fooled around that night."

Riley frowned and shook his head. "Kollin—"

"Dude, I'm telling you, I haven't jizzed that quickly in ages." Kollin sat back in his seat. "I was actually wondering if you were blowing me off because I sucked at pleasing you. I felt pretty good about it that night. You were so into it, and when you took charge… I mean, really, Riley…."

Kollin realized he'd gotten a bit overzealous in trying to reassure Riley. He didn't want to sound desperate, but he wanted no doubt left in Riley's mind that he'd been just as into their dry-hump session as Riley. Kollin was no therapist, but a bit of confidence couldn't hurt the situation.

Riley studied Kollin for several moments, and Kollin would have given up dibs on movie choice at the next ten family nights for a peek inside Riley's unfiltered thoughts.

"I have scars on my chest," Riley blurted out. "They're faded, but you can still see them."

"You think I didn't know you'd have scars?" Kollin waited until Riley met his eyes again. "I don't care about those. I'm more concerned about the ones no one can see, Ri. I know we're in this strange place, and I don't mind waiting until you've gotten all your shit straightened out, but please know I'm ready to move forward. You gotta tell me what you need from me, though."

Riley nodded.

"Really?" Kollin teased. "Or are you just trying to get me to shut up?"

"Yes. Okay." Riley sounded exasperated, but at least he laughed. "I hear you."

Only time would tell. Between Adam's and Eli's warnings and Riley's shady behavior, Kollin figured it wouldn't be that easy. But he hoped he'd at least gotten his point across. Nothing to do but wait and see.

# CHAPTER 13

RILEY SAT in the chair that Kollin pulled out for him and then nudged the chair next to him so Kollin had room to sit too. Before Riley left for college, he and Kollin had often spent time people watching, and they decided go to a local bookstore coffeehouse and reinstate the tradition. More often than not, they ended up creating scandalous stories that gave the drama in *Desperate Housewives* a run for its money.

"Oooh… look at them. I bet that's not his wife. It's the nanny." Kollin's eyes widened, and he gently swatted Riley's arm. "Did you see that? He just grabbed her ass."

"Ass grabbing means she's the nanny?"

Kollin shrugged. "Sure. Why not?"

"Where's the mom, then?"

"She's probably off having an affair too." Kollin took a sip of his coffee and pointed to a man browsing in the New Releases section. "That guy. He's spying on the husband and nanny so he can catch him in the act. Then the wife will have proof of his cheating ways and can sue the bastard for everything he has."

"Wait, I thought the wife was off with her lover."

"Well, not right now. Duh. She's waiting in the car." Kollin rolled his eyes. "What happened to you? You used to be good at this."

"Guess I got too swept up in my own drama to keep up the practice." Riley sipped his coffee and waited for Kollin's next quip. When none came, he looked over at Kollin, who was fiddling with the top of his coffee cup. "What's wrong? Why're you nervous?"

"Well." Kollin drew the word out, and Riley groaned internally. "I was hoping you'd tell me some more about your parents. Maybe I can help you figure out whether or not you want to try to see them again."

Riley sighed. "What do you want to know? They're parents. My mom was old-fashioned—took care of most of the cooking and cleaning but never seemed to mind. My dad was sarcastic and protective of his little girl."

"But like…." Kollin twirled the top of his cup around as he thought. "Before you went off to college, I remember you used to say they were okay parents. They just didn't get you and refused to use male pronouns. Did you guys talk about it a lot?"

Riley shrugged. "Some. We had a couple fights about it."

"So they knew how serious you were about transitioning?"

"I guess." Riley huffed. "I don't know. It was a long time ago."

Kollin grabbed Riley's hand. "I'm not trying to make you mad. I'm just trying to understand."

"I know." But Riley didn't love where Kollin was going with his questions, especially given how nervous Kollin looked.

"You really never told them you were quitting college or had a job or anything?"

"No. Because they had a long sit down with me over Christmas break and told me if I insisted on carrying on with dressing like a boy and acting like a boy, they weren't going to pay my way any longer. I didn't see the point."

"You know I think that was a shitty thing to do. They should've listened to you and supported you. I'm just wondering if they would've been more receptive if they understood how serious you were." Kollin drew both of his feet onto his chair and propped his chin on his knees. "Eli used to hate his dad because he didn't want Eli to publicly date men. But Adam's always told us at the center to cut our parents some slack because sometimes all they need is a little time to adjust. They've had this one perception of us our entire lives, and when it changes on a dime like that, they have to let go of all the future dreams they had for us, ones they'd been forming in their minds and in their hearts since the moment they found out we would be born—before then even—and change them.

"And you know what? Eli's dad is fucking awesome. He was an asshat to Eli when he found out he had a boyfriend, but after some time, he came around and realized his son's happiness was more important. He just had to let go of his expectations."

Kollin's words settled between them, and Riley frowned. Maybe he had a point, but weren't parents supposed to love and support their kids unconditionally?

Kollin grabbed Riley's hand. "I just don't want you to miss out on something with your parents because it took them a little longer to let go of their daughter than you would've liked."

"And if they have no interest in having a son?"

Kollin squeezed his hand. "Then we'll deal with that together."


"WHY'RE YOU acting like you don't want to be here?" Kollin asked as he pulled Riley toward Legends. "This was your idea."

Riley rolled his eyes. Kollin was right. He'd thought a night of dancing and a few drinks would snap him out of the downward spiral of doubt he'd fallen into. He needed to remember what it felt like to loosen up and have fun—to stop worrying all the damn time. But at that moment, all he could think about was what might happen later that night at Kollin's house. Neither of them voiced it, but the air was heavy with expectation when they made plans to crash together in Riley's room after their night out.

"I want to go. I'm excited." He forced a smile.

Kollin laughed. "You really look it."

Riley stopped in the middle of the parking lot and pulled Kollin back to him. He loved the wild look Kollin got in his eyes whenever his enthusiasm took over. Riley couldn't resist planting a kiss on his lips. "I am. Just, you know… big crowds. I'll be good once I have a drink."

Kollin's eyes lit up even more. Taking a step outside of his comfort zone always paid off when he was with Kollin. Even if his only reward was a smile, it was always worth the anxiety.

The club was packed. They'd arrived much later than before, and Riley had to wait almost five minutes for their drinks while Kollin scouted out a table. When he found Kollin, he was talking with two other guys around a small, round, standing table. One of the guys had his shirt off to showcase his impressively toned, chocolate-colored chest. The other guy looked a bit rounder, but it was hard to say for sure, since he was obscured by Kollin. What Riley *could* see were the guy's hands all over Kollin.

Unsure of what to do—he and Kollin had never agreed to be exclusive—Riley held back for a minute. Surely Kollin wouldn't ditch him to hook up with someone else while they were on a date….

Tendrils of doubt crept around the sides of Riley's heart. He tried to listen in on the conversation, but the music was far too loud. Kollin's smile seemed friendly. He didn't move the guy's hands off of him, but he didn't reciprocate the touch either.

Then the black guy stepped closer to Kollin to grab his hand, and Riley's stomach plummeted. He was clearly interested in Kollin, and even from the side, Riley could see the guy was far and away above his league. Riley took a step backward, but then Kollin shook his head and scanned the crowd. When his eyes met Riley's, they lit up again, and Kollin motioned him over.

Riley let out a small sigh of relief and approached the table. Kollin took his drink in one hand, slid his arm around Riley's waist, and thanked him with a kiss to his cheek.

"This is Chris and Steve." He gestured toward the touchy-feely guy to indicate he was Steve. "Guys, this is my boyfriend, Riley."

A smile Riley would normally have to fake when meeting new people spread of its own accord. If Riley expected Steve to back off just because Kollin claimed he had a boyfriend, he was mistaken. Rather, Steve turned his attention to Riley.

He ran his hands down Riley's chest and back up again and finished with a squeeze of Riley's pecs. "Mmmm… aren't you cute as a button. And you work out too, I'd say."

Riley's eyes widened, and if Kollin hadn't been holding firmly to his waist, he would've fled without another word. Thankfully the much more sober and personal-space-respecting Chris tactfully pulled his friend away.

"Take it easy, buddy. Not everyone's as friendly as you."

Steve poked out his bottom lip in an overly exaggerated pout but replaced it with a grin and a wink as he shimmied up against Chris. "Nobody comes to the clubs except to get freaky, Chrissy-poo. Don't be ridic."

Chris laughed. "Yeah. But not everyone comes to the club to get freaky with *you*."

"All's the more's a pity," Steve said and rested his head on his friend's shoulder.

Chris grabbed the drink out of Steve's hand and placed it on the table next to them. "I think it's time for you to take a break from these."

Kollin squeezed Riley's hip and made him jump. Kollin winked. "Is your drink good?"

Riley sighed, grateful Kollin had taken a moment to check in. "I'm about to find out." He chugged down half the drink, forcing the burn of the alcohol to warm his throat and stomach.

"That's what I'm talkin' about, baby." Steve whooped and shimmied again. "Drink the rest of her down, and let's get that cute ass out on the dance floor."

Kollin looked at Riley, shrugged, and gulped down the rest of his drink, apparently ready to dance with their new "friends." Panic crept in, but Riley finished his drink and set it on the table to follow Kollin. He hoped to God no one but Kollin got too close to him. He wasn't wearing a packer in his briefs, and there was a good chance anyone who pressed up against him would know he wasn't normal. Logically he knew it didn't matter. He had no intention of going home with anyone other than Kollin, but any time he could avoid that awkward "what the fuck is wrong with you" look was fine by him.

Riley should've known better than to worry. Kollin kept Riley's front to him at all times. He allowed the other two to dance around them, but never to come between them. Riley briefly thought Kollin probably looked the part of a jealous boyfriend, but rather than making him uncomfortable, the thought warmed him. No one had ever cared about him enough to be jealous before. Riley loosened up after a couple of songs, and a few songs after that, he even began to enjoy the feel of Kollin in front of him and one of the other two behind him.

"You having fun?" Kollin had to shout directly into his ear to be heard.

Riley nodded. "You?"

"Yeah. You don't mind dancing with these guys? They seemed harmless enough. Drunk, but harmless." Kollin screwed up his face and stuck out his tongue to make Riley laugh.

"It's fun, but I'm glad we're staying together."

"'Course we are." Kollin tugged Riley closer again and kissed him, not briefly but not too seriously either.

They danced for a while longer, until Chris decided he needed another drink. With a quick grope of Kollin's ass, Steve danced away and shouted something incomprehensible over his shoulder.

"Are they together, you think?" Riley asked Kollin.

"Nah." Kollin leaned in closer. "Chris told me Steve just got dumped, so he's drinking away his sorrows. Chris is making sure he doesn't do anything too stupid. Looks like he's got his hands full, if you ask me."

"I thought Chris was into you before. I thought both of them were, actually." Riley avoided Kollin's gaze. He didn't want him to see how scared he was that Kollin would decide he wanted someone better.

Kollin shrugged, neither confirming nor denying the suggestion.

"He's like... crazy hot." Riley said and met Kollin's eyes.

Kollin laughed. "Yeah. He is. But I got a man."

Riley threw his arms around Kollin and pulled them close together as he buried his face in Kollin's neck. The position forced them to slow their dancing some. The music hadn't changed, but Kollin didn't seem to care. They slow-danced while everyone around them twerked and dabbed, but Riley had no plans to back away until he could wipe the stupid-happy grin off his face.

When he finally looked up, any remnants of the smile vanished. Across the room, staring directly at him while he danced with another guy, was Tony. Riley pulled away from Kollin and moved toward the door, but it was too late. Tony was already chasing him down.

Riley grabbed Kollin's hand and tugged him across the floor. He stumbled and almost ran into a couple dancing. When they reached the short hallway to the bathroom, Kollin spun Riley around to press him against the wall and block him off from the rest of the crowd.

"What's wrong?"

Riley shook his head. "We need to leave. Now."

Kollin narrowed his eyes but didn't question Riley's request. He grabbed Ri's hand and started toward the door. Tony called Riley's name, but Riley didn't stop. Instead he sped up, but Tony caught up to them just as they were about to walk out the door.

"Hold up, Riley." Tony grabbed Riley's arm, and Riley flinched. "I've been calling you. Didn't you hear me?"

Just seeing Tony brought back a host of unwelcome memories. But standing beneath his sleazy, scrutinizing gaze, Riley felt dirty and unworthy to even be near Kollin. Riley hunched his shoulders in a lame attempt to hide himself, but he forced a smile onto his face and hoped

Tony wouldn't catch on to his humiliation. "Hey, Tony. We were just on our way out."

"Let me buy you a drink." Tony jerked his hand toward the bar. There was no question that Tony expected him to follow. Riley took a step forward, but Kollin gripped his hand and held him back. Tony eyed Kollin for a moment and then pressed again. "Both of you a drink, then. What're you even doing in Raleigh, anyway?"

Riley figured the quickest and most painless way out of the conversation would be to answer Tony's questions until he could escape. "Drummond's has a contract in Cary."

"Nice. I'm visiting my cousin. Figured I'd check out the scene here. It's way better than back home." Tony popped his eyebrows up and down a few times, and Riley winced, embarrassed that Kollin had to see the type of man he'd given so much of his life to. "So how about that drink?"

"I don't think so. Like I said, we were just leaving." Riley took a step backward and bumped into someone, startling himself so badly that he jerked to his side and bumped into someone else. Both men turned to see what had just happened. Neither appeared upset, but Riley's embarrassment tripled.

Kollin pulled him closer. "You're okay," he whispered in Riley's ear. Thankful to Kollin for grounding him, Riley stared at the floor and took a deep breath.

"Come on," Tony pressed again. "It's been forever. Maybe we can find somewhere to go after this… you know. For old time's sake. I've missed you."

Geez, Tony was such a douche. He didn't even care that Riley and Kollin were clearly together. Disgusted, Riley shook his head. "That's not a good idea."

Tony stepped forward and grabbed Riley's hand. "Come on, Riley."

Riley jerked away and bumped into Kollin. His voice carried a flare of anger. "I said no. Leave me alone." He spun on his heels and hightailed his way out of the club, leaving Kollin to follow or not.

Riley didn't stop running until he reached Kollin's locked car. He stood next to the passenger door and waited. He hoped Kollin would decide to follow him, but even the brutal August heat couldn't stop Riley from shivering as he waited. He crossed his arms over his chest in a futile effort to control his body. Kollin jogged up moments later, but Riley refused to look at him. As soon as he heard the doors click, he jerked his door open and sat in the car without uttering a word.

After several minutes of riding in silence, Riley noticed they weren't heading back to Kollin's house.

"Where are we going?"

"Don't know." Kollin sounded pissed, and when Riley peeked at him from the side of his eye, he could see Kollin's jaw twitch each time they passed beneath a streetlight. Had Tony said something to piss Kollin off, or was Kollin mad at him?

Riley just wanted to go home, get in bed, and hide for the rest of the weekend, but clearly Kollin had other intentions. As the passing scenery became more rural, he suspected Kollin knew exactly where they were going, but Riley didn't dare ask again. They drove for a few minutes, and then they pulled into the lot beside the very same park where Kollin had once gotten caught kissing a guy. It was late as hell, so the park would be closed for the night, but Kollin didn't seem to care as he parked haphazardly across three spots.

They sat in silence for a long time. Riley had no intention of speaking first, and he became so lost in his own thoughts that he jumped when Kollin finally spoke.

"Why haven't I heard Tony's name before tonight?" A surge of guilt rushed through Riley, but hot on its heels were shame and indignation. At no point had he agreed to tell Kollin every detail of his past. "I mean, I have no idea who he is, of course, but I'm smart enough to gather the guy's a dick, and you had some kind of romantic or sexual history with him. But that's kind of strange because you act as if you never dated anyone. Seems like he's important enough—and not in a good way—that I should've heard his name by now."

Riley shook his head. "I didn't want you to know he existed." His voice sounded hoarse... weak. "He represents everything in my past that I'm ashamed of, and I didn't want to disappoint you. He doesn't even know how much he messed me up."

Kollin looked at Riley in disbelief. "From the way you just reacted, how the hell could he not? He'd have to be the most self-absorbed jackass in the world."

Riley shrugged. "You're not far off. He never knew how close he came to destroying everything I'd been working toward."

From the look on Kollin's face, Riley's vagueness wasn't going to fly that time. Riley couldn't think of when he'd ever seen Kollin so angry—at least not at him. Headlights bounced in the side mirror as another car pulled into the parking area and stopped several spaces down from them. The driver cut the engine and immediately leaned across the console toward the person in the passenger seat. The windows would be fogged up in minutes. Riley huffed out a humorless laugh. That's how he thought his night would end. Instead he managed to piss off the boyfriend he didn't even know he had until a few hours earlier.

Riley sighed. "Tony always took me to places like this. We were friends in public, but when he wanted to fool around, we had to go to the middle of nowhere. I had my own place, but he didn't want people to see us going in or out alone."

"Riley—"

But he cut Kollin off. "I mean, he never actually said that, but I'm not stupid. Most guys who hook up with me only do it the one time. Or if they come back, they just want a blow job. But Tony seemed to be into having sex with me. I thought he liked it." Riley looked at Kollin, and everything else tumbled out. "He had a girlfriend. She was really sweet. Way too good for him, and I felt guilty that I helped him cheat, but I thought Tony was in the closet and… I don't know. I knew being with him was wrong, but I justified it because I'd finally found someone who wanted me. Or so I thought.

"And if that wasn't bad enough, Tony had a nasty drug habit. I should've been stronger, should've told him no, but when he was with me, when it was just the two of us… I would've done anything he wanted." Riley blinked back tears and hated how small his voice sounded. "I know that's awful. But he was the first person who ever seemed to care about me. Who ever seemed to *want* me. I thought once he got his shit together and came out of the closet, we would be together."

Riley's voice cracked as he continued. "I couldn't see how he was destroying my life. Greg's the only reason I got out. He figured out what was going on and pretty much severed all ties between Tony and me. Then he helped me get clean."

DEVASTATION FILLED Kollin's soul, and still no words came to mind. He was so angry at Riley. After everything they'd been through, did he really think so little of Kollin? Did he really think Kollin would've looked down on him? Did he really expect Kollin to treat him the same as that douchebag? The last thing Riley needed right now was Kollin's anger, but he'd held it in for months. He'd ignored his instinct to be honest about his own feelings and instead put Riley's first, to make sure he didn't scare him off.

Riley reached for Kollin's hand across the console, but Kollin jerked away. It was too much. Tony. Riley's drug problems. The secrets. The constant worrying and reassuring. Putting all of his own issues aside to focus on Riley. At that moment Kollin couldn't handle Riley, couldn't deal with everything that being with him entailed.

"We should get home." He turned the key in the ignition without looking at Riley. If he did, he knew he'd reach out for him and tell him he understood, tell him he'd always be there. And Kollin couldn't do that. Not then.

They remained silent the entire ride home. Kollin got out of his car as soon as he turned the engine off and was halfway to the door when he heard Riley call his name.

"Can you please say something?" Riley pleaded.

Kollin shook his head and looked at the ground to avoid the look of raw pain he knew would mar Riley's features. "Not tonight. I need some time."

He turned back to the house, but Riley grabbed his arm. "Kollin, please."

Kollin stopped but didn't turn back. "I said not tonight, Riley."

"But you can't just leave me hanging like this." Riley's voice broke. "After everything I just told you."

Kollin didn't say anything but kept walking to the door.

"This," Riley shouted. "This is why I didn't fucking tell you. I knew I'd get nothing but rejection. Why the fuck would I want to subject myself to that again? Fuck that, Kollin."

Kollin whirled around. "Fuck that? Fuck *that*? Fuck *you*, Riley. I've done nothing but support you since the moment you walked back into my life after *four fucking years* of nothing. You could've been dead, for all I knew. Found in some ditch and tagged John fucking Doe because no one cared enough to identify you. All that time you were gone, and the only thing I asked for from you when you waltzed back into town was a little respect.

"I understood that you didn't want to be seen with the flamer while on the job. I understood that you didn't want to move our physical relationship forward. I fucking understood that there were some things you wanted to keep quiet. And every single time I worried about you, every single time my feelings were hurt because you didn't trust me enough to confide in me, and every single time I got pissed off because I could tell you were lying to me about something, I shoved it aside, determined to be not only a supportive boyfriend but a supportive friend. And the first time I ask you for five fucking minutes to process the fact that you're a drug addict, dated some fucktard whose bullshit lies still affect you today, and lied to me about it for months, *you* somehow end up pissed?"

Kollin screamed into the night and tugged at his hair.

"Dammit, Riley. And now I'm even more pissed at you for making me act like such a fucking asshole when I know you need me right now. I know you do, but I just can't." Kollin shrugged his shoulders, He felt more helpless than ever before. He wished he could offer Riley better. "I just can't, Ri."

Kollin turned back to the door and unlocked it. He took one step in the house and half turned back to Riley, who hadn't moved since Kollin's outburst. "Just… don't take off tonight. Please come inside."

Riley didn't move, so Kollin walked inside and left the door open behind him. He climbed the stairs quickly and waited at the top until he heard Riley quietly click the door closed behind him. With a small sigh of relief, Kollin trudged into his bedroom and flipped on the light.

"I take it Riley finally came clean?"

Kollin jumped back and automatically grabbed for some kind of weapon but came up empty. "Shit, Adam. What the hell?"

Adam sat on the corner of Kollin's bed. He looked surprised that he'd startled Kollin and turned the corner of his mouth down. "Sorry. Figured you'd expect me after all that racket you made outside."

"I need my own place," Kollin mumbled as he toed off his shoes and then collapsed on the bed behind Adam.

"Good luck paying for it."

Kollin grunted and closed his eyes. He knew Adam would wait until he was ready to talk. He'd even leave if he asked him to, but Kollin didn't want to put off dealing with the matter. As angry as he was at

Riley, he still worried about him. Dragging the situation out wouldn't solve anything.

"Tony, who I assume you know about, was at Legends tonight," Kollin finally said. "He cornered Riley. Acted like a jackass, which is apparently just his normal self."

"Ah," Adam said. "So he didn't tell you willingly."

Kollin shrugged. "I wasn't holding a gun to his head, but willingly would definitely be a strong term to use. How much did you hear?"

Adam fell back on the bed beside Kollin. "Oh, pretty much everything after 'fuck you.' That was quite the rant. Impressive. I think my favorite part was when you acknowledged that you were acting like an asshole and then didn't apologize."

Kollin sighed. "I will tomorrow. I asked him not to leave."

"There's something, at least."

"If you're in here just to make me feel worse, feel free to head back to your room at any time."

Adam tucked his hands behind his head. "I'm waiting on you, kid."

Kollin rolled his eyes. Why couldn't Adam be a little less Mr. Miyagi and a little more Madea and just tell him what to do?

"He doesn't owe me anything," Kollin said, his voice soft.

"No. He doesn't."

"He still should've told me." Kollin looked at Adam. "If nothing else, when we started dating, so I could understand everything he was trying to deal with."

"Yeah." Adam agreed. "He probably should've."

"I have every reason to be mad at him. Right? Everything I said is true. All those years of nothing, and then he comes back. I forgive him like it was nothing, even though he devastated me, and he can't even be honest with me. That's not some bullshit reason to be pissed."

Adam hesitated and then asked, "Didn't you already tell him you forgave him for that?"

"Well, yeah. But it was still a shitty thing to do."

"Of course it was, but you gotta pick one or the other. Either you hold it against him forever, or you forgive him and let it go."

Kollin huffed. "I don't want to hold it against him forever, but it's only been a few months."

"You wanna know one of the most amazing things about Elijah?"

Kollin side-eyed Adam and wondered where the abrupt subject change was going to lead. "Uh, okay."

"After my mom came back, and I had all those issues, he never once held it against me. He told me the first day I came back that he forgave me. I will never forget standing in his office and hearing those words, wondering how he could mean them after everything I'd done to him and to you." Adam shrugged. "But he did. He never mentioned it again. For the next two years, every single fight we got in, I kept waiting for him to throw that back in my face as proof of how unreliable I was or what a shitty husband or father I was, and it never came."

"Sooo… your brilliant plan for helping me fix this is to point out how much better of a human being Eli is than me?"

Adam nudged Kollin's side. "No. My point is, I can't imagine how difficult that must've been for him. I'm not sure if I could've done it. It would've been on the tip of my tongue so many times, but I never heard the slightest bit of resentment from him. You know, to this day I've never thanked him for that." Adam sighed. "Part of me thinks if I point it out, he'll be reminded and use it against me in our next fight, but I know he wouldn't."

Kollin covered his face with his hands and groaned. "If you're not trying to make me feel bad, then I still don't get how this relates to me and Riley."

"Maybe it doesn't. But it popped in my head while we were talking, and I felt like I needed to confess my secret. Even though it's one I'm ashamed of."

Kollin's eyes widened, and he sat up and pointed at Adam. "Oh… you're good. You are *good*." Adam laughed and Kollin fell back onto the bed. "I get why he didn't tell me. And I tried to avoid the clusterfuck we had outside, but he kept pushing me. And he sounded so dejected, and I knew it was because of me, and I hated myself for making him sound like that—especially after opening up to me tonight. But I just kept thinking how he only did it because he was backed into a corner.

"If Tony hadn't shown up, we'd be in the basement right now doing God knows what. *That* is scary as fuck to me after hearing how that piece of shit treated him. Nobody deserves to be used like that, and certainly not Riley. How the fuck can anyone know Ri and not see how amazing he is?"

"Probably because Riley can't see the good in himself."

"That's my fucking point. It's mostly because of that idiot." Kollin's voice trailed off and he sighed. "I should've known."

Adam sat up and patted Kollin's knee. "I know it hurts right now, but I think in the end, this will be a good thing. No matter how much we know Riley's entitled to keep certain things to himself, if you two are serious about being in a relationship, you're better off being up front and honest about all your emotional baggage. You're just as guilty for keeping all of that pent-up anger to yourself as he is for not telling you about Tony."

"Ugh." Kollin covered his face with his hands. "I know."

"I know you do. That's what makes it so hard." Adam stood. "You good?"

"Good enough."

"You gonna sneak down to the basement tonight?"

Kollin laughed. "Not quite that good yet. Besides, I'm probably the last person he wants to see."

Adam started out of the room but paused at the doorway. He looked back at Kollin. "I wouldn't be so sure about that."


WITH TEARS streaming down his face, Riley pounded down the stairs. He flipped on the light, grabbed his duffel bag at the end of the bed, and began stuffing his clothes into it. He swiped some of the wetness off his cheeks and went into the bathroom to grab his toothbrush. When he came back out, Elijah stood at the bottom of the steps with a bottle of liquor in his hands.

"Care for a drink?"

Humiliated enough for one night, Riley tried to cover up the fact that he was crying. "No thank you."

No hiding that quake in his voice.

"Mind if I have one while you pack?"

Guilt flooded Riley. All Kollin had asked him to do was not run away again. Everything he'd said had been right, yet still Riley wanted to flee in the middle of the night, without a word. He shook his head and shoved his toiletry bag into the duffel. Then, understanding he wouldn't be leaving until Elijah had his say, he sat on the bed.

"I'm not going to lie, Riley," Elijah said. "This isn't really my thing."

"*This?*"

He took a swig of the amber-colored drink. "You know. Talking shit out. I'm more of a fix-it type guy."

"I've noticed," Riley muttered.

Elijah nodded. "Most people do."

"If I promise not to leave until morning, can we skip this, then?"

Elijah shook his head. "Ah, ah, ah. Afraid not. You're not getting me in trouble with Adam that easily."

"So? What? You drew the short straw and had to come find me while Adam's consoling Kollin?"

"Actually, I wanted to come down here." Elijah took another sip of his drink and eyed Riley the entire time. It was intimidating as hell.

"To scare the shit out of me? 'Cuz if so, job well done."

Elijah grinned. "Maybe a little. You hurt my kid."

Riley nodded. "I don't really need a reminder."

"So why'd you do it?"

"Do what?" Riley figured he was treading a thin line, but he half hoped he could piss Elijah off enough to get himself kicked out. Then he could blame his morning absence on Elijah instead of his own insecurities.

"That's fine. We can do this the slow and painful way, if you want. I got all night."

Riley sighed. "I didn't mean to hurt him. Okay? It's just… there's this part of my life that's so embarrassing, and I didn't really see a point in telling him. I never expected to see my ex again, and I never thought he would be so upset at me just for not mentioning it."

"Damn, son." Elijah set the bottle of liquor down on the nightstand. "The past always, always, *always* comes back to bite you in the ass, at some point. How could it not? It's part of who you are."

"Yeah. But it's a pretty shitty part of who I am."

"Doesn't matter," Elijah insisted. "If whatever happened tonight hadn't happened, would you be here today? I mean, assuming being here today with Kollin is where you want to be, doesn't that make it at least a little worth it?"

"Yeah. But I did some pretty terrible things."

"Yeah, but," Elijah mimicked, and Riley sort of wanted to punch him. "Kollin is, hands down, the greatest kid I know. You can't tell me you think he wouldn't have understood, wouldn't have had compassion for your situation."

Frustrated that Elijah wasn't listening to him, Riley shouted. "He shouldn't have to, though. That's my point."

"And why not? He chose you, Ri. And from what I hear, he practically bullied you into this relationship. He wanted you and everything that comes with you." Elijah pointed up the stairs. "That boy is not an idiot. He knew you were hiding something, and he wanted you anyway. I need you to understand that before I walk my ass back up all those steps. If you run out of here tonight and we never hear from you again, I need to be sure you understand that, regardless of whatever fight you two had tonight, Kollin wants you in his life—as a friend and as more than that."

"But why?" Riley stood and paced around the room. "It doesn't make any sense. I'm broken—physically and emotionally. There were plenty of guys at the club tonight who would've loved to dance with him, sleep with him, date him, whatever. And then he wouldn't have to deal with my bullshit drama."

"Doesn't matter why," Elijah insisted. "What matters is that you know."

Riley sighed and flopped back on the bed. "Yeah, I guess I know," he mumbled.

"What was that?" Elijah asked as he cupped his ear.

Riley rolled his eyes and then looked directly at Elijah. "I said I know that Kollin wants me in his life."

"Good." Elijah picked up his bottle of liquor. "So we're both in agreement that if I wake up in the morning and your ass is gone, you will never ever grace the steps of my house again?"

Riley felt as if every ounce of energy in his body drained right out, and he cast his eyes toward the floor. "Yes, sir," he said quietly.

Elijah turned back toward the stairs and paused at the bottom to flip off the light switch. "For what it's worth, I hope to see you for breakfast. And not just because it'll break Kollin's heart if you're gone."

Riley sighed. He wanted to scream and shout and throw things, but it was way too late. Lizzie had slept through all the drama so far— he hoped at least—and he had no intention of waking her up. Instead he threw his packed duffle bag on the floor, slipped off his shoes, and climbed into bed, fully clothed. It was too hot for a blanket, but he covered up with his sheet and tucked one arm behind his head.

He lay in bed, his head buzzing, going over every mistake and bad decision he'd made in the past ten years. Maybe he should've taken Elijah up on the offer of a drink. Lost in his demons, he didn't register that the basement door opened or clicked shut, but he did hear the footsteps padding downstairs. Assuming Adam had decided to take his turn with him, Riley closed his eyes and feigned sleep.

Instead of the retreating footsteps he expected to hear, though, he felt the edge of the bed dip down. He cracked one eye open and was shocked to see Kollin squeezing into bed next to him. He lay on top of the sheet and wrestled with the blanket. Once he had the covers where he wanted, Kollin settled down, gently grabbed Riley's hand, and laced their fingers together.

"I wish I'd known," he whispered. "I would've done something. I would've come to get you."

"Koll—"

"Shh…," Kollin hushed him. "Can we please do this in the morning? After sleep. And after food."

Riley squeezed Kollin's hand and nodded. "Can I just say I'm sorry?"

Kollin nodded and then nestled his head closer into Riley's neck. "Me too."

# CHAPTER 14

WHEN RILEY woke the following morning, Kollin was no longer in bed. He grabbed the alarm clock that had magically appeared one weekend and pulled it in front of him. The bright red numbers read 10:07. He slammed the clock back down and rubbed his eyes, which were crusty from all the crying he'd done the night before. He also had a killer headache that felt too much like a hangover for his liking.

No noise floated down the steps, which was strange. Saturday morning meant Saturday-morning brunch, which usually meant enough ruckus to wake the dead. He groaned as he sat up and tilted his head to the left and then the right to release the tension in his neck with a pop on each side. He got out of bed, brushed his teeth, and headed up the stairs. He paused at the top and listened for sounds coming from the kitchen, but he heard none, so he took the plunge and opened the door.

Kollin sat at the kitchen table, a cup of coffee and his computer in front of him. A slow smile spread across his lips when he saw Riley, and he sat up a little straighter.

"Morning." Kollin's voice was hoarse, and Riley wondered how long he'd been awake.

"Hey." Riley looked around the kitchen. "Where is everyone?"

Kollin grabbed a slip of paper Riley hadn't noticed and held it up. "Apparently no one felt like making brunch this morning, so the three of them went out. We're to text them if we want them to bring us something back."

"Oh." Riley scratched his head. "I thought missing Saturday brunch was like committing a felony."

Kollin slammed the paper back onto the table. "So did I. But don't worry. They won't come back until they hear from us. You know, to make sure we don't go hungry." Kollin rolled his eyes.

"Wait." Riley flopped down in a chair next to Kollin. "My brain isn't working yet. They're just giving us time alone?"

"Looks like it." Kollin pushed his chair back and got up to walk over to the coffee pot. "Just cream. Right?"

"Uh, yeah. Thanks," Riley said, but he felt a little dumb. He could've made his own coffee.

Kollin set the coffee cup in front of Riley and nudged his knee as he sat down. "You're welcome."

"I'm sorry your family felt like they had to run off on my account."

"Don't be." Kollin grinned. "Lizzie is probably eating this up. I can't tell you how many times she's begged for us to just go out for brunch. I think half the reason Adam and Eli insist on us fixing it ourselves is to annoy her."

"I don't know if that's brilliant or mean."

Kollin shrugged. "Both, probably. You want me to ask them to get us something to eat?"

Riley shook his head. "I'll just make some toast or something. Or it's so late now, I'll just find something for lunch."

Kollin closed his laptop. With his ankles and arms crossed, he offered Riley a sad smile. "I'm sorry I exploded on you like that last night."

Riley waved him off. "Don't be. It's—"

"It's not fine, Ri. My feelings were valid, but I should've told you in a civilized way. For that, I'm sorry."

Riley nodded. "Can we just call it even, and I forgive you?"

"Yeah, but… can we get everything out, first?" Kollin ran a hand through his hair, tugged on the ends, and then leaned forward in his seat and jiggled his foot.

Riley leaned forward and steadied Kollin's knee. "Don't be nervous. I'm not gonna run away. Promise."

Kollin's eyes met his, and he grinned sheepishly. "Okay." He sat back in his seat again. "Can we start from the quasi beginning?"

"Sure."

"Why didn't you call us for help? Even if I don't agree with it, I think I understand why you cut off communication… at first. But why didn't you call when you got in trouble? You know we would've been there in a heartbeat."

Riley shook his head. "There's no way. I'd just gotten my top surgery, and every bit of confidence that came with my new look left after the first few guys rejected me because I didn't have a dick. Tony, though, the first time we were together, he told me how hot it was that I looked like a man but still had a pussy. I hated that he called it that, by the way. I know I'm not huge, but in my mind, what I have down there is a dick. And I hated that he only thought I *looked* like a man. I *am* a man."

"Damn straight, you are," Kollin said, and he grinned.

Riley leaned farther forward. Now that he was telling Kollin everything, he wanted to be sure Kollin understood. "He was the first person who seemed to accept me just like I was. Not only did he accept me, but he was also turned on by me. I figured pussy was just a word, and I was reading way too much into everything he said. I mean, someone like me... I can't be too picky. Right?" Riley shook his head and sat back. "But after a while, after enough of his comments, I started thinking I'd never be good enough for anyone else.

"And you know, I'm still not sure he wanted to intentionally hurt me. You saw how clueless he was last night. He thought he was doing me a favor, bestowing me with the gift of his presence and lousy sex. And I believed it all, at the time. Even after I disappeared from his life, it took me a long time to understand that he slowly poisoned me—my thoughts, my emotions, even my body."

Kollin leaned forward and rested both of his hands on Riley's knees. "Why didn't you call me?"

Riley shifted away. Kollin's touch made everything harder to confess. "Don't you see? I'd left you hanging in the wind. For all I knew, you hated me at that point. I couldn't come crawling back as a bigger failure than I was when I left. Hell. If it hadn't been for the perfect timing of this job and needing a second reference, I don't know if I ever would've. Even after I pulled myself together, I never felt like I was good enough to make up for ditching you like that."

"Well, good thing we've already forgiven each other for that debacle." Kollin's tone held a hint of sarcasm to lighten the mood, and Riley had never been more grateful. They sat in silence for a while as Kollin apparently chewed over everything Riley had just said, and Riley gave him the time and peace to do so. After the night before, he'd learned his lesson. "You're a drug addict?" Kollin suddenly asked.

Riley winced but nodded. Thinking about his drug addiction made him feel weak and pathetic, but at the same time, if Greg hadn't recognized the symptoms in Riley, he may've never pulled Riley away from Tony. If Riley had stayed with Tony—and there was no doubt in his mind that he never would've had the guts to leave—Riley feared where his depression would've taken him.

"At first he just offered me some pot, which, since I'm being honest, I still smoke from time to time if I don't have to work for a few days. But never more than a few hits to relax, and I swear I haven't touched it since I've been back in town."

Riley spared a glance at Kollin, who grinned and rolled his eyes. "If you think I haven't smoked a little weed, you're mistaken. It's not my thing, but I don't have anything against it." Kollin laughed. "Well, aside from the fact that it's illegal."

Riley smirked. "Minor detail. Well, it didn't stop there. One night he gave me some pills. He said they would make me feel good all the time. And they did. I dunno, Koll. I'd rather not go into a lot of the details, but it grew from there. I didn't mess much with acid, but I liked mushrooms when we could get them. Mostly, though, I was addicted to the pills. I functioned better on them than without them, after a while. But see, prescription meds are expensive on the street. When I couldn't afford them, I was a real pain in the ass, and I started messing up at work."

"And that's when Greg noticed?"

Riley let out a long sigh. Fuck. Confessing his past sins was hard. "Sort of. I dropped a ton of weight pretty quickly. The pills… it's hard to eat on them. I could go an entire weekend and eat nothing but a sub. Everything I ate made me sick to my stomach. And then, whenever Tony told me to stay home from work, I obeyed. Between the weight loss, my attitude, and the calling in, it raised a red flag with Greg.

"He already knew my situation, and I'm lucky as hell he wanted to help me out, or who knows what would've happened to me. He pulled me aside one day, told me he knew how hard it was to go through everything I had to deal with, but that if I didn't quit the drugs, he'd have to let me go. He reminded me of everything I'd been working for and what I had to lose. He should've fired me on the spot. Instead he stayed with me during the first few days. And when he found out about Tony, he got me a new phone and found me a new place to live."

"Ri...." Kollin grabbed Riley's chair to pull them closer together. He wrapped his arms around Riley's neck and bumped their foreheads together, which forced Riley to look at him. "Remind me to buy him a fuckawesome muffin basket. Okay?"

Riley nodded.

"I'm not even shitting you. The biggest one there is. With the fancy muffins that have the crumbly shit on top."

Riley laughed. "I don't think he likes muffins."

Kollin's mouth dropped open. "Who the hell doesn't like muffins?"

Riley shrugged, which was difficult, considering the way Kollin was wrapped around him.

"You know I'm talking about muffins so I don't think about what could've happened to you. Right?" Kollin's voice broke. "Where you'd be right now if it weren't for him?"

Riley looked up at Kollin and saw the raw emotion shining through Kollin's tears. "I'm sorry, Koll."

Kollin shook his head and sat back in his chair again, but he left their legs tangled together. "I'll shut up about the damn muffins now. Finish your story.... Greg stayed with you and got you sober."

"Oh God." Riley buried his head in his hands. "It's the worst feeling in the world, coming off those things. Your entire body aches. Your mind tells you that you can't function without them, that you need them. And every second is consumed with the thought that if you just eat one more pill, it'll all go away. Your mind lies to you and tells you it'll be easier the next time if you just take one now, and you hurt so much...."

Kollin growled. "Two baskets. Two huge baskets. Of beer. Does he like beer?"

Riley grinned and looked up from his hands. "Yeah. He likes beer."

"I'm sorry. I'm an idiot." Kollin pulled at his hair. "I wanted to hear all of this, and now I don't know what to say."

"Don't say anything." Riley clutched Kollin's knee between his own and squeezed. "You were right. You're my best friend, and I needed you to know. I might've told you sooner if we hadn't started dating. Maybe." Riley shook his head. "Probably not. Seeing Tony was never on my to-do list, ever again, so I didn't think it was a big deal."

"So you have no idea how he took the breakup, for lack of a better word?"

Riley shook his head. "I basically ghosted him. Something I should probably be ashamed of, but after everything he did to me, I'm not. For all I know, he's still dating that girl."

Silence filled the kitchen while Kollin processed again. Finally he met Riley's eyes. "You know this doesn't change how I feel about you?"

Riley sucked in a long, slow breath and then let it out just as slowly. "I do now."

Kollin grinned. "Good. Now we just have to figure out how to move forward. I mean"—Kollin's face fell—"do you still want to move forward with me?"

"Yes," Riley said immediately. "You're nothing like Tony, and I know that. Clearly I have some self-esteem damage from him. Although to be fair, I've nearly always had that, thanks to my dysmorphia. But you've never once hidden me, and when we're together, you make sure to take care of me… you know, physically."

Kollin waggled his eyes. "Yeah I do." He grabbed Riley's hand. "I realize this is none of my business, so feel free to tell me to fuck off, but does Dr. Maggie know about all this?"

Riley slouched into the seat. "Yes. It's why she wants me to hold off on bottom surgery. She doesn't think I've dealt with my residual anger properly. She wants me emotionally healthy before surgery, instead of relying on the surgery to fix my issues for me." Midway through Riley's speech, he'd pitched his voice to mimic Dr. Maggie's. He appreciated everything she was doing for him, for free no less, but it was hard not to hold a little resentment toward her for slowing up his plans—even if she did have a valid point.

"So…." Kollin paused and wiggled the skin on Riley's fourth knuckle while he thought. "Should we hold off doing anything physical until after your surgery?"

"Oh God. Please no." Riley shook his head vehemently. "I mean, if you don't mind what I have now, we don't have to wait. Maggie actually suggested that since I'm with someone I trust, taking our relationship a step or two further might help, since I've never orgasmed with anyone else."

"Wait. What?" Kollin's eyes widened. "You've never had an orgasm?"

Riley jerked his hand back and buried his head again. "Not with a guy. Although I guess I did that time with you, but it wasn't technically sex, since all of our clothes were on."

"So she wants me to see how you like it?" Kollin's voice pitched high, and he bounced his foot up and down again.

"No. I mean, she didn't exactly say it like that." Riley backpedaled. "I told her how worried I am about taking my clothes off in front of you. She said I should trust you to be honest and kind about my body the same way I trust you to be honest and kind about any other aspect of my life. And—" Riley stopped. Judging by the tone of Kollin's voice, that moment didn't seem like the best time to admit everything he and Dr. Maggie had talked about. "Well, anyway. I might've extrapolated a bit. We talk about a lot of stuff. Sometimes it blends together."

"Wait." Kollin held up his hand. "What were you going to say just now? You started and then stopped."

Riley winced. "Nothing. It was nothing."

"Are you sure? We just established that the more I know, the more I can help. I mean, hell. For weeks I've been swimming in a shark tank with a mangled, bloody leg and the lights off, except I had no idea, Ri."

Riley huffed. "Fine. But don't blame me if you hear more than you want to."

Kollin held up two fingers. "Scout's honor."

"Yeah right. They never would've let you in Scouts. Girl Scouts, maybe."

Kollin shrugged. "I'd've rocked the Brownie skirt with pride."

"You probably would have."

Kollin nudged his knee. "Stop stalling. Lay it on me."

Riley took a deep breath. "There are lots of different ways to get bottom surgery. I've never been willing to disfigure myself to get a penis, so that's one option gone, but that still leaves me with some decisions to make. If I want a hysterectomy, if I want to close up the vagina completely, if I want testicle implants. I don't have to do it all at once, but some of them can be done together. Maggie didn't tell me to, but she suggested that since I'm in a trusting and committed relationship, and that if we were both on board for taking that step, that maybe having vaginal intercourse before I made a decision one way or another wouldn't be the worst idea in the world."

Riley peeked up at Kollin, who looked somewhat dumbfounded. "That's a lot of, that's a lot of… something right there."

"You're freaking out."

Kollin shook his head. "Nope. No. I'm not. I'm just thinking. What if I'm horrible, and you make the wrong decision, and it's all my fault?"

Riley stared at Kollin. "How will I know you're horrible? Or that I've made the wrong decision?"

Kollin glared right back. "Not the point, Ri."

"Well, it's obviously up to you." Riley fiddled with the bracelet on his wrist. "We haven't even really talked about sex, at all, so I don't know if you like to top or bottom. If you do top, you might not even be willing to do it in my vagina, which would be totally understandable, of course."

"Whoa, whoa, whoa." Kollin held up his hands. "We're doing this now? I figured we'd just go for third base or something and work our way up."

Riley shrugged. "We're already uncomfortable now. Might as well get it over with."

Kollin sighed. He looked more uncomfortable than Riley felt. "I'm not… so sure… that I feel comfortable being a deciding factor in what parts you do and don't keep." Riley opened his mouth, but Kollin cut him off and continued. "Reason being, my decision, my desire, to be with you is not dependent on what you look like down there. And even though I adore you and I can see this going white-picket-fence amazing, we've only been dating a few weeks. And for a big chunk of that time, you were actively trying to avoid touching me. Last night, when I called you my boyfriend, I was terrified you would rabbit away on the spot." Kollin sighed. "I'm so fucking glad we're having this conversation, and I'm not saying no, but I think it'll be better for both of us if we table the rest of this discussion for now. Can we do that?"

Riley nodded. Kollin had a point. He hadn't meant to spill the beans like that or make it sound like Kollin was responsible for his decision, but he understood that's how it sounded. Riley's explanation would keep, though. Kollin deserved time to process everything.

"What do you say I text Adam and let them know we're ready for them to come back? I'll ask them to bring us a couple of sandwiches?"

At the mention of food, Riley's stomach grumbled. "Sounds perfect. Just don't order me that nasty-ass bourbon chicken sub you like so much."

"Tell you what. We can have whatever the fuck kind of sandwiches you want from now until we figure this shit out. Deal?"

Riley grinned. "Deal."

"Seal it with a kiss?"

Riley sighed and exaggerated his eye roll, which made Kollin laugh. "If you insist."

Kollin cupped the side of Riley's face. "I really, really do."

"Good." Riley stood and smacked a kiss on Kollin's forehead. "Now order me a turkey on rye with no mayo while I go change."

# CHAPTER 15

"WHO ELSE wants turkey bacon?" Eli shouted over the general commotion in the kitchen.

"Uh… once again, no one but you eats that shit," Kollin said as he mixed pancake batter.

"Yeah, Dad. I dunno how you eat that shit."

Lizzie didn't even flinch when Adam and Elijah both yelled, "Language."

"Kollin gets to cuss," Lizzie whined, but she continued to cut the fruit in front of her and dump it into a large bowl.

"Kollin is an adult," Adam said and pulled a carton of eggs out of the fridge.

Apparently when Adam told Kollin Saturday-morning brunch was canceled, he meant it was postponed. Until Sunday. Which Riley found out when the clanging of pots and pans woke him early that morning.

Not that Riley minded. He actually loved the ritual and had quickly discovered that each person had a specific task, no matter what was on the menu. Lizzie nearly always cut up fruit. Kollin made the pancakes or waffles. Elijah was in charge of the breakfast meat, and Adam handled the eggs. The feeling of family and love that settled in the kitchen every Saturday was almost unbearable sometimes.

From day one they'd all taken every opportunity to make Riley feel welcome, but he still felt like an outsider when he sat there watching everyone work. The only job he'd claimed as his own was setting the table, and that took all of fifteen seconds. He once persuaded them to let him wash the dishes, but since they normally rinsed and stuck everything in the dishwasher as they cooked, he just ended up in the way.

Riley watched Elijah lean into Adam and whisper something in his ear that made Adam's cheeks turn pink. It was almost sickening how perfect their family was.

"Hey, Ri," Kollin said. "You want to make us a couple of sandwiches so we can head out as soon as breakfast is over?"

"Sure," Riley agreed quickly, grateful for the busy work.

Kollin winked. "Whatever kind you want to make is fine with me."

After spending most of the day before doing their own things, which for Riley equaled rotating between watching TV and lifting weights, Kollin suggested they spend Sunday afternoon hiking. Riley jumped at the chance to get out of the house and to spend time with Kollin doing something familiar.

"Where are you going?" Elijah asked.

Kollin shrugged. "I thought maybe we'd go to Umstead Park, since they have so many different trails."

"Ooh," Lizzie squealed. "Can I go too?"

"No," Kollin said. "And don't even try to pull 'the face' on me. I taught you that, and it won't work."

"But *why* can't I go?" Lizzie whined.

"Because Riley and I want to be alone. One with nature and all that shi—crap."

"All you two ever do is be alone, anymore," Lizzie said. She stuck out her bottom lip and crossed her arms. "You haven't done anything with me in forever."

Kollin frowned and looked at Lizzie. "I'm sorry, Liz. You're right." He placed his spatula down and leaned against the counter next to her. "I really need to do this with just Riley today, but why don't you and I do something special tomorrow night? Just the two of us."

"Really?" Lizzie practically squealed. "But can't Riley come too?"

Kollin smacked a loud kiss on the side of her face and returned to his pancake making. "That's up to you and him, I guess."

Warmth spread through Riley's chest. It felt nice to be included, to have people *want* him to be where they were. "I think I can drag myself away from my lonely hotel room if Her Highness requests my presence."

"Riiiiiley, don't call me that," Lizzie complained, but the bashful grin on her face gave away how pleased she was with his attention.

While the smell of sizzling bacon filled the air, Riley slapped their sandwiches together. He decided to go with simple peanut butter and jelly so they didn't need to worry about how to keep them cold. Every so often the butterflies in his stomach reminded him how it would feel if Kollin decided to reject him after all. But from the way Kollin kept finding reasons to drag his hand across Riley's ass or peek at him from the corner of his eye with a sly smile on his face, Riley felt optimistic about their outing.

Everyone lingered over breakfast, mostly discussing the antics at the center during the week. Elijah asked Riley how he felt the crew was progressing at Home for Hope, and Riley marveled at how Elijah was able to so effortlessly act as if he hadn't all but threatened Riley two nights before. He supposed, since he hadn't taken off, Elijah had no issues with him—though that hadn't stopped Riley from avoiding Elijah at all costs the day before.

By the time they got on the road, it was just after eleven o'clock—damn near making it the hottest part of the day by the time they stood in front of the trail map. They decided to hike one of the shorter trails and save something more challenging for later on in the evening when the sun wasn't quite so unforgiving. Riley considered Kollin and himself to be in pretty good shape, but he questioned that assumption an hour later as they each gulped down a bottle of water.

"Hoooo-lyshit," Kollin said and trudged toward the trees. "We gotta find somewhere out of the blazing sun."

"When did Umstead relocate to the pits of Hell?" Riley panted and fell onto a shady patch on the ground. He took off his hat and covered his face as he lay back. "It's gotta be at least a hundred degrees today. What the hell were we thinking?"

A warm finger grazed across the bottom of Riley's stomach. He jumped at first but settled quickly. "We were thinking you'd look sexy as hell sprawled all over the ground and finally showing some skin."

Riley laughed and shook his head. He took the hat off his face to look at Kollin. "I still can't believe you think of me like that."

Kollin rolled onto his side and kissed Riley's cheek. "Well, believe it, baby. I'm in for the long haul."

Riley shook his head. "No. I don't mean like that. I mean, sometimes I mean it like that, but…." Riley looked at Kollin. His face was relaxed and happy, and he knew what he was about to admit would delight Kollin no end. Unrequited romances were right up his alley. "I can't believe I'm about to tell you this."

"Oh?" Kollin's face lit up. "Tell me, tell me, tell me."

"Please don't make a big deal about this."

Kollin held up his hand and stuck out his pinky. "Pinky swear."

They linked fingers and twisted, but instead of letting go, he rested their joined hands on Riley's stomach. Nervousness fluttered through Riley, and he glanced around, but no one else was in sight.

Riley took a deep breath. "When we were younger... I had a wee little bit of a crush on you."

"You what?" Kollin's voice rose several octaves as he squealed out the last word. His smile was as wide as Riley had ever seen it, and his eyes twinkled. Oh yeah. Totally worth the humiliation.

"Maybe it was a little more than a wee bit of a crush." Riley covered his eyes with his free arm. "I was pretty much full-on in love with you. That's why I always hung around you. I wasn't quite so cynical back then. I had visions of going on T, getting surgery, and then suddenly you'd fall in love with me, and we could be together."

"Shut. The front. Door." Kollin could not have sounded more shocked.

"I'm so serious." Riley peered out at Kollin, who was still grinning. "God. I was so stupid. Then all the stuff with your parents happened, and it seemed shitty to tell you I had a crush on you. And anyway, my parents were so against me doing anything to become a male, it never would've happened."

"Riley Meadows." Kollin's voice was so loud he scared one of the animals in the woods. Riley watched the squirrel scuttle up a nearby tree while Kollin continued to gape at him. "I cannot believe you never told me. What the hell, dude?"

"Come on, Koll." Riley looked away. "Can you really see that conversation going over well? You didn't think of me like that, at all, back then. All you did was talk about how much you wanted to suck dick, and I sure as hell couldn't help you out there."

Kollin winced. "Well, shit. A minute ago, I thought the crush was cute, but now I'm realizing what a total ass I was. Why in the world did you even have a crush on me when I was such a jerk?"

Riley shrugged. "I'm telling you, man, I had it all worked out in my head. Someone could've written a book about our story. It was *that* heartbreakingly perfect. Besides, you're the best person I know. You may have been preoccupied with things every guy your age was, at that time, but when you weren't, all you ever wanted to do was help other people. Even back then, you were the only one at HOPE who took time to befriend the only trans kid there. How could I not crush hard on you?"

"I cannot even believe this." Kollin laughed. "It's almost more surprising than everything you told me last night. Even if someone had asked me, I never would've guessed you liked me back then." He leaned over and kissed Riley again, this time slowly, deeply, and with intention. "I am so sorry you had to listen to me complain about so much stupid shit back then," he said without moving away, so their lips touched with each of Kollin's words.

Kollin kissed him again. When he finally pulled away, Riley couldn't stop the smile from spreading on his face. Better yet, he didn't want to. "Maybe my fairy-tale ending can still come true."

Kollin bit his bottom lip. "Maybe so."

They lay in silence for a while, and Riley marveled again over the fact that Kollin had somehow become interested in him. Following Elijah's advice Riley decided not to question it anymore. He'd never understand, and if he tried to force himself to, he'd only make himself miserable.

After a while Kollin said, "Should I be worried about you doing drugs again?"

Riley closed his eyes and took a deep breath. He let the sounds and smells of summer soothe him as he searched for an honest answer.

"It's been a while. I don't crave them or anything. But I don't know what will happen if I need meds after surgery." His voice dropped. "You don't even realize you're addicted until it's too late."

"What about the drugs that weren't pills?"

Riley shook his head. "No. There's no part of me that wants to take anything like that again—aside from the occasional bowl anyway."

"You don't worry about getting addicted to weed?"

This time Riley snorted. "You can't get addicted to weed."

"Umm. Every DARE officer I know says differently." Kollin grinned.

Riley laughed. "Know a lot of DARE officers, do you?"

"Oh yeah. I'm on a first-name basis with most of them. Something about those hats just gets me going. Really does it for me." Kollin propped himself up on one elbow to look at Riley. "Maybe we can see if we can find one for you."

Riley ignored him. "I get that you feel so good when you're on it, you never want to stop, but it's not like I get the shakes or something." He nudged Kollin's foot. "I thought you smoked before. Shouldn't you know this?"

"What you did sounded like it was a little more serious than the occasional joint I had." Kollin shrugged. "I'm so old now, my partying days are done, so I guess I'll never know unless I ask the master."

Riley laughed. "Oh my gosh. You're barely twenty, first of all. And second of all, smoking weed every now and then is hardly considered doing drugs. It's safer than drinking."

"Oh really? Wanna take out a billboard to spread your message to the masses?"

Riley's stomach soured. Was he making himself sound like some kind of pot pusher? "I'm not saying you should start smoking all the time. I mean, if it's a big deal to you, I won't ever do it again."

"Of course it's not a big deal. I'm just teasing. I thought you knew that."

"Yeah. I did." Riley hesitated. "Until I didn't, anyway. Doesn't matter. It's all in the past."

Kollin fell quiet again, so Riley closed his eyes.

"Did you have any help?" Kollin asked. "I know you said Greg stayed with you at first, but what about after that? How did you deal with the rest of the shit Tony did to you?"

Riley sighed. He hadn't expected to talk about it on their outing, but he'd promised himself he'd be honest. "Not really. I have a therapist back in Boone, but I just told him what I needed to get on T and then sign off for top surgery. Dr. Maggie already knew me, though. She didn't buy my bullshit for a minute."

"Fuck," Kollin whispered. "Who took care of you after the first surgery?"

"No one, really. But it's not a bad surgery." Kollin started to interrupt, but Riley cut him off. "I swear, Kollin. I didn't really need anything but a week off from work. Greg knew what was going on, so he brought me Subway that night and gave me easy jobs for a while, once I was back on-site."

Kollin fell onto his back and stared into the trees. "I keep thinking your past can't get any worse, and then I ask another question and you prove me wrong. Is there anything else I should know?"

Riley thought about Kollin's question for a moment. "I don't think so."

"Thank fuck." Kollin rolled over to his side and rested his head on his hand. He grabbed Riley's hand again. "What do we need to do now?"

"Well…." Riley took a deep breath and looked into Kollin's eyes. "I spent a lot of time yesterday thinking about everything, and maybe it wouldn't be a bad idea to reach out to my parents."

"Yeah? That's great, Riley. I hope, no matter what happens with them, you can find some peace there."

Riley nodded. "I'm usually too busy falling apart to be the one who has to have his shit together. That's the goal. I was wondering—hoping, I guess—that maybe you'd go with me. If they slam the door in my face, I don't want to be alone."

"Of course." Kollin didn't hesitate. "Whatever you need."

A sigh of relief escaped. "Thank you. Are you sure, though? I can't guarantee I'm not gonna end up a hot mess."

"Not gonna lie. I'm terrified I'm going to fuck something up and end up hurting you somehow. But I'll do my best to hold you together. I don't want you to do this alone."

"If it'll make you uncomfortable—"

"No," Kollin said, his voice louder than he probably intended. "That's not what I meant at all."

"Okay. I'll mention it to Maggie on Tuesday. See what she thinks we should do, and go from there." Riley picked up a stray leaf and twirled it between his fingers.

"You know what I was thinking?" Kollin asked.

Riley turned to look at Kollin. "What's that?"

"This might be a little off-topic, but when you mentioned Maggie, it reminded me of a new kid at the center who's trans. What do you think about talking to him sometime? Might be good for both of you."

Riley looked back into the trees. He'd heard Adam mention the kid before, and he'd been curious. "Yeah, maybe. Dr. Maggie told me to join a trans group—even if it was an online one. She thinks I should talk to more people like me, so I don't feel like an outcast. I've been putting it off. Kept hoping everything going on between us…. I thought maybe that would be enough. *Obviously* I was wrong about that. Talking to him would be a good first step, I guess."

"I think that's a great idea. You know how much I care for you and want to help, but I don't know exactly what you're going through." Kollin wiggled Riley's hand in his own. "Talking to people who are going through similar issues.... I bet it's going to make a world of difference just to not feel alone anymore."

Riley grunted. "That's what Dr. Maggie said."

Kollin raised Riley's arm in the air and scooted under it to lie back on Riley's chest.

"Can I ask you something now?" Riley waited for Kollin to nod. "Is there ever a time Lizzie doesn't whine when she doesn't get her way?"

Kollin laughed. "Uh, no. I don't know if that came from her stint in foster care or if her parents caved every time she pouted or if it's typical of twelve-year-old girls. But it's annoying as hell."

Riley snuggled Kollin in closer and closed his eyes. No one had ever used him as the big spoon, and he wanted to memorize the feeling. He knew it was stupid to put so much importance into something so insignificant, but in his mind, being the big spoon equated to being a man.

"I can't believe she almost walked in on us the other week," Riley said. "I wanted to crawl into a hole and die."

"She's never met any of my other boyfriends." Kollin played with a patch of exposed skin on Riley's stomach. "She just doesn't know how to act. But then she's boy crazy herself, so.... I heard Adam tell Eli they should let her invite some boy she likes over to the house. Eli is totally against her even thinking about a boy, but Adam doesn't want her to sneak around."

"Oh geez." Riley rolled his eyes. "I can imagine how well Elijah took that."

Kollin huffed. "Yeah. He wasn't exactly on board with that plan. But it's in his head now. So whenever she finally asks to go out with someone, more than likely Eli will be the one to suggest he come to the house."

Riley laughed. "Oh my gosh. Adam's some kind of evil genius."

Kollin agreed. "He knows how to work Eli. I've never seen him take advantage before, though."

"Elijah is so... unique."

"What do you mean?" Kollin asked as he laughed.

"I've just never met anyone like him. There's that old adage about hurting the ones you love most. But Elijah's completely the opposite.

His entire being shifts when he's home with you guys. He's definitely more relaxed and friendly at the center than anywhere else I've seen him, which, granted, isn't much, but at home…? I dunno. It's pretty cool. Instead of expending his energy to be nice to the people who don't really matter, he saves the best bits of himself for you guys."

Kollin lifted his head to look at Riley with a wide smile on his face. Then he lightly kissed the bottom of Riley's chin. "I love that you see that. It's a really beautiful sentiment."

"Not that Adam isn't amazing too."

Kollin snorted. "Obviously. Adam's a fucking saint. I don't know how he puts up with the shit he does every day and still comes home with a smile on his face almost every night."

"Oh, hey. Whatever happened with his birth mom?" Riley asked. He felt a twinge of guilt for not asking sooner.

"He hasn't heard from her since. Good riddance." Kollin's tone was bitter, and Riley couldn't blame him. Kollin had been devastated when Adam took off when his birth mother deceived him in a lame effort to get her hands on some money.

Riley had stopped answering Kollin's calls around the same time, but he'd read some of the e-mails. The twinge of guilt magnified, and Riley shoved it away. They'd agreed to put all of that behind them.

Kollin continued. "It took Adam a while to really get over everything that happened. I'll cheerfully tie her to a tree and then start a fire around it if I ever see her face again."

Riley blinked. "That was oddly specific. Remind me to never piss you off."

"You'll do well to remember that," Kollin teased.

"I know we're over this, but I'm sorry I wasn't around longer for you, back then. I was such a mess that it seemed like the best thing for everyone, at the time."

"I want to say you did the right thing, but you fucking didn't." Kollin poked him in the stomach. "You should've told me what was going on. I would've still been there for you too."

"I didn't want to drag you back down, though. Besides, if I'd done that, we might not have ended up right here." Riley squeezed Kollin. "And I kind of like right here."

Kollin ghosted his hand along the bottom of Riley's shirt and touched his skin from one hip to the other. "Speaking of… we have one last thing to talk about."

Riley's heart fluttered. "Mmm… and what's that?"

"When do I get to see you with your shirt off? And when do we get to do all this exploring you were talking about yesterday?" He slipped his hand under Riley's shirt to graze his palm over Riley's toned stomach. Riley shivered. "I'm seriously tired of jacking off in the shower every morning."

Riley looked around, but they were deep enough in the woods that no one had even come near them while they lay there chatting. Quickly, before he could talk himself out of it, Riley shimmied out from beneath Kollin, sat up, and quickly grabbed the back of his shirt to pull it over his head. He ignored the urge to ball the shirt up in front of his chest and threw it to the side instead. Kollin, in all of his Kollin-ness, eyed Riley's chest with a small grin.

"I didn't exactly mean you had to strip here in the middle of the woods." He sat up and placed his hand on Riley's stomach. Riley fought not to tense his abs to make them look more six-pack-ish and less feminine. "I had no idea you were hiding anything this good under there. I'm embarrassed to take my shirt off now."

Riley laughed. Thank fuck Kollin always knew how to put him at ease. "You're crazy. You don't have an ounce of fat on you."

"Dude—" Kollin trailed his fingers up and down Riley's stomach. "There's none on you either. All I feel is muscle."

Riley looked away. "I'm working on it. My hips are still kind of round and doughy. I want a V."

"Holy geez. Now I'm seriously never getting naked in front of you. I'm a fucking twig compared to you." Before Riley could respond, Kollin trailed his hand up to Riley's chest and lightly fingered each of his scars. "You can hardly see these. And you got a tattoo. You never told me."

Riley shrugged. The scars were always the first thing he saw when he looked in the mirror. When he compared what they currently looked like to a picture taken just a few weeks after his surgery, Riley could see the improvement. They'd gotten smaller and healed over well. They weren't bright pink, but instead an unobtrusive dark reddish brown. But without the side-by-side comparison, he usually only noticed a screaming, jagged reminder of everything his body wasn't. The tattoo had been a desperate attempt to draw his—and everyone else's—attention away from the scars.

"Seemed like the thing to do at the time," Riley said as Kollin traced the edge of a tiger's paw. "Hurt like a bitch."

"It's pretty, but I think I like these better." Kollin trailed his finger back down to the scars. "They're proof of how tough you are."

Riley laughed and shook his head. "Almost every trans guy out there has scars like these. Doesn't make me tough. Just means I'm going through the motions."

Kollin growled. Then, shocking the hell out of him, Kollin swung one leg over Riley to straddle his lap. He forced Riley to look into his face. "I don't want to hear you say anything like that again. You hear me? Stop thinking like that right now."

"Koll—"

"I mean it, Ri. You must know the statistics. Probably better than I do. Not everyone makes it this far. And I'd bet a lot of the ones who do don't do it alone like you did." He slid both hands down Riley's chest and ran his thumbs over each scar. "This is strength to me. And determination. And pure fucking willpower to be who you are. To be your true self. Other people may look at the muscles in your arms or your defined chest or even your washboard abs and see those things. But this is where I see all of your best qualities." Kollin leaned in and kissed Riley. Kollin groaned, and Riley sensed he was holding back even as his teeth tugged on Riley's lip ring. Finally Kollin pulled back and rested his forehead against Riley's.

Emotions Riley couldn't identify consumed him, and he fought back tears as he wrapped his arms around Kollin's waist and tugged him closer. No one had ever seen him the way Kollin did.

"And you wonder why I had a thing for you back then," Riley said, his voice thick.

Kollin laughed. "I didn't spout poetic shit like that back then."

"Poetic *shit*, huh? You had to go and ruin it." Riley pulled away to look at Kollin again. "You've always made me see things differently. It's good for me."

Kollin kissed the tip of Riley's nose. "I'm glad if it means you're seeing yourself more clearly. Because the way you normally view yourself is flawed."

Riley rolled his eyes but didn't protest. "About the other thing you mentioned…. I don't know if it's better to let things happen naturally or to plan something. I'm scared if we try to just go with the flow, I'm going to freak out, and that won't be fair to you. But if we plan a night ahead of time with the intention of you seeing me completely naked, I'm going to be a nervous wreck."

Kollin nodded. He had a slight frown on his face.

"I'm sorry," Riley said. "I know dating me already comes with sacrifices on your part. I'm sorry I'm making this so awkward."

Kollin groaned and climbed off Riley's lap. "Will you stop? Dating you does not come with sacrifices. And I'm happy to do whatever I can to make this easier on you. We just need to think about it first. What're you most worried about?"

*That's easy.* "That you'll be grossed out by my vagina."

"Okay." Kollin peered at Riley from the side of his eye. "You've been really honest with me, and I want to do the same for you, but I don't want you to freak out. Can you do that?"

"Oh God. Just tell me now and get it over with."

"That's my biggest worry too. But—" Riley fell back on the ground and covered his face, and Kollin shot out a hand to grab his arm. "I really don't think it'll be an issue. I care about you a lot. More than that—I think you're really sexy. And not in the ways that matter, like the fact that you're really smart and compassionate and hard-working, but in a totally shallow way. Like your ass looks amazing in that pair of jeans with a hole in the left knee, and when you wear your Superman T-shirt, the one that stretches across your chest, not gonna lie, dude. I get a little chub."

Riley barked out a laugh. "Shut up."

"I'm serious." Kollin laughed too. "I had one a minute ago until you said some bullshit about me sacrificing things. I wanna take you back to Legends and parade you around with your shirt off, but you think I'm missing out or some shit."

Riley didn't know what to say. Kollin spoke lightly, even though he probably meant every word, but to him… to have someone *want* to show him off…. Riley never thought he'd have that. So he just nodded and choked back the tears he really didn't want to shed right then.

Kollin grabbed his hand again. "Why don't you let me plan something and let it be a surprise for you? That way you get some security in knowing I'm prepared without having to worry."

Riley nodded. "I can do that. Just… don't wait too long. I'll go insane."

"Ha! I don't think you have to worry about me putting this off any longer than absolutely necessary." Kollin stood and held out his hand. "Wanna tackle the seven-miler or eat something first?"

Riley grabbed his shirt off the ground and then allowed Kollin to pull him up. "I'm still stuffed from breakfast. I'm not used to eating that much food on my PB&J and ramen noodle budget. Can we do the hike first?"

Kollin winked. "As long as you leave your shirt off."

"Uh, no. But nice try." Riley shook his hand free from Kollin's and put his shirt back on.

Kollin sighed loudly but grinned. "Worth a try. Will you at least hold my hand?"

Riley's cheeks flushed and then warmed even more when he realized how smitten he was acting. He threaded his fingers through Kollin's and pulled him closer for a kiss. "That, I think I can handle."

# CHAPTER 16

"Soooo...." KOLLIN sat back in Adam's chair. "Do you want me to warn you ahead of time that we're about to have an awkward conversation, or do you just want to be surprised?"

"Uh, I think you just warned me." Adam's fingers flew over his keyboard for a few more moments, and then he turned to give Kollin his full attention. "Let's go."

"I'm coming to you because you already know a lot of the stuff Riley went through before."

Kollin waited for Adam to nod. "I'm glad you two worked everything out. He needs someone else he can trust. Someone who isn't a paid professional."

Kollin shifted in his seat. "Right. Well, it's put us in a strange place, where we want to move forward but don't really know how."

Adam stared at him and waited, but Kollin didn't know what to say next, so he stayed quiet and hoped Adam would catch on.

"I'm gonna need a little more to go on than that, buddy."

Kollin eyed Adam for a minute and then spit the words out as fast as he could. "He wants to have sex to see if he wants to keep his vagina, and I'm fucking freaked out that I'm going to be shitty at it, and then he'll end up making the wrong decision when he gets his surgery, and then we'll break up, and he'll hate me for the rest of his life."

"Whoa." Adam scratched the back of his neck and took a deep breath. "That was a lot of information in five seconds."

"Sorry," Kollin said, feeling more and more idiotic by the minute.

Adam closed his eyes and looked down so that he spoke to the desk. "First of all this isn't something I ever wanted to say to you, but I think *you* know, at least, that you're not really shitty at it. And not because I know anything about your sex life but because you care so much about Riley that I would anticipate you'll be thinking of his needs first and foremost the entire time. And even if it's kind of clumsy and awkward, that's okay. That's good because you two are still learning each other. And Riley's not stupid. He knows you've never worked with his equipment before. He's not going to expect you to be an expert. We both know, when it gets right down to it, he needs someone who truly respects and cares for him more than he needs someone who knows exactly what button to push." He peeked up at Kollin. "Did you get everything I was saying, or do I need to be more explicit?"

"Please don't get explicit," Kollin begged.

"Oh, thank God." Adam rubbed both hands over his face. "I know it should be easier to talk about sex with you, since it's part of my job, but it's really not."

Kollin smirked. "I hope it's never easy for you to tell a kid that he's good at sex."

Adam narrowed his eyes. "Funny. *Next*," he said pointedly, "it's dangerous for you to take any part of Riley's burden onto yourself. He has to make these decisions, not you. Supporting him is one thing, but whatever decision he makes is on him, not you. Feel me?"

Kollin huffed. He knew that. Of course he knew that. But knowing that didn't lessen any of the monumental pressure he felt weighing him down.

"Have you talked to him about this?" Adam asked.

"Trust me, we've done plenty of talking."

"So what's your real question?"

Kollin shrugged. "I don't know. I guess I'm nervous I'm going to screw it all up."

"I think that's a perfectly normal feeling. One Riley would likely understand." Adam leaned forward and cupped his hands together in a faux megaphone. "Tell him."

"And what if he runs away again? What then?"

"What if he does? Do you want to be with someone you can't depend on?"

"It's different with Ri—"

Adam cut him off. "No, it's not. Maybe his reasons for running are more complicated than someone just being an asshole, but he's still being an asshole if he bails on you again. You're asking him to be open and honest with you, but you don't trust him not to run again. You say he's your best friend, but you come to me every time you have a problem with something he's done."

Kollin stared at his hands. Adam was right. He'd told Riley he'd forgiven him for all those years of silence, but he hadn't. Even after Adam's little speech about how amazing Eli was, Kollin couldn't bring himself to reach that point.

"Look. If Riley told you everything he's been through, you know how strong he is. And surely there've been times he's led the relationship forward too. If nothing else, he fully opened up to you about his past. That's a huge sign of faith in where you two are going." Adam paused, but Kollin could tell he wasn't finished with his thought by the way he tugged on his hair.

Shame washed over Kollin as he waited for Adam to continue. He'd told Riley over and over that he believed in Riley's strength, and then he failed to show him. "I know you've talked this thing to death, but every relationship requires a ton of communication to be successful. Add to that Riley's complicated past and transition and your desire not to hurt him, and that means even *more* talking."

Kollin groaned. "Ugh. You're the worst."

"That's what they say. I'm planning to make it the tag line on my new business cards. Adam Lancaster—The Absolute Worst. Here to encourage you to do all the things you don't want to do but know you should." Adam sat back in his seat. "You get what I'm saying, though?"

"Yes. I think you want me to talk to him some more."

Adam grinned. "I don't know what gave you that impression, but if it's what you think is best…."

Kollin snorted and then sobered again. "I don't want to mess this up."

"I know you don't. And I'd be willing to bet all of Elijah's money that whoever Riley's talking to about this stuff—if he's talking to anyone, that is—he's telling them the same thing." Adam paused. "You guys will get there eventually. Life won't always be this cumbersome."

"Yeah. I guess."

"Delightful attitude. Now is there anything else I can do for you?"

"Fuck. I sure as hell hope not," Kollin grumbled.

"Hey." Adam waited until Kollin looked up. "I'm sorry I can't give you an easy-button solution."

Kollin shrugged. "Adulting is hard."

"Oh, kid." Adam sighed. "You don't even know the half of it. But it gets better. Promise."

AS RILEY fiddled with his hair in the mirror, he watched Greg's reflection shove an entire Dorito in his mouth.

"Haven't you been dating this guy for a while now?" Greg asked, chip crumbs falling out of his mouth. "Month or two?"

Riley swept his bangs to the other side of his face and hoped that would do something to hide the ginormous cowlick that forever plagued him.

"Something like that," Riley said and flipped his hair back the other way.

"So why you got your panties in a twist over tonight? Fixin' to get lucky?" Riley opened his mouth to answer, but Greg held up his hand. "Wait. Don't answer that. I don't want to know."

"I'm coming back here when we're done, so unless you plan on watching…." Riley spun around to look at Greg. His hair was a total loss. "Nothing like that will be happening tonight."

"Then what's got you in a tizzy?" Greg turned up his bottle of beer and chugged half of it down.

"I dunno. Who says I'm in a tizzy?"

Greg rolled his eyes. "Me. You're fluttering all over the place. Changed shirts four times and then put the first one back on. Brushed your teeth twice and took a thirty-minute shower." Greg popped another chip in his mouth and waggled his eyebrows. "I don't know how things work in your world, but in my world, a thirty-minute shower equals bow-chicka-wow-wow."

Riley shook his head and gestured toward the beer. "Dude. How many of those have you had?"

"This is only my third one," Greg said, derision lacing his voice.

"I'm just saying. You've hardly said this many words to me the entire time I've known you."

Greg shrugged. "Rough day, man. Hell. Rough week. Needed to take the edge off. And I miss my wife. I'll be glad when this job is over."

"Yeah." Riley couldn't say the same thing, but he wouldn't point that out to Greg.

"You gonna be coming back with the rest of us after we're done here?"

Riley looked up, surprised. "Of course. Why wouldn't I?"

Greg tried to sound casual but failed miserably. "Seems like you got a good thing going on here. Why would you?"

Riley stared at him. *Wasn't it obvious*? "My job is back in Boone. I wouldn't leave you hanging like that after everything you've done for me."

"You don't owe me nothing, kid. It's just a job. Life's more than who signs your paychecks."

"What're you trying to say?" Riley asked. "You think I should stay here?"

Greg burped. Loudly.

Riley rolled his eyes and tried not to laugh.

"I've just never seen you this… content in Boone. I'd hate to lose you, kid." Greg waved his bottle toward the wall, where some of the other crew had rooms. "You're a hell of a lot more dependable than most of these bozos, but you don't smile like that back home. You don't seem to have much purpose there either."

"Uh, thanks?"

"Don't mean it like that." Greg shook his head. "This is why I never say much of anything. Nothin' ever comes out right. You got a good thing going here. Friends. Things to do. People who care about you. You got me in Boone, and that ain't saying much of nothing."

Greg's words made Riley smile, not only the ones about everything Riley had here, but also how Greg, in his own roundabout and subtle way, let Riley know he cared. Riley knew any form of reciprocation would make the uncomfortable moment even more unbearable, but he couldn't resist his own roundabout admission of appreciation. "I dunno. Says something, I reckon. Besides, it's not so bad. Your mom's cooking is worth the three-hour drive to see my friends here."

"Might have to agree with you there." Greg cast a side-eyed glance at Riley. "Just don't tell my wife I said that."

"Mum's the word."

Riley started cleaning up the mess he'd made while he was choosing his outfit. Greg was right. He had no idea why he was so nervous about his date with Kollin. They were just going to a movie—an early one at that, because Kollin had class first thing in the morning and, of course, Riley had to work. There was absolutely no chance that he and Kollin would do anything more than kiss good night.

But it was the first time they were going out on a real date *not* at a gay bar. They'd be out together. In public. Like a normal couple.

Even though they were anything but normal.

Riley shoved that thought aside and, instead, pondered everything Greg had just said. Could he really stay in Cary? Where would he work? Where would he live? He couldn't camp out in Elijah's basement forever, and the area wasn't exactly known for its cheap real estate. Asking for a transfer when Drummond's opened up a Durham office was one thing. Moving back home without a steady income was another ball of yarn entirely.

Riley tucked his discarded shirts back in the dresser drawer and looked at Greg. "When do you think Drummond's will make a decision on the Durham office?"

Greg wrinkled up his nose. "Decision's made as far as I can tell. I guess they can still change their minds, but they're looking for a place to set up base."

"Do, uh… do you think they'd let me transfer here?"

Greg didn't look at Riley, but he smiled into his beer as he took a sip. "I might could make that happen, if it's what you want."

Riley shrugged. "I'm not saying it is. Just wondering, is all."

"Mmhmm…. Gonna miss seeing you around, kid."

Riley grinned and looked down. He could feel his cheeks warming.

"Me too." Riley turned back to the mirror and grinned. "I mean, *if* I move, that is."

A knock at the door interrupted their conversation. "Am I supposed to make myself scarce?"

"So I can answer the door?" Riley rolled his eyes. "I think it'll be fine. Besides, he wants to meet you."

Greg grunted. "Why the hell would anyone want to meet me?"

Riley grunted back. "What can I say? You're one of a kind."

He walked to the door and opened it. Then he laughed out loud when he saw Kollin, holding the biggest muffin basket he'd ever seen in one hand and a basket full of beer in the other.

Kollin flashed a sheepish grin. "Figured I'd cover all my bases. I refuse to believe the man doesn't like muffins. You've just never seen him eat one." He stepped through the doorway, crowding Riley, and he planted a kiss on his cheek as he passed by.

"Sure. Come on in," Riley muttered as he closed the door.

Kollin hefted the beer onto the desk and set the basket of muffins on Riley's bed. "Nice to meet you, sir," he said and approached Greg's bed while holding out his hand.

Riley covered his mouth to hold in his laughter at the look of bewilderment on Greg's face. Always full of surprises, though, Greg took a moment to brush off his Doritos-powdered fingers on his shirt and took Kollin's hand. Then he looked around Kollin at Riley. "He think I'm your dad or something?"

Unable to speak from trying not to laugh, Riley shook his head.

"I'm not old enough to be his dad," Greg insisted, looking back at Kollin.

Kollin shook his head and looked at Riley with wide eyes. "Of course not. What...."

No longer able to take it, Riley burst out laughing.

"Will somebody give me one of those beers and tell me what the hell is going on here?" Greg demanded, which only served to make Riley laugh harder.

Kollin jumped at Greg's words and hurried to take the cellophane wrapping off the basket of beer.

"Aw hell, kid. I wasn't being serious." Greg looked at Riley. "He's a bit skittish, isn't he?"

Kollin held a bottle of beer in his hand and looked back and forth between Riley and Greg while Riley composed himself. "You're a horrible person," Riley finally said.

Greg shrugged.

Kollin held up the beer. "So... I should put this back?"

Riley snatched the beer out of Kollin's hand and put it back in the basket. "I think he's had enough for tonight. Can you please be nice to my boyfriend now?"

Greg huffed but apologized to Kollin and tacked on, "Thank you for the... goody baskets."

"Yes, sir," Kollin replied, seeming to gather his wits again. "I know it seems strange, but Riley recently told me how much of a help to him

you've been over the past several years. I wanted to thank you, and…
well, I don't know anyone who doesn't like muffins. Or beer."

Greg's expression softened as Kollin spoke, and this time when
he thanked Kollin, his voice held more sincerity. "That was very
thoughtful of you. Thank you. And I'm glad I was able to help Riley.
He's a good kid."

Kollin looked at Riley and smiled. "Yes, sir. He is."

Greg grunted and waved his hand toward the door. "Y'all get on
out of here now."

Clearly not needing to be told twice, Kollin grabbed Riley's hand
and pulled. Riley barely had time to snatch his wallet off his bed on the
way out. Kollin didn't slow down until they were outside of the building,
where he rounded on Riley.

"Dude."

Riley grinned. "Yeah?"

"*Dude*." He pointed at the hotel in the general direction of
Riley's room.

"*Yeah?*" Riley intoned his voice to match Kollin's.

"I thought Greg was the strong and silent type," Kollin screeched.
"What the hell was that? He made fun of me."

Riley laughed. "Technically he didn't make fun of you. He poked
fun *at* you."

"You said he's the most serious person you know. You *said* he'd be
nice to me."

Riley grabbed Kollin's flailing hands. "First of all I've never seen
him have more than two drinks. Apparently any more than that brings
out his fun personality." Riley wiggled their joined hands. "Second of
all I didn't think you were *actually* going to bring a muffin and beer
basket."

"Okay." Kollin held up their hands, popped up his first finger, and
then mimicked Riley. "First of all there are two baskets—a muffin basket
and a beer basket, not a muffin and beer basket. Second of all"—he held
up another finger—"you haven't hugged me yet today."

A slow grin spread over Riley's lips, and he closed his eyes.
Kollin's off-the-cuff romantic gestures never failed to surprise him or
make his insides turn to mush. With a quiet chuff, he leaned into Kollin
and wrapped his arms around Kollin's waist to hug him in the middle of

the hotel parking lot. When he pulled away, he said, "I still can't believe you brought muffins. I told you he doesn't eat them."

Kollin grabbed Riley's hand and pulled him toward the car. "There are over twenty different kinds of muffins in that basket. If he can't find one he likes, I'll find a basket of scones." Kollin opened the driver's side door and looked over the roof at Riley. "But you're going to have to give it to him on my behalf because I never plan on being in the same room with that man again."

Riley laughed and settled into his seat. "You're being a bit dramatic. He's just a big teddy bear."

"Nah, ah, ah." Kollin backed up and pulled out of the parking lot toward the movie theater. "Eli is a teddy bear. There's no way you can honestly tell me Eli is worse than that man. He made me get him a beer two seconds after I met him."

"He was joking." Riley lay back against the headrest and grinned. "Besides, Elijah—your *dad*—threatened to ban me from your house while waving a bottle of scotch around. I'd say that's a mite scarier than my boss teasing you for all of thirty seconds."

"Eli threatened to ban you from our house?"

Riley shrugged. "I deserved it. And worse. He came down the night after we got in that fight and found me packing everything."

Kollin frowned and cocked his head to the side. "So the only reason you didn't leave that night is because of him?"

Riley's heart sank. *So much for a perfect first real date.* "In a roundabout way, I guess. I'm not saying I would've definitely left if he hadn't come down, but I'm glad he did, and I'm glad I stayed. Running again would've been the biggest mistake of my life, and I owe you—and myself—better than that."

"Huh," Kollin said.

Riley remained quiet. He figured silence was always his best bet whenever Kollin learned new, possibly troubling information. Eventually Kollin glanced over at Riley and smiled. He reached across the console and took Riley's hand in his own.

"What movie do you want to see?"

Riley let out a low sigh of relief. Maybe it was taking longer than either of them liked, but he and Kollin were finally on the right path to balance their proven and faithful friendship with their budding new romance. For the first time, Riley truly believed they might actually have a shot at making it. Together. As a couple. In the happily-ever-after type of way.

With that thought in mind, he smiled and squeezed Kollin's hand. "Whatever you want is fine with me. I'm just glad to be along for the ride."

# CHAPTER 17

"ARE YOU nervous?"

Riley cast a side glare at Kollin. "Are *you*? Because you're the one who won't stop fidgeting."

Kollin stilled his legs and folded his hands in his lap. "Why am I nervous?"

"I dunno, but could you stop? You're making me nervous, and this is nothing to be nervous about."

Kollin grabbed Riley's hand. "I'm sorry. I just want this to go well."

Riley sighed and looked at Kollin. His face held so much sincerity, Riley couldn't doubt how much Kollin cared for him. "It's not a big deal if it doesn't. I'll still join the group thing. I want to get better too. I promise."

Kollin's answering smile made Riley's heart flip, and when Kollin laid his head on Riley's shoulder, he thought maybe he knew what Greg meant when he said Riley looked content.

"There he is," Kollin whispered and raised his head from Riley's shoulder.

"I know what he looks like," Riley whispered back.

Joe, the trans male who had recently started to show up at the center, walked across the playground as Kollin and Riley stood. He held out his hand when he reached them. "Hey, Riley… Kollin."

They all shook hands, and Riley figured he better take the lead, since he'd invited Joe to their little shindig. He waved toward the bench. "You want to sit or take a walk around the trail?"

Joe looked around the park. "I'm up for a walk."

Kollin squeezed his hand. "I should probably head out, actually. I don't want to be late to class, but thank you for lunch." He planted a quick kiss on Riley's cheek and turned to Joe. "Good seeing you again, man."

"You too. See you around the center." Joe waved as Kollin retreated to his car, and then he shoved his hands back in his pockets. They walked around the trail in silence until Joe looked sideways at Riley. "Was Kollin trying to mark his territory or something? Because I'm straight. He's got nothing to worry about."

Riley tripped over his own feet and stopped to gape at Joe. "What? No." He shook his head. "No. We have lunch together here sometimes, so he decided to hang out until you got here. He just wanted to say hi."

"If you say so." Joe shrugged.

"I do. Trust me. Kollin is not like that." *Was he*? Truth be told, Riley didn't know if Kollin was a jealous person or not. He'd never had the opportunity to find out, but the emotion didn't really fit the rest of Kollin's personality.

Joe held up his hands. "I believe you. I was just trying to put your mind at ease."

Riley fell silent again and anxiety began to creep in. The little meet and greet wasn't going as well as he'd hoped so far, and once again, he felt stupid. Did he really expect them to bond instantly and be lifelong buddies because both of them had been born in the wrong body? Joe had barely said ten words, yet Riley already found him a bit too abrasive.

"Sorry." Riley wasn't sure why he was apologizing, but he felt like he needed to. He took a deep breath and looked at Joe as they walked. "Thanks for meeting me. I'm not really sure what to say or where to start."

Joe frowned at Riley and then asked, "Is there anything specific you want to know?"

*Everything*. Riley wanted his entire life story so he could compare and contrast, but how would that help him? According to gossip around the center, Joe's parents were very supportive of him and allowed him to start transitioning at an early age. Riley's own experience couldn't have been any more different.

When he asked Adam to help him approach Joe about getting together to chat sometime, Adam had basically taken over and handled the entire meet-up. Riley had no idea where to go from here.

"I'm not sure," Riley admitted after a few moments of silence. "I've gone through most of this alone. I don't know what's okay to talk about and what's not."

A jogger passed them by, and Joe waited until she was out of earshot to continue. "Have you transitioned below yet? Or are you going to?"

"No. Dr. Maggie wants me to deal with some shit first. Hence her encouraging me to speak with other trans people."

Joe nodded. "Probably a good idea. My parents are awesome. They've always supported me. And I still went through a period of depression after my bottom surgery. It's better than what it was before, but it's still not what I picture in my head. It took me some time to accept that and then some more time to be okay with it."

Riley frowned. That wasn't what he wanted to hear. "Do you do any of the trans group things?"

"I have in the past. Most of the people in those groups were older than me, though. It felt good to know I wasn't alone, but... I still felt alone because I was so young. That's why I started coming to HOPE. I thought I'd be more likely to meet trans people closer to my own age, but you're the first to show up." Joe laughed humorlessly. "And apparently you're some kind of legend or something there."

Riley scoffed. "I doubt that."

"You shouldn't."

Joe didn't offer any further explanation, and once again, Riley became frustrated with his lack of inclusion and empathy. Wasn't that the point of the whole meet-up?

"I'm not sure I understand what you mean," Riley said, hoping Joe would elaborate.

"Oh, you know, golden trans boy heads off to college with his entire bright and shining future ahead of him and then drops off the face of the earth for years before suddenly turning back up to save the day and help build on a new addition to the inn." Joe waved his hands around in the air as if that helped explain everything. Curiously enough there wasn't a hint of derision or sarcasm in his voice. Joe just stated the facts, maybe warped a bit, but facts, nonetheless... as he knew them.

"I guess," Riley mumbled. "I didn't realize anyone other than Kollin actually remembered me."

"Who else needs to?" Joe asked. "Everyone there loves Kollin. I've not had much chance to interact with him yet, but everyone I've talked to only has good things to say about him. It's not like you took off and he forgot who you were. They say it was years before he stopped talking about you as if you would still drop by any day."

Riley's heart ached. He felt as if one of the passing joggers had punched him in the gut. Aside from the time Kollin exploded at Riley when he found out about Tony, Kollin hadn't mentioned how much it hurt when Riley cut off all contact. How did someone who didn't know him or Kollin know more about how Kollin felt than Riley did?

"Who is 'they'?" he asked, weakly.

Joe shrugged. "Different people around the center. You know how everyone gossips, and they're all so protective of Kollin, seeing as how he's Adam's son."

No. Riley didn't know. Outside of his appointments with Maggie, he'd only been to the center a few times since he'd come back into town, and then only at Kollin's insistence.

Joe continued as if he hadn't just destroyed Riley's heart. "There's even an unofficial pool over whether or not you'll stick around this time."

Riley stumbled again and stepped off the trail. "Can we sit for a few minutes?"

Finally Joe seemed to realize Riley wasn't taking his lackadaisical attitude toward Riley's past very well. He grabbed Riley's elbow and led him to the nearest bench. "Are you okay? I said something wrong, didn't I?"

Riley gaped at Joe. Were they not just in the same conversation?

"I didn't mean to upset you." Joe sat next to Riley. "My mom always tells me I'm too blunt. I have Asperger's, and it can make social situations difficult."

Riley's head swam with everything Joe had just said. He had no idea where to start, and none of it was related to what he originally wanted to talk to Joe about. He figured it was best to start with the easiest topic. For him, at least.

"I didn't realize you were on the spectrum."

Joe shrugged. "Most people don't. It's not like I wear a sign."

*Made sense.* "Was it hard? Dealing with Asperger's and being trans?" Riley rolled his eyes. "Obviously it was hard, but do you think it was harder?"

"It's the only thing I've ever known, so I don't know if it's more or less difficult. One of my doctors mentioned my autism might have made accepting the fact that I'm trans easier." Joe looked at Riley. "But sometimes it just feels like one more thing to overcome."

Riley nodded. "I'm glad you have such awesome parents. Must've been a huge help."

"They were."

They stayed silent for a while, and things began to click into place for Riley. His earlier anxiety about Joe not liking him evaporated, and he mulled over his comments about Kollin. He didn't need to wonder why Kollin never told him how hard he took Riley's absence. Kollin never would. He'd absorb the burden into himself and deal with his negative feelings alone, at least until something triggered everything loose. Kollin's outburst when he found out about Tony made even more sense after Joe's accidental gossip session.

Riley cleared his throat. "I'm glad you told me."

Joe nodded once. "Things aren't always easy to hear, but sometimes it's better to hear them anyway."

Riley snorted. "Yeah. That may be the understatement of the century."

"I'm sorry I upset you. I realize this isn't what you want to talk about today. I wasn't expecting to see Kollin, and it threw me off."

"It's fine." And Riley meant it. If Joe hadn't spilled the beans, Riley might never have known. "Are people really betting on me?"

Joe actually appeared mortified. "That was rude of me to say."

"Wow." Riley sat back against the bench. "Am I at least winning?"

Joe looked at Riley. "Depends what you call winning."

Riley laughed. "Touché. If you want to get in on the action, you best vote that I stick around."

Joe tilted his head to the side and grimaced. "Betting's not really my thing."

Riley grinned. "I just meant that I plan on staying. Assuming Kollin wants me here, anyway."

Joe peered at Riley. "I think he does. He talks about you all the time." Joe cracked a grin. "So they say, anyway."

Riley's laughed at Joe's joke. "We all know they know best. Right? Wanna walk again?"

"Sure." Joe stood and waited for Riley to join him. They spent the next hour at the park, and while they had to awkwardly stumble through a few conversations, Riley enjoyed himself. Talking to Joe was sort of like talking to Greg. Riley sometimes had to guess at the root cause of whatever was being said. Except where Greg was often incredibly vague, Joe cut to the point quickly—it just didn't always make sense. Between his autism and his transitioning, Joe was picked on a lot by his peers, but his parents went to bat for him every time it became an issue. The end result.… Joe was confident in himself and needed almost no validation from anyone else.

Riley wasn't sure his meeting with Joe helped him in the way Maggie or Kollin hoped it would. He liked Joe and could see them hanging out again, but they would never be great friends. Meeting Joe *had* given Riley a clear picture of where he should be, mentally and emotionally, before he took the next step in his transition. He finally—truly and fully—understood why Dr. Maggie had been hesitant to recommend him for bottom surgery. Maybe Riley wasn't quite as emotionally stable as he needed to be yet, but for the first time in a long time, he no longer felt as if he were just floundering. With help from the few people he had in his life and a kick in the ass from himself, he knew he could get there sooner rather than later.

"YOU WHAT?" Kollin looked over his shoulder and then again over Riley's shoulder. "Are there hidden cameras in here? Is this some kind of prank show?"

Riley laughed and punched Kollin lightly. "No, idiot. I thought you'd be excited. After all, *you* love *your* parents."

"I do," Kollin agreed. "But you're terrified of them. I can't believe you set up a double date for us with my dads."

"I like that I can surprise you." Riley tugged Kollin close and kissed the tip of his chin. "Especially when it's in a good way."

Kollin wrapped his arms around Riley and leaned in for a more satisfying kiss. Riley's usual, woodsy scent was masked by his soap and cologne.

When Riley had stopped by HOPE earlier, he came straight from the site. He was grungy and sweaty, his hair an oblong-shaped mess from his hard hat. Kollin thought he looked cute as hell. Apparently Greg, either from exhaustion or more likely from missing his wife, had given his entire crew Friday afternoon off so they could return to Boone early.

Excitement flooded Kollin when Riley suggested spending the afternoon together at HOPE. Kollin readily handed over his keys so Riley could go home to wash up, and when he saw Riley pull back into the parking lot, Kollin met him outside and dragged him around to the side of the building.

Kollin broke off from the kiss and nuzzled his face into Riley's neck to take a deep breath and search for more of the smell he loved.

"Your dad is going to kill us if he finds us over here like this," Riley said as he tightened his arms around Kollin.

"Don't care." Kollin nipped at Riley's shoulder. "Besides, we're volunteers, not students, *and* you're buying them dinner tonight. That's got to give us a little leeway."

Riley laughed and pulled away. "Not sure any of that will get us off the hook if we're caught making out. We're supposed to set a good example."

Kollin sighed. "Fine, Mr. Goody Two-shoes. Let's go inside and keep a respectable two inches between us at all times."

Riley clucked his tongue. "What's gotten into you? I don't seem to remember you ever having a problem with center rules before."

"That was before I had a hot-ass boyfriend who likes to wear shirts that are one size too small and jeans that cup his perfectly bubble-shaped ass."

Riley gasped and opened the door for Kollin. "My shirts are not too small."

Kollin eyed Riley's impressive chest and shoulders, which were on prominent display due to the aforementioned too-small shirt. But it was Riley's face that really made his heart flutter. Riley looked so relaxed and carefree. His smile came easily, and his eyes held a spark Kollin hadn't seen in a long time. Like, a really long time.

"It's so good to see you again," Kollin said. He wished he could convey everything he felt with those simple words.

Riley shot Kollin a puzzled look as he stopped by the front desk, where HOPE's longtime receptionist, Chloe, watched them. "I was just here an hour ago."

"I know," Kollin said with a shrug.

"He means," Chloe said, "it's good to see you happy again. That's the first real smile I've seen from you in months, Riley."

Riley glanced at Kollin, who offered a small smile and then turned back to Chloe. "If you say so."

"In fact, I do." Chloe grinned. "May I ask what brought its return? Or is it the obvious?" She pursed her lips and pointedly looked at Kollin.

Riley flushed, and his cheeks turned a lovely shade of pink that contrasted with his platinum hair. "I guess it might have a little something to do with seeing your shining smile on this beautiful Friday afternoon."

Chloe laughed and waved him off. "Go on out of here, you charmer."

Riley winked, and Kollin grabbed a handful of the M&M'S that Chloe kept out for everyone. He dumped them in his mouth as he and Riley walked toward the multipurpose room, where they were immediately dragged into different activities. Kollin helped a couple of girls with their homework while Riley watched a few rigorous games of ping-pong and handed out tips whenever he could. When Joe showed up, he went straight to Riley and engaged him in a lengthy conversation that involved a lot of hand gestures and laughter on Riley's part.

Riley hadn't given Kollin many details of his chat with Joe earlier in the week—only that it went well, but he didn't think they'd be best friends any time soon. Kollin couldn't help but notice that Riley seemed ten pounds lighter since their conversation, though. Whatever they talked about must have done something good.

When Eli walked in, still dressed in one of his dark suits, Kollin looked at the clock on the wall and was surprised to find it was after five. He handed his controller over to one of the other boys on the couch and excused himself from the game.

"Got out early for a Friday, didn't you?" Kollin asked him.

Eli threw a lazy arm around Kollin's shoulders. "Didn't want to miss the super secretive double date. What's this all about?"

Kollin shrugged. "He didn't say much to me about it. I kinda thought he was trying to do something nice for me."

"If having dinner with your parents is your idea of a fun evening, you two need to broaden your horizons."

"Ha, ha, ha. Maybe my parents are just super-duper cool. Didja ever think of that?"

Eli scoffed. "You need money or something?"

Kollin rolled his eyes. "You're so jaded."

"And proud of it," Eli said and squeezed his arm tighter around Kollin's neck. "How much time we got? Want to play a quick game of twenty-one?"

Kollin looked up at Eli. "Gotta change of clothes, old man?"

Eli grunted. "Maybe I'll just loosen my tie and we can play to ten."

Kollin whacked Eli's stomach with the back of his hand. "You're on. Let me tell Ri."

Twenty minutes later Kollin laughed as Eli bent over and propped his hands against his knees to keep himself up. Sweat rolled off his face, and Kollin knew his shirt had to be soaked. He looked like he might fall over at any second, but Kollin knew better.

"Please don't tell me you're letting me win." Eli gulped in air.

"Wouldn't dare, but one of these days, I'm gonna beat your ass out here." Kollin dribbled the ball a few times and took a shot while Eli caught his breath. They'd been playing hard, and though Eli wasn't quite as formidable as he was when Kollin first showed up at the center, he was still no match for Eli's size and skill.

"Nuh uh." Eli held his hands up for the ball. "As soon as I turn forty, I'm done. I'm going out on a high note so everyone can remember me in my glory."

"Hell. You're just vain enough to do it too." He jumped for the rebound when Eli missed, but Eli got there quicker and went in for the easy layup.

"That's game," Eli shouted, raising his arms in victory.

"No way," Kollin argued. "You never said we were starting again. I was being respectful to the elderly and giving you a chance to catch your breath. No one called times in."

"Kollin." Eli shook his head. "It's a bit pathetic to argue semantics. You should've learned how to be a gracious loser after all these years."

"But you didn't say times in," Kollin shrieked.

"And you never said time out." Eli was already gathering his jacket from the bench. "Besides, I need a few minutes to change. I'm all sweaty."

Kollin grabbed the ball off the court and stalked toward the door. "One of these days, you're not going to get away with this shit."

"I know." Eli flashed a grin over his shoulder. "But that day isn't going to be today. Give me ten minutes to get cleaned up, and we'll be ready."

Kollin followed Eli inside but broke off toward the bathroom so he could splash some water on his face. He hadn't gotten nearly as sweaty as Eli, but a quick rub down with a paper towel wouldn't hurt.

When he opened the door to the bathroom, he saw Riley at one of the sinks, washing his hands. "You win?" he asked.

"No," Kollin grumbled, "but he cheated."

"Doesn't he always cheat?"

Kollin huffed. "Yeah. I guess he does. But he'd still win if he didn't, so I don't know why he does it."

Riley dried his hands and leaned against the sink next to where Kollin bent down to wash his face. "Probably because it pisses you off."

Kollin swiped the excess water off his face and reached for a paper towel. "Surely Eli wouldn't be that childish.... Okay. I just heard that come out of my mouth. That's definitely why he does it."

Riley quirked his head to the side. "How'd it take you five years to figure that out?"

"I dunno. He's my dad. He's not supposed to intentionally make me mad, is he?"

Riley shrugged. "That's what mine did to me."

"Yeah. But yours is an asshole. Or was. And maybe still is...." Kollin let the sentence trail off. He hadn't meant to go there. Riley still hadn't gone to visit his parents, and Kollin didn't want to push the issue. He didn't want to cloud Riley's perception of them either way while Riley was still trying to decide what to do.

Fortunately Riley ignored the huge foot in Kollin's mouth. "And yours are more like friends than dads, so I guess you're going to have to deal with it."

"Not a bad trade-off, I guess." Kollin dried his face. "You gonna tell me anything else about this dinner tonight?"

Riley sighed. "It's really not a big deal. I don't know why everyone is making it out to be."

Kollin nodded. "Okay. That's fine. Keep your little secret."

Riley grinned and looked at the ground. "Thank you."

He had a strong urge to grill Riley for more information, but Kollin ignored it, and an hour later they were all seated at a four top at The Cowfish near downtown Raleigh. They'd just ordered their food, and Riley had become obviously more nervous. He kept moving his fork around, and Kollin felt Riley's right leg bouncing up and down. With no idea what was going on in Riley's head and no desire to force it out of him in front of Adam and Eli, Kollin simply placed his hand on Riley's knee and squeezed.

Riley immediately stopped his knee and flashed Kollin a grateful smile. He flipped his fork over a few more times and then cleared his throat. "I know you guys have already figured out I initiated this whole thing for a reason." His knee bounced up and down again, and he looked up at Adam and then Eli. "I want to thank you guys for everything you've done for me since I've been back in town. You've gone out of your way to make me feel welcome in your home, even though I managed to complicate everyone's lives."

The sincerity in Riley's voice was palpable, and Kollin resisted the impulse to lean over and hug him. He glanced at his parents instead and saw a look of proud admiration on Eli's face, while Adam was all smiles.

"Don't even mention it, Riley," Adam said. "We're always glad to help."

Riley nodded. "I know, but taking me into your home goes above and beyond your usual measures of awesomeness, and I really am so thankful, especially after everything that happened with Kollin." Riley looked at Kollin. "Recently and four years ago."

"Riley...." But Kollin didn't know what else to say.

Riley continued as if Kollin hadn't said anything. "I guess you all know we'll be done with the work on H4H in a few weeks. I can't—" Riley took a deep breath. "I can't stay when we're done. I want to, but my job is back in Boone, and I know a job isn't everything, but I've worked my ass off there to move up the ranks. I'd have to start all over if I stayed. Greg says the Durham office will be opening soon, though. Maybe even by the end of the year. And he's going to do everything he can to get me transferred over here." Riley cleared his throat and started flipping his fork again. "I just wanted to tell each of you that. And I promise I'm not going to disappear again."

Kollin prepared to defend Riley, to tell him there was no need to reassure them, that of course they knew he wouldn't leave again, but Eli spoke before he could.

"Thank you, Riley." Kollin looked at Eli, who was smiling toward Riley with a hint of admiration in his gaze. "It's not easy to say something like that, but I appreciate hearing it."

Riley nodded and looked at Adam.

"We'll help any way we can," he said. "If you need a place to crash when you get back, let us know. And if Drummond's doesn't work out for some reason, I'll put some feelers out for other job opportunities if this is where you want to be."

Kollin opened his mouth once again to add his reassurances, but Riley's hand clamped down on his leg. Rather than look at Kollin, Riley stared at his plate, intentionally avoiding eye contact with him. So Kollin closed his mouth and sat back in his seat.

The rest of dinner passed much more pleasantly, if somewhat strangely. Riley interacted with Kollin, but he didn't allow Kollin an opportunity to direct the conversation. Kollin had no idea why Riley was so determined to prevent him from asking about his plans, but he tried not to let it bother him while they were all out together.

When Adam and Eli started making noises about rescuing Adam's sister, Kirsten, from watching Lizzie longer than necessary, Riley attempted to pay for dinner. Eli just rolled his eyes and handed the waiter his card. Once they parted ways, Riley didn't give Kollin time to say a single word. Instead he pulled them close together and rested his forehead against Kollin's.

"I know you have something to say to me, but I didn't want to have to talk about this with you in front of them."

Kollin smiled softly. "You could've warned me what was coming, then."

Riley tilted his head down to look at the ground, but he stayed connected to Kollin. "I know. But it felt important. It felt like something I should tell you guys together. I don't want your parents to be worried about me or about us—or for you to worry about us, for that matter."

Kollin tilted Riley's head back up and pressed a firm kiss to his mouth. He wanted to vocalize what he hadn't been able to say during dinner, to reassure Riley he had full and complete faith in him. But once the moment had passed and he had time to think about Riley's words, his gut reaction was gone. Kollin wanted to more than anything, but he didn't quite trust Riley's promise just yet. He couldn't get rid of the nagging feeling that, at the first sign of something difficult, Riley might run for the hills. Whether it was something personal in his own life or something between the two of them, Kollin didn't know. But that uncertainty only made his hesitation stronger.

Kollin felt Riley's smile against his lips, and a small pang of guilt shot through him. He needed to talk to Riley about his concerns, but doing so when Riley seemed so happy felt cruel. He shoved it all aside and kissed Riley again. He was ready to suggest they head back to his house when a woman walking by with her date scoffed, "Can't you do that in private?"

Kollin rolled his eyes. Though never pleasant to endure, he'd heard worse over the years. Riley, on the other hand, jumped back. His eyebrows rose as he watched the retreating couple walk into the restaurant, and he took another step backward.

"Ri?" Kollin asked.

"Shit," Riley whispered and covered his mouth with his hand.

"What's wrong?" Kollin looked back toward the door, but the rude woman and her date had already disappeared inside. "That wasn't another douchebag ex, was it?"

Riley shook his head. "No. But I think the guy she's with is on my crew."

"Oh." Kollin stared back at the restaurant door for a moment and then back at Riley, who looked positively terrified. Surely he wouldn't bail an hour after his little speech? Out of all the issues Riley had overcome in the past few weeks, Kollin knew coming out at his job wasn't one he felt ready to conquer yet. "He probably didn't even see who you are, you know? The girl was just being a bitch. Most people who pull shit like that don't afford us more than a passing glance." Kollin waved his hands around. "Besides, it's already dark."

Riley cut a withering glare at Kollin. "It's light enough for me to recognize him."

Frustrated, Kollin snapped. "Well, he wasn't sucking face with his date like you were with yours, so maybe he didn't get a good view."

Clearly taken aback, Riley let his shoulders slump. Without another word he turned toward Kollin's car.

Heaving a big sigh—and refraining from shouting in frustration—Kollin followed. Once they were both in the car, Kollin immediately started driving in the direction of his home. He was halfway there before he spoke again.

"Please don't leave."

"What?" Riley asked. He sounded confused.

"Don't bail on me just because that guy might have seen us. There's a big possibility he didn't, and if he did, we can deal with the fallout together."

"What the hell are you talking about?" Now Riley sounded angry. "Didn't I just tell you in front of your parents that I wouldn't run again?"

"Well, yeah, but—"

"Do you not trust me at all?" Riley asked, apparently unwilling to hear Kollin's side of the story.

"Of course I do, but—"

"Then what the hell, Koll? I thought we were finally on the same page, but it sounds like you expect me to flee any second."

Kollin growled. "Stop putting words in my mouth."

"Am I wrong? Were you thinking something else when you asked me not to leave?"

Kollin sighed. Riley wasn't wrong. And the worst of it was, even listening to Riley's ire didn't erase Kollin's doubt. He managed to ignore the pit in his stomach most of the time, but the anxiety over whether or not Riley would be there the following morning always lurked.

"I just need some time." Kollin spoke softly, determined not to become defensive or accusatory. "I want to believe you'll always be there, but please take a moment to look back over my life. I know you've had it worse than me. I know you've been alone for years, and I had two amazing people save me the second I lost my birth parents. But I was still not only abandoned but also beaten by two of the people who were supposed to love me unconditionally. Adam promised he'd never leave me, but then he did. And you might not have made any explicit promises, Ri, but damn it, I didn't think we needed to say the words to believe we'd never just flounce our friendship. I've gotten pretty fucking adept at covering up my insecurities about my abandonment issues over the years. Just… give me time to see you're not leaving me again, and I promise I'll get there."

The words tumbled out—confessions he'd only uttered to his therapist for fear of upsetting Adam or Eli. Kollin knew Adam would never leave them again, but it had taken him nearly a year to trust that. He had to see Adam stick around and struggle through his issues before he truly started to trust him, to believe that nothing would ever keep Adam away from him and Eli again.

Kollin wanted to forgive Riley the moment he'd walked back into his life, and in a way he had. But he hadn't forgotten his feelings of despair when he wondered where Riley was, if he was okay or not, and what part Kollin might have played in making him leave. He hadn't forgotten that, for years, he'd held on to hope that Riley would come back or that he finally accepted that he'd never see his best friend again.

They were nearly home, and Kollin hoped like hell that Adam and Eli had stayed at Kirsten's for a while when they picked up Lizzie. One of their father and son talks was the last thing he wanted. If he and Riley could retire to their respective rooms without being seen, Adam and Eli would never know their night had taken a turn for the worse.

Relief washed over him as he pulled into the empty drive. Riley hadn't said anything, but Kollin didn't know if it was because he was pissed off or because he was trying to give Kollin the space he'd requested.

Kollin got out of the car but stopped at the sidewalk and waited for Riley to catch up. He grabbed Ri's hand and forced Riley to look him in the eye. "You have to know how important you are to me, Ri. And I feel like it's pretty obvious that I'm falling in love with you, which is terrifying all on its own. Add in the fact that we're best friends and how much I stand to lose if this doesn't work out *and* my own abandonment issues, and the terror factor multiplies by about a bajillion and a half. Not to mention all the shit you're going through. I mean, hell, I'm amazed we've made it this far."

Riley's eyes were solemn, but he smiled at Kollin. "I get it. I'm willing to take the time to prove to you that I'm serious."

"I want that more than anything." Kollin scratched the back of his neck. "I don't know what I thought would happen when I bullied you into going out with me, but this wasn't it."

Riley laughed, but it didn't hold any humor. "I was certain it would end in disaster."

Kollin tilted his head and grinned. "There's always still a chance, I guess."

Riley shook his head. "No. Not anymore." He grabbed Kollin's other hand. "Maybe it turns out we can't make the romantic part of our relationship work, but I believe in us, and I know we won't let *us* be ruined. And I'm willing to believe enough for the both of us until you catch up."

Kollin dropped Riley's hands, wrapped his arms around Riley's neck, and tugged him in for a tight hug. Riley couldn't have uttered more perfect words.

When Riley's arms circled around his waist, Kollin had never been more grateful for a hug from his best friend. He pulled away but left one arm over Riley's shoulders. Suddenly being alone in his room didn't sound like such a great plan after all. "Wanna watch a movie in the living room? I bet they'll be home soon. We can make popcorn, and maybe Lizzie will want to join us."

Riley rested his head on Kollin's shoulder. "Sounds perfect."

# CHAPTER 18

"OH GOD." Kollin tried not to shout as he slammed his head back against the wall. Riley held both of Kollin's hands in one of his and Kollin's pants were down around his ankles. With Riley's mouth engulfing Kollin's dick, Kollin had run out of outlets for expressing how fucking amazing he felt. Riley cupped Kollin's balls and rolled them around while he circled Kollin's tip with his tongue and then plunged his mouth back over Kollin's dick and forced the head to squeeze down Riley's throat.

Kollin closed his eyes and bit his bottom lip. Riley's mouth felt like sin and sweetness rolled into one gloriously wet package. Even Riley's teeth scraping along Kollin's shaft sent shivers through Kollin as Riley sucked him in quickly and then slowly pulled out. Kollin wanted to thrust into his mouth and chase down the orgasm that he was teetering on. But Riley, who no longer had issues taking control in the bedroom, loved nothing more than to drag out Kollin's ecstasy, to make him work for his release. Not giving Kollin time to take off his pants had nothing to do with their lusty rush to get off and instead had everything to do with Riley knowing that restraining Kollin aroused him ten times over.

Riley's other hand, wet from jacking Kollin off, trailed up Kollin's stomach to tweak his nipple. Electricity shot straight to Kollin's groin and his balls tightened up, but Riley gripped the base of Kollin's penis and held it tightly. Kollin slinked away from the edge again, and then Riley's tongue was on his balls.

Over and over again, Riley tortured Kollin, bringing him to the brink of insanity and then pulling him back instead of letting him jump. When Kollin's balls ached from a need to release, he whimpered out a pitiful, "Please."

Riley released Kollin's hands and finally allowed him to grip the back of Riley's head and pump in and out of Riley's mouth. Riley held still and played with Kollin's balls until Kollin's grip tightened. Then Riley slipped a wet finger inside Kollin's ass, and Kollin exploded. His orgasm swept through him and drained the blood from his head so quickly that Kollin thought he might pass out. When the fuzz cleared away, he realized he was still standing with his dick inside Riley's mouth. Ever so gently he pulled out and tugged on Riley's shirt. "C'mere."

Still panting, Kollin crushed his mouth against Riley's. His taste on Riley's mouth turned him on more and bolstered him for what he wanted to do next. So far, every time they fooled around Riley managed to distract Kollin from reciprocating. Kollin didn't want to force himself on Riley, but at the same time, they'd agreed to move forward, and Kollin thought they were both ready.

He gently shoved Riley onto the bed, crawled on top of him, and lifted Riley's shirt as he did. They'd done it enough that Riley no longer had issues with Kollin seeing him shirtless, especially given how emphatically Kollin appreciated his torso each time. He didn't give Riley time to get nervous. Instead he went right for the sweats Riley wore and tugged them down to reveal a pair of dark green boxers.

Riley tensed beneath him, but Kollin climbed back up his chest and kissed his mouth. Between kisses, Kollin reassured Riley.

"I'm ready for this." Kiss to the side of the mouth. "I've been ready for this for a while." Kiss to the hollow of his neck. "Please." Back to the mouth for a longer, deeper kiss.

Kollin ground his hips against Riley while he begged Riley to let him continue. When Riley clutched Kollin closer and nodded, Kollin didn't hesitate. He snuck his hand beneath Riley's boxers and ghosted over coarse hair until his fingers found what was considered Riley's dick. He was stiff, and Kollin fumbled around as he tried to blindly get a feel for Riley's different anatomy. Ri's breathing picked up as Kollin rubbed up and down his length and eventually drew a low moan from Riley.

Building up his courage, Kollin ventured farther south and immediately found warmth and wetness. *Holy fuck. That's wet.* Kollin's dick ached, seeming to understand that his fingers were somewhere it wanted to be. Riley's breathing slowed while Kollin explored, and he stopped squirming, so Kollin moved his slick fingers back to Riley's cock.

He studied Riley's face and searched for clues to see what felt good and what didn't. Riley smiled at Kollin and gripped the back of Kollin's hair, but Kollin could see he wasn't hitting any kind of magical spot. Kollin felt like an idiot for not knowing what to do next. He'd never taken Eli's advice and talked specifics with Riley, and now Kollin wished he'd sucked it up and just asked.

Filled with desperation to please Riley, Kollin leaned in to pepper kisses up his jawline. "I'm sorry. I don't know what to do. Will you show me?"

Riley stared at Kollin for a moment, clearly unsure, scared even.

Kollin nuzzled their noses together and placed a soft kiss on his mouth. "Please."

Riley sighed into the tender gesture and wiggled his boxers off. Kollin sat back on his haunches, his heart racing, and looked at a completely naked Riley for the first time.

Riley used the crook of his arm to cover his eyes, but he allowed Kollin time to look at him. Kollin's heart sank. He grabbed Riley's other hand and linked their fingers together in an effort to ease Riley's anxiety. His scars, which Kollin hardly noticed anymore, stood out against Riley's pale skin, still proudly showing promises of Riley's strength. Kollin brushed his thumb over each of them and then trailed his hand down Riley's side. Riley flinched and sucked in his stomach, and Kollin tucked the ticklish spot away for future endeavors. When he reached Riley's thigh, Kollin gently massaged the muscle and allowed his thumb to drop between the crease of his leg and his groin.

Riley let out a long, slow breath and spread his legs just enough for Kollin to see his dick poking out. Kollin slid his thumb farther over to trail the length of Riley's penis. He wasn't as wet as he'd been earlier, so Kollin wet his thumb in his own mouth and returned to stroking Riley. He jerked his other hand free of Riley's and nudged the inside of Riley's leg.

Still covering his eyes, Riley spread his legs apart completely. Kollin drank in Riley's body spread out before him and wondered why he'd ever been so nervous. Riley was so fucking gorgeous it almost pained Kollin to look at him. Riley's scars, his tattoo, the lip ring that sent shivers through Kollin every time Riley had his mouth on him, even that stupid nose ring that Kollin would've hated on anyone else—they were pieces of Riley that made him Riley. That made him a survivor.

His bottom half was no different. He might not have a "regular-sized" penis or testicles, but seeing Riley laid out on the bed, baring his entire self to Kollin, left no question in his mind whether or not Riley was male.

Relief overwhelmed Kollin, and he fell on top of Riley and pressed their naked bodies together from chest to groin to hairy ankles. Kollin tugged Riley's arm away from his eyes.

"I don't want this to come out wrong or ruin the mood or anything, but you're gorgeous."

Riley shook his head and opened his mouth to say something, but Kollin shushed him.

"I'm serious. I could've just kept going and not said anything, but I need you to believe me on this one. Your parts are different than mine, and it might be awkward the first few times while I figure out what to do, but I find you just as sexy with your clothes off as I do with them on. When I look at you, I don't see anything but an incredibly sexy man. I mean it, Ri. You're hot as fuck. The sexiest guy I've ever been with, by far."

Riley pursed his lips, and, horrified, Kollin watched as tears trickled from his eyes.

"I'm so sorry," Riley whispered as Kollin swiped a tear away with his thumb. "I'm being so dramatic. It's embarrassing."

Kollin shook his head. "After everything you've been through, I would be shocked if you didn't need a moment to start rewiring your brain."

"Rewiring?"

Kollin brushed a clump of platinum-tipped hair out of Riley's face. "Yes. You need to forget everything negative anyone has ever told you about your body, including yourself, and listen only to me."

"Listen to you, huh." Riley grinned. He wrapped his arms around Kollin's bare waist and drew small circles on his back with his thumbs, which made Kollin's cock take interest. Kollin held his breath and tried to stop himself from getting hard. The moment still felt too serious for him to pop wood, but then he saw Riley's eyes light up and his grin widen.

"I'm so sorry," Kollin blurted out. "I know this is important, but it's your fault for being so freaking hot, and now you're touching me, and he's down there, nestled in where it's all warm, and oh, God—" Kollin tried to pull his hips—and dick—away from Riley, but Riley grabbed his ass and pulled him back in.

Kollin tilted his hips up and rubbed his shaft against Riley's slick cock. Riley shuddered and clutched Kollin closer, and Kollin groaned into Riley's ear.

"We can talk later," Riley panted.

"Good idea."

Kollin slid back down Riley's body and forgot to be apprehensive after the sudden change of events. He rubbed the tip of his penis against Riley's cock, and Riley shuddered again but batted Kollin's hand away and moved it farther down, so his fingers slid easily into Riley's vagina. Momentarily stunned, Kollin stared as Riley grabbed Kollin's dick and started jerking him off while furiously rubbing his own cock. Riley groaned—clearly turned on by something he was doing to himself, since Kollin had yet to move—and Kollin snapped out of his haze and gently fingered Riley.

Falling back onto what he knew from being with men, Kollin pumped in and out of Riley and slowly added more fingers as he searched for the elusive G-spot he'd heard so much about. He knew he found it when Riley's whimpers turned into moans and his entire body started to shake. Eager to draw Riley's pleasure out as Riley always did to him, Kollin teased Riley, never focusing on anywhere long enough to bring him to completion.

Riley became insistent and begged Kollin to bring him relief, and Kollin realized his own orgasm was approaching. Feeling Riley squirm beneath him and watching Riley touch himself turned out to be a bigger turn-on than anything Kollin had ever experienced. Kollin still felt like a fumbling idiot, but he must have been doing something right, given the obscene sounds coming out of Riley. His sexual energy was overwhelming, and Kollin had a sudden urge to bury himself in Riley for real.

With that thought Kollin leaped over the edge. His orgasm was shorter and not nearly as intense, but given Riley's state beneath him, Kollin enjoyed it a hell of a lot more. Jizz spurted out of Kollin's cock and landed on Riley's stomach just as Riley folded into himself, and his entire body spasmed with the force of his orgasm. Kollin fingered him through the end, until Riley flopped back on the bed and groaned.

Kollin collapsed on top of him and buried his face in Riley's neck.

"Wow." Riley's voice was hoarse, and he sounded completely surprised. It made Kollin laugh.

"Yep."

"I mean—"

"I told you we'd be good together."

Riley shook his head, which jostled the top of Kollin's. "There's no way you knew it would be that good."

Kollin propped himself up to look at Riley and shrugged. "Maybe not, but it's us. How could it not be that good?"

"You're amazing." Riley grinned. "I still have moments where I think to myself, 'Holy shit, I'm dating Kollin Haverty,' or 'Holy shit, I just had Kollin's dick in my mouth. Kollin, my best friend. Kollin, the guy I crushed on for years.'"

Kollin frowned. "I guess I don't spend a lot of time overanalyzing stuff. I feel good when we're together. That's good enough for me."

Riley sighed. "I wish it was that easy for me."

"It's not always a positive thing. Sometimes I rush into things without thinking through the outcome. Or make rash decisions that I later regret because I'm too in the moment to see all the sides." Kollin rolled off Riley and shoved his legs beneath the covers. "I've even been known to lose my shit and scream at people I care about."

Riley gasped. "No."

"Shocking, I know." Kollin studied Riley's relaxed face. His eyes were closed and a small smile played on his lips, and Kollin's heart filled, knowing he'd help put it there. "So, you're okay with everything I did?"

Riley's eyes fluttered open, and he turned to face Kollin. "Yeah. I was pretty nervous, especially at first. It felt so awkward to know you were so focused on me. I didn't really like it, if I'm being honest. But I guess I forgot to be self-conscious after a while."

"Good. You shouldn't be." Kollin cleared his throat. "I know you've been worried about us having sex. I guess we've both worried about it, and I hope you don't take this the wrong way, but I really wanted to be having sex with you. Like real sex. My penis and your...." Kollin hesitated and frowned. "I don't know what you want me to call it."

Riley laughed. "It's okay to call it a vagina. Just don't use the p-word, please."

Kollin scrunched up his face. "Noted. So yeah, my dick is ready to have sex with your vagina."

Riley burst out laughing, and Kollin grinned.

"I'm serious. And I want to do more than just finger you next time, so you have to show me how to touch you. I was kind of scared I'd hurt you, but you weren't exactly gentle."

Riley covered his face, but Kollin pulled his hands away so he could see his eyes. "I have big feelings inside me right now, Ri. All for you. I'm ready for us. Is that okay with you?"

A slow smile spread over Riley's face. "More than okay."

Kollin made a face and stuck out his tongue. "Is that it? I get no reciprocation after that huge confession of big feelings?"

Riley rolled his eyes. "I have big feelings too. Okay? Like the biggest. They're huge."

"Thank you. Was that so hard?"

"You're ridiculous."

"Maybe. Maybe not."

They lay together and stared at one another for a while. Kollin felt drunk in love, even if he wasn't quite ready to take the leap and confess anything more than big feelings. There were too many obstacles in their way to make that jump, and Kollin didn't want to force them three steps back when he finally felt like they were on the edge of getting everything right.

Riley grasped Kollin's hand. "I know this may not be the best time…."

Kollin looked at Riley. "Oh boy. Should I be scared?"

"No. It's just… I really want us to stay in this place we're at now. It's a good place, don't you think?"

Kollin nodded and waited for Riley to continue.

"Right. So I was thinking I'm ready to go visit my parents. I want to heal and let go of resentment and let go of wondering what if. So, I had Greg drive me by their house last week, and it doesn't look like they've moved. Same car in the drive, anyway."

"Wow. That's great, Ri." Kollin squeezed his hand. "Like I said before, I don't know how they'll react, but finding closure can only be a good thing in the long run."

"I know. It's just such a scary step, you know? You think I should call or just drop by?"

Kollin blew out a long breath. Calling might give his parents a chance to refuse to see Riley, but telling Riley that felt cruel. Adam's voice popped into his mind. Kollin needed to start backing up his words with his actions. He'd told Riley over and over again that his scars represented his strength, so why didn't he trust him to handle his opinion? After everything Riley had been through—on his own, no less—Riley deserved the truth.

"Honestly I'd just drop by. If you call first, they may not agree to see you, and I don't think that route would offer you as much closure." Kollin rolled over to look at Riley. "This way at least they'd be able to see everything you've accomplished on your own. I've never met your parents, but I can't imagine they wouldn't be proud of the way you've taken care of yourself all these years."

Riley snorted. "I don't think they'll be proud of anything having to do with me transitioning. Or leaving like that."

"Maybe not, but I hope they can look past that, eventually. What are you planning on telling them?"

"I don't know." Riley looked up at the ceiling. "I just want to know how they feel about me. I can't *not* be who I am. At least not the man part."

"Good. It's good you know that."

"They used to tell me that everything I was going through was just a phase." Riley closed his eyes, and Kollin knew that whatever Riley wanted to say was difficult. "I hope when they see me like this, they'll understand how hard it was for me to live as a girl."

Kollin placed his hand on Riley's cheek and gently caressed his skin. When Riley opened his eyes, Kollin could see the fear in them. "Why would I do this to myself if I weren't already more miserable? I just want them to get that."

"I know." It wasn't enough. He wanted to tell Riley they would get it, that they would welcome him with open arms, that they would love their son as much as they had loved their now defunct daughter, but he knew better than anyone that parents didn't always come through in the end. Sometimes, and more often than not, the people you love the most let you down the hardest. Instead he gathered Riley in his arms and whispered the only thing he knew for certain would hold true. "Whatever happens, I'll be there."

Riley nodded. The scruff of his face tickled Kollin's neck, and he tightened his arms around Kollin's waist.

# CHAPTER 19

RILEY STARED out of the car window at his parents' house. Sunrays blazed behind it and almost cast a halo around it. Through the front window of the house, Riley could see the flickering lights from the television and what looked like the kitchen light on in the background. It was too late for his parents not to have eaten yet, but maybe they were doing the dishes.

Kollin slid his hand down Riley's arm and grabbed his hand. "You okay?"

Riley looked over at Kollin and nodded. "Feels surreal."

"You ready or you want to wait a bit?"

"Let's just go. It's not going to get any easier." Riley squeezed Kollin's hand and opened the car door. The wind blew and its chilly bite reminded Riley that summer was truly over. He waited for Kollin to come around to his side of the car, and together they walked toward the house.

"Um… quick question," Kollin said.

"Yeah?"

"Are we dating?"

Riley raised his eyebrows and looked at Kollin. "I thought we were."

"No. I mean to your parents. Are we dating?"

"Oh." Riley hadn't really figured out how to explain Kollin yet. How could he until he saw how they took the news of his transition? "I don't know. I thought I'd just play that part by ear. But I promise, if I don't tell them today, I will soon." Riley stuttered for a moment. "I mean, if I see them again, anyway."

"Okay." Riley couldn't tell if Kollin was truly okay with his decision or not. He knew Kollin well enough that he wouldn't make an issue of it, either way, but he couldn't worry about hurting Kollin's feelings as he walked up to the front stoop of his old house.

With a deep breath, Riley knocked on the door. Barking immediately erupted from behind it. Riley looked at Kollin. "We didn't have a dog before."

Riley's dad screamed, "Lorraine, will you shut that damn dog up?"

"You're the one who wanted a dog, Bob," his mom's voice called back.

The dog continued to bark, and it sounded as if it were pawing at the door.

"I didn't want a crazy dog who barked every time someone knocks on the door." Riley could tell his dad was walking to the door as he spoke. Shit. He'd hoped his mom would answer.

"All dogs bark, hon." Riley could picture his mom rolling her eyes as she spoke, a small smile on her face even though exasperation laced every word.

That simple thought made his heart ache. He really wanted the evening to go well. He missed his parents. They hadn't understood him or what he was going through when he was in high school, but they'd loved him and showed it often. They broke his heart when they made their last-ditch effort to keep him from transitioning by threatening to stop paying his college tuition, and he'd held on to his anger and resentment for years. Every obstacle and poor decision he'd made over the past several years, he'd blamed on them. Even everything that happened with Tony became their responsibility.

The door opened, and Riley's knees buckled, but Kollin grabbed his arm to steady him.

"Yes?" his dad said, looking expectantly from Riley to Kollin as he held a small dog back with his foot.

"Uh…." Riley's heart raced, and he frantically searched for what he'd planned to say if his parents didn't immediately recognize him.

His mother appeared over his dad's shoulder. "Who is it, Bo— Riley?" She pushed past Riley's dad and grabbed Riley's face. "Riley?"

Unbidden, tears popped into Riley's eyes. "Mom."

She gripped Riley's shoulders and pulled him in to her chest. Riley wrapped his arms around his mom and held on as the tears fell freely. She held him through his heaving sobs, and did nothing more than cling to him as fiercely as he clung to her. Riley wasn't aware enough to know what Kollin or his dad were doing, but when he finally pulled away, his dad was holding the overexcited dog and Kollin stood awkwardly to the side.

He swiped most of the tears off his face and looked at his dad, who stared back without saying anything. The silence grew awkward until Riley's mom grabbed his arm and tugged him inside.

"Why don't you two come in?"

Riley vaguely noticed that Kollin followed behind him as everyone shuffled into the living room. Not much had changed from what he remembered. In fact pictures of Riley still hung over the fireplace.

Riley's dad sat in the recliner. His mom gestured toward the couch and sat right next to him, so she and Kollin flanked either side of him. The dog immediately ran to Riley and Kollin, sniffed at their shoes, but didn't jump up.

Riley still didn't know what to say. He hadn't expected his mom to react so viscerally. It threw him off his already-wobbly balance. Relief flooded him when Kollin gently nudged his knee.

"Oh. Right." He turned to Kollin. "This is my best friend, Kollin." He gestured toward his parents. "Lorraine and Bob Meadows."

Kollin smiled his easy grin and reached around Riley to shake his mom's hand. "I spoke to your husband at the door. It's nice to meet you, Mrs. Meadows."

Riley's mom smiled politely. "Likewise." But she immediately turned her attention back to Riley as though she couldn't believe he was sitting on her couch.

Riley cleared his throat. "I, uh... I didn't know if I'd be welcome, so I asked Kollin to come with me." Riley's mom covered her mouth with her hand, and tears slipped down her cheeks.

"I can't believe you're here," she whispered and placed her hand on Riley's knee.

Riley stared at it. He supposed it was meant to be a comforting gesture, but instead, it only ramped up his nerves. His dad still hadn't said a word to him.

"Riley," his mom said.

He looked up to meet her gaze, and she placed her palm on his cheek to graze over the scruff on his face.

"I didn't think you'd approve, so I stayed away," he said softly.

Riley's dad cleared his throat but didn't say anything, and his mom slowly lowered her hand. "I never meant to push you away from us. I just...." She paused. "I'm so sorry, Riley. I'm so very sorry I didn't listen."

Lorraine clutched Riley's hand in hers and started to cry again.

Riley's dad cleared his throat again, and this time Riley gathered the courage to look at him. His face was red, but the glare on his glasses prevented Riley from seeing his eyes. His mouth was set in a stern frown, though.

"You shouldn't have worried your mother like that," his dad finally said.

His words knocked the wind out of Riley's chest—so much said in that short sentence. His mother had worried over him for years. His dad had not.

"I'm sorry." Should he say more? He felt stupid, unable to believe he'd spent so many years running from his family, and here he was sitting next to his mom, who didn't seem to be able to stop touching him. "I thought you were done with me."

Lorraine shook her head. "Never, Riley. You're our dau… our only child."

Her slipup didn't go unnoticed, and some of Riley's anger returned. "You cut me off unless I swore to stop moving forward in transitioning, and I couldn't do that. What was I supposed to think?"

"Don't take that tone with your mom." Bob's voice was stern, and Riley shrank back into his seat.

"Sorry, Mom."

"Hush, Bob. Give Riley a chance to talk." She turned back to Riley. "I didn't know how serious you were about all of this."

"But I told you, Mom. I *told* you something wasn't right. I told you exactly what was wrong. I begged you to listen to me. And all you ever did was tell me I needed therapy. And when my therapist encouraged me to transition, that still wasn't good enough for you."

"We just thought you should get a second opinion," Riley's mom pleaded. "You were my daughter, Riley. I used to braid your hair and dress you in frilly lace dresses. I spent years picturing how I'd help you get dressed in a beautiful white dress on your wedding day. I didn't understand your desire to suddenly become a male."

Riley sighed. "I didn't want to *become* a male. I *am* male. Look at me, Mom." Riley sat up straight as his mom looked him over. "It doesn't matter what you thought. I'm a man. I know it would've sucked to reframe your future with your child, but it was hard for me too, and I didn't want to do it alone."

Tears streamed down his mom's face, and his dad's anger poured out as he shouted, "Then why the hell did you cut off all contact with us? It's been over four years. We should be punished for four years because we couldn't understand you?"

"I thought you were done with me," Riley repeated.

"We're your parents," Bob yelled. "Of course we weren't done with you."

Riley bit back his retort that not all parents felt that way. It was on the tip of his tongue, but saying it in front of Kollin felt cruel, and to insinuate that his parents were as shitty as ones who would, could only drag their progress eight steps back.

Riley remained quiet and clueless as to how to make the situation better. There were too many hurt feelings on his side and apparently on his parents' as well. And there were still a lot of unanswered questions— like if his parents cared so much, why they hadn't found him after he left college. At least Riley no longer doubted that his mom, and maybe his dad too, had missed him and were happy to see him again—even if they still thought of him as their daughter.

"I'm sorry I hurt you," Riley said, surprised at how true his words were once they slipped out. "I was hurt too, and I felt rejected. I thought it was what you wanted. I thought it would be easier on all of us if I made a clean break of it instead of forcing you to do it."

Silence followed Riley's apology until his mom began fluttering. "Oh my. Do either of you want something to eat or drink?"

"No thank you, ma'am," Kollin said as he absently patted the dog's head.

"No thanks, Mom," Riley echoed. He wondered if the moment could get any more awkward. He could tell his mom wanted to ask him questions, but she seemed uncertain. Whether because she didn't know where to start, or feared she'd run him off, or some other reason, Riley couldn't tell. But she hadn't taken her eyes off of him for more than a moment since they sat.

"I don't know what to do," she finally whispered.

"What do you mean?"

"I prayed for this moment—every night for years." Lorraine wiped a tear off her cheek. "You're so different. Grown up and… look what you've done to your hair, and you have so many piercings. And…." She folded her hands in her laps and looked down at them. "Did you have a mastectomy?"

Riley's dad shifted in his seat, and Riley ignored the urge to fidget as well. He knew his parents would want to know everything that he'd gone through. He'd rehearsed what he would say, intending to be as clinical and brief as possible.

"I lucked out and found a job in construction at the end of my freshman year. It paid pretty well, so I had enough to start taking testosterone and support myself. After a while I saved up enough for top surgery. I had some ups and downs over the years, but I found a couple of people who supported me and helped me get through. I've been saving again, hoping to get bottom surgery sometime in the next year or two."

Lorraine nodded slowly when Riley finished speaking. "So you're a man now. Officially."

Riley almost laughed. She was trying, at least. And if he put himself in her shoes, he could see how difficult it would be to process.

"This is the strangest fucking thing I've ever seen in my life," Bob muttered. "Are you sure this is what you want?"

Riley sighed, and in a brazen act that seemed to come from someone else, he stood up and lifted his shirt to show his scars. "I'm pretty fucking sure, Dad."

"Oh God." Lorraine stood and raised her hand toward Riley, as though to touch his scars. She seemed to realize what she was doing and immediately jerked her hand back to her chest and clutched it in her other hand. "My poor baby."

"It's okay, Mom," Riley said and dropped his shirt. "They don't hurt anymore."

She sat there shaking her head as tears fell steadily out of her eyes. She looked around Riley at Kollin. "Were you the one who helped him through this?"

"Ah… no, ma'am. I didn't know Riley back then," Kollin said, obviously stumbling over his words. Riley grimaced. He'd talked about Kollin often when he still lived there. They knew he and Kollin were friends before he left for college. Kollin had just unknowingly opened up another can of worms.

"Oh," Lorraine said as she sniffed out the lie, like any good mother. "I thought you were the same Kollin he used to talk about."

Kollin looked up at Riley with his mouth open. Clearly he didn't know how to respond.

"He is, Mom." Riley felt stupid saying her name so many times, but after so long without saying "Mom," he couldn't seem to stop. "He's just trying not to make me feel bad by pointing out that he didn't know where I was for all those years either. We ran into each other when I was back in town for a job, and he helped me decide to come see you guys again. He, uh, persuaded me that I'd acted rashly when I cut everyone off."

"Thank you." She reached around Riley and squeezed Kollin's hand. Then she looked back to Riley. "We looked for you when you didn't come home that summer. When we first stopped hearing from you, I assumed you were just pouting, and we'd work it all out when you got home for summer break. But there was nothing. No one at the school knew where you'd gone. We tracked down the girl we thought was your roommate, and she said you'd requested a transfer after the first day, and a week later you were gone."

Riley sank back into the couch and lowered his head as shame crept through his veins. "I spoke with someone at housing and explained my situation. She helped me get set up in a single."

"But you used to tell us everything you and she did together."

Riley shrugged. "I lied."

Kollin's leg pressed against his again, and he glanced over at him. Kollin raised his eyebrows and looked toward the door. Riley scrunched up his face in question.

Kollin leaned in a little closer and whispered, "Do you want me to leave?"

Riley shook his head. Maybe it was selfish to ask him to sit through that torture, but he still wanted Kollin there. "Not unless you want to."

Kollin smiled and sat back in the couch. "Just making sure."

Lorraine's eyes flickered from Kollin to Riley and back again. "You two are... friends?"

Riley swallowed hard. He never would've dreamed reuniting with his parents would turn out as well as it had. He could possibly ruin the entire evening by also coming out as gay. His parents had already endured a huge shock. Should he really put them through another one?

But if not now, when?

"Uh, yeah," Riley said. "We are friends, but we're also dating. Have been for a few months."

"Oh," his mother said. His dad leaned forward in his seat and buried his head in his hands. Riley resisted the urge to apologize. He'd made a lot of mistakes—some pretty fucking huge mistakes—but being gay wasn't one of them.

"I don't suppose this is a phase?" his dad asked from behind his hands.

"No, sir. I've always liked guys. I don't think it's going to change now."

Bob chuffed and looked up. "Worth a shot."

*Did Dad just make a joke?* Riley glanced down at Kollin, who raised his eyebrows a couple of times and grinned.

"I know me showing up out of the blue like this is six kinds of awkward. I didn't know if you guys would be okay seeing me, so I don't know what else to say. The job that brought me back to town is about to end, but I'll be moving back to the area soon. The construction company I work for, Drummond's, is opening a branch in Durham. My boss thinks he can get me transferred here. If you're willing to accept me like this, I'd like to try to fix things."

"Yes," his mom said instantly and grabbed his hand again. "Of course. We just want you back. Do you need somewhere to stay? We haven't changed your room, but you can do whatever you want to it. Stay as long as you like."

And just like that, with his mom's immediate and easy acceptance of him, tears filled Riley's eyes. He looked at his dad, who, while not exactly rude, hadn't been very welcoming either.

Bob nodded. "If you ever pull this shit on me or your mother again, though, I will hunt you down and wring your neck myself. You hear?"

Riley felt Kollin's hand on his back, and his mother gathered Riley into her arms. "I'm so sorry, Riley. I'm so, so sorry. It might take me some time to get used to it, but I just want you back. You're still the same inside. That's all I want."

Riley nodded, and her shoulder soaked up his tears. He felt as if he might explode any minute, given the jumbled feelings raging around inside him. But the overwhelming feeling was relief. His parents still loved him. They looked for him. They prayed for his return, and were willing to work zhrough their issues to accept him.

# CHAPTER 20

BEFORE KOLLIN and Riley left his parents' house, Riley's mom had shoved a wad of cash into his hand and told him to buy some new clothes and whatever he might want to put in his room should he decide to move back in.

Riley was hesitant at first, knowing his mom only gave him the money out of guilt, but he eventually realized she would feel better if he just took it. And he could use some new clothes. For the past several years, nearly all of his clothes had come from Walmart or Goodwill, and Riley was excited to get something nice for a change.

Riley was an emotional mess the remainder of that night, so Kollin dropped him off with a long hug and a plea to call if he needed anything. Some sort of construction catastrophe kept Riley from their Friday night dinner plans, and as usual, Kollin spent Saturday morning preparing and eating brunch with the whole family.

Eager to spend some quality time shopping with his man, Kollin grabbed Riley's hand as they walked into the mall that afternoon. The place was packed, even for a Saturday. Only the thought of shopping without having to spend his own money made Kollin eager to power through the huge crowd.

"You going to get new stuff for your room too?" Kollin asked.

"I don't know." Riley looked through the windows of each store they passed. "You think I should move back in with them? It's been so long since I lived with anyone. Ugh, and the thought of living with my parents again…."

"I live with my parents," Kollin said. "Hell, you live with my parents on the weekends."

Riley shook his head. "It's different."

Kollin sighed. "How? They're still my parents."

"I don't mean it in a bad way. But they're Adam and Elijah—Savior and Benefactor. They're cool as hell."

"Umm, not too long ago you were telling me how scary Eli is."

"You know what I mean." Riley wandered into a store and started browsing through the jeans.

"Fine." Kollin huffed as he trailed behind him. He didn't necessarily agree with Riley. Living with Adam and Eli might sound like a dream, but they were still meddling parents who constantly wanted to interfere in Kollin's life. Kollin never complained. He knew just how awful parents could be, through first and secondhand experience, but that didn't mean his life was perfect.

"What if all we do is fight?" Riley looked at Kollin then. "What if they keep calling me 'she' or their 'daughter'? Riley is a unisex name, so I never changed it, but now I wonder if that wouldn't have made it easier for them to accept."

"I don't think what they call you is going to make this easier or harder for them to accept." Kollin picked up a shirt, held it up in front of Riley, and then put it back. "What's important is that they're willing to try. More than that they seem to want nothing more than to have you back in their lives. I mean, for fuck's sake, Ri. Your mom gave you money, knowing you could take it and never see her again."

Riley threw the jeans he was holding back down. "I wouldn't do that."

"Of course you wouldn't. I'm just saying, I think she really wants better for you than what you've had over the last few years. That's gotta mean something."

"So you think I should move in with them?"

Kollin shrugged. "Why not? At least at first. They want you there. It's a free place to live. They'll be forced to see you every day, and greater exposure generally leads to greater acceptance in the people who are willing to try. And your mom looked like she'd be signing up for PFLAG if it meant having you home again. What's not to like about any of that?"

Riley groaned. "Living with my parents is what's not to like about that. Having to answer to them whenever I want to do something. What if I want to spend the night with you? They'll freak if I'm out all night. Or worse, what if you end up staying over? I would die if they caught us together in bed."

Kollin laughed. "That last one is your issue, man. But I think they'll recognize that you're four years older now, and you've been taking care of yourself for that long. And if they don't, talk to them."

Riley shook his head and motioned for Kollin to follow him out of the store, apparently unhappy with everything the store had to offer after looking at two racks of clothes. "My parents and I don't talk like that. They talk, and I listen."

"That's not how it went down the other night. Look. If you don't want to live with them, then don't. But at least be fair, and base your judgments of them off who they are now." Kollin hesitated and then continued. "What they did back then was wrong, but you made some mistakes too, and assuming you're the only one who learned from this is foolish. Especially given the lengths they're willing to go to get you back home. Your mom might pay you to do nothing just so she could stare at you all day long."

"Yeah." Riley remained quiet after that, and Kollin wondered if he'd overstepped his bounds. As far as he was concerned, the more ties Riley had to the area the better.

After a few moments, Riley tugged Kollin into a clothing store, and they spent the next couple of hours trying on clothes. Six shopping bags and one box of shoes later, they trudged out of the mall and stowed their new clothes in Kollin's trunk.

"Where to now?" Kollin asked as he settled into the driver's seat.

Riley sighed with exasperation and looked at Kollin with a smile on his face. "Take me to Bed Bath & Beyond, Jeeves. I guess I've got new bedding to buy if I'm going to be crashing at my parents' house soon."

Kollin grinned over the console at Riley. "For what it's worth, I think that's definitely the right decision."

"Yeah, yeah," Riley muttered. "Just drive."

KOLLIN SLAMMED his book bag down into the passenger seat of his car. Mondays should be banned. Not only had his normally flaky lab partner "forgotten" to do her part of their assignment over the weekend—meaning Kollin had to either pick up the slack *again* or accept a subpar grade—but his psych partner's grandmother had passed away over the weekend, and she would be out of town for the remainder of the week, dumping the rest of their assignment solely in Kollin's lap. He'd missed lunch when he stayed after class to beg his professor for an extension on their project, and he was supposed to be at the center in forty-five minutes to relieve Adam.

All Kollin wanted to do was go home, crawl under the covers, and pretend as though the day had never happened. Instead he banged his head against the steering wheel a few times and took off for the nearest drive-thru. The only upside Kollin could find was that, if he rushed, he'd have just enough time to drop by H4H and see Riley for just a few minutes. Knowing Riley's love for ice cream, Kollin tacked on a Frosty to his order at the drive-thru and drove off, his spirits slightly higher at the prospect of surprising Riley.

Kollin parked on the completed side of the building and walked around back toward the construction zone. He peeked through the open windows of the nearly completed building and spotted Riley immediately. Kollin wasn't technically supposed to be on site without a hard hat, and after Riley had been so hesitant to even touch Kollin the first time, Kollin had avoided speaking with him at all while there. With a daunting week of extra work ahead of him, Kollin was willing to risk raising suspicions just for dropping by.

Kollin snagged the arm of a worker walking past him. "Would you mind asking Riley to come out here for a minute?"

The man stared at Kollin with a strange look on his face and then stuck his head in the window and shouted, "Hey, Riley, your boyfriend's here."

Fear sliced through Kollin, and he gaped first at the guy next to him, who smirked and walked away, then looked back at Riley, who had dropped whatever he was holding and stared at Kollin with his jaw dropped.

Kollin recalled the guy who had seen them kissing in the parking lot. He'd completely forgotten about the incident and assumed Riley had too, since he never brought it up. Could this be the same guy? Had to be.

A few of the workers surrounding Riley started to laugh, but one of them shouted, "You're such an asshole, Jenson."

Jenson shrugged from his position near the door. "Call it like I see it."

There was some more laughter, but no one seemed surprised by Jenson's sudden outing of Riley. A light bulb switched on in Kollin's brain, and he realized the crew thought Jenson was making a joke, giving Riley a hard time. Relieved, he let out a deep breath and looked back at Riley to offer a smile. Riley still looked terrified, though, and he hadn't taken his eyes off Kollin. Everyone else had returned to what they were doing except for Riley, who seemed frozen in place until Greg entered the room and drew Riley's attention.

Kollin backed up a few steps, feeling confident that he wasn't welcome and desperate not to make life worse for Riley.

"Kollin," Riley called out. "Wait."

Kollin stopped his retreat but remained where he stood.

When Riley spoke again, his voice was strong. He was accustomed to speaking to these men, to being in charge of them. Only someone who knew Riley as well as Kollin could detect the slightest hint of nervousness. "Listen up, everyone. Jokes like that aren't going to be tolerated on this site. You may not mean anything by it, or you may be trying to be intentionally cruel, but you knew going into this job the type of youth who might be hanging around the site, and you agreed to be respectful."

A few of the men nodded, unperturbed by Riley's speech, and went back to work. But Jenson wasn't going to let it go so easily. "Wasn't being rude, boss. Just speaking the truth. Maybe you should keep your private matters indoors."

If not for the derision in his voice, the rest of Riley's crew might have blown off Jenson's comment. Clearly homophobic, Jenson teetered on the line of disrespect without using the specific words that would automatically get him fired.

"I don't ask who you're dating on the weekend, Jenson, so I don't see how it's any of your business who I spend mine with." Riley looked around the room. The men seemed to have caught on that it was more than a misunderstanding or a lame attempt at a joke. "If anyone has a problem with me, you can take it up with me after five. Until then, we have a job to finish."

Greg cleared his throat. His quiet presence was formidable, and Kollin felt a rush of gratitude that he had Ri's back. "Or better yet, you can take it up with me. I'll even be happy to send you packing now."

A mumbling of "yes, sirs" went around the room, and Riley nodded at Greg. "I'll be back in a few minutes," he said and walked out. He kept walking when he got to Kollin until they were out of sight on the other side of the building.

Riley put his back against the wall, slid down to the ground, and buried his face in his knees. Kollin kneeled before him but didn't lay a hand on him. He was so proud of Riley he thought he would burst, but first he needed to make sure Riley wasn't about to have some kind of panic attack.

"Are you okay?"

Riley left his head buried but shook it. "Am I still alive? Did that just happen?"

"Damn skippy it just happened," Kollin said, unable to hide the glee in his voice. "You were amazing. Oh my God. You've got to use that voice in bed. Where did you learn to do that?" He pitched his voice low to mimic Riley. "'You can take it up with me after five'…. Get on your knees and give me a blow job. Gah."

Riley raised his head, and a weary smile graced his face. "You have a one track mind. I just outed myself to the whole crew, and you're thinking about sex?"

Kollin's grin grew bigger, and even though they were both half sitting on the ground, he still somehow managed to tackle hug Riley. "I'm so damn proud of you, Ri."

"Thank you." Riley's words were muffled by Kollin's arm, so Kollin let go. "I may not be able to walk back in there ever again, but it felt good."

"Don't be silly. That Jenson guy's a douche, but everyone else seemed okay. You must be a damn good boss, because it's obvious how much those guys respect you. Fuck, Ri. That was incredible. Who knows how many people you influenced just now by standing up for us. This is huge."

Riley shook his head. "I don't think it's that big of a deal."

"It is, though," Kollin insisted. "Just a few months ago, you didn't even want to give me a bro hug in front of them. And we weren't even dating. And who knows how many of them will think twice before making judgments on someone in the LGBT community now. All because of you."

Riley laughed. "Don't get ahead of yourself. It's not like I'm going to tell them I'm trans."

Kollin shrugged. "Doesn't matter. That's none of their business, anyway."

"Yeah?" Riley peeked at Kollin. "Doesn't make me a wimp for not telling them?"

"Of course not. Your job is to live your life as authentically as possible. That doesn't mean you have to be an advocate for the entire community, just because you're trans."

Riley nodded. "That sounds better than me being scared shitless to tell people."

"Hey." Kollin grabbed Riley's hand. "If you ever get to the point where you want to be an advocate, I'll be there. But honestly it's no one's business but yours and who you share a bed with. And since that's me, you're covered there. You're a man, Riley. Whether cis or trans doesn't matter."

"Thank you," Riley said softly. They sat in silence for a few moments, and Riley looked at Kollin again. "Why're you here, anyway? Is everything okay?"

"Oh shit," Kollin gasped. "Your Frosty. I bet it's all melted now."

Riley grinned. "You bought me a Frosty? I love Frosties."

"I'm aware." Kollin stood up. "Do you also love really cold chocolate milk? Because that's probably all I can offer you right now."

Riley hoisted himself off the ground. "After all of that, I'll take all the chocolate I can get."

Kollin grabbed Riley's hand and leaned in to gently graze his lips across Riley's cheek. With a light squeeze, he dropped Riley's hand and headed back to the car. He wasn't stupid enough to think Riley would want to flaunt their relationship just because he'd come out.

"I'm afraid I have some bad news to go along with your ice cream." Kollin filled Riley in as quickly as he could on the walk back to his car. Riley understood and was appropriately sympathetic. With a little subtle suggestion on Kollin's part, Riley even mentioned spending some time with his mom and dad during the week.

They parted with an awkward wave to one another, but Kollin pulled out of the parking lot feeling considerably lighter than he had when he pulled in. Maybe Mondays weren't so bad, after all.

# CHAPTER 21

"OH MAN. I forgot how good these are." Riley grabbed another grilled cheese fry off the plate his mom had placed in front of him.

"Well, eat up. I made plenty. And when your father gets home, we'll have chicken and dumplings. Do you still like them?" Lorraine asked.

"'Course I do, Mom." Riley took a bite of the gooey, cheesy fry and moaned. "You didn't have to go to all this trouble, though."

She waved him off. "I wanted you to have your favorites. I know it's not exactly a well-balanced meal, but I couldn't help myself."

Though Lorraine smiled every time she looked back at him, she still sounded as if she might break down in tears at any moment. Riley totally got the conflicting emotions, but he didn't know how to fix it. Kollin was probably right. Only time and consistency would move his family out of their awkward phase.

"Thanks. I really appreciate it."

"Anytime," she said and returned to her dumpling dough.

Riley ate a few more of the fries and pondered whether he should tell her about the new bedding still in the trunk of Kollin's car. Living between a hotel and Kollin's house left him with very little storage space, especially since he didn't have a car of his own. He hated relying on everyone else to get around, but he didn't have any other choice. Once he finally had bottom surgery, he could focus on saving for a car. He could move forward in life without the stress of transitioning attached to every decision he made.

God. He couldn't wait.

"Hey, Mom," he said, still partially unable to believe what he was about to do. "I thought about your offer—to live here."

"Oh?" His mom's voice sounded shaky, filled with anticipation and trepidation.

"I bought a new bedspread the other day. And some sheets."

Lorraine spun around and flung flour all over the floor. Hope shone in her eyes. "That's wonderful," she said, clearly trying to stifle her excitement.

"I'm still going to be at the hotel during the week. We'll actually be packing up soon. The job's almost done. But I thought I could stay here at least one weekend before I go back. See how it goes." Riley flipped one of his cheese fries over and over. "I've gotten used to living on my own and not answering to anyone. I don't want to come home and ruin our relationship before we even fix it because I'm suddenly expected to follow a curfew or something."

Lorraine dusted off her hands and came to sit at the table with Riley. She grabbed Riley's hand in both of hers. "I feel like I'm constantly walking on eggshells with you because I don't want to upset you and have you disappear again. But please know that you coming home and not having a curfew is going to be the very easiest change for your father and me to deal with."

Riley burst out laughing and his mom smiled.

"I missed you." Riley's confession tumbled out easily.

"We missed you too. So much." She squeezed his hand and went back to her dumplings. "I meant what I said. I'm working on this whole transition thing, but you might have to be patient with us. I went online yesterday and watched I don't know how many videos about all of the ways I can accidentally insult you. Seems to me after everything someone like you has been through, you shouldn't be so sensitive, but what do I know?"

Riley grinned and shook his head. Of course she researched it— and still somehow managed to be a little insulting in her delivery. He couldn't deny she was trying, though, and some of the doubt he harbored fell away. "How about we make a pact? You keep making me grilled cheese fries, and I'll tell you whenever you insult me."

Lorraine laughed and peeked over her shoulder at Riley. "You know, when I look at you or hear you talking, it's very obvious to me that you're a man now. But when I think about you, I still see my little girl." She turned her back to Riley again. "I don't want to erase my little girl from my memories, but I do want to get to know my son. I'm bound to mess up sometimes."

Riley choked up and wondered how many tears he'd shed before he was finally in a good place with his parents again. "I can live with that." They sat in silence for a few minutes, until Riley pushed his chair back. He went to his mom and wrapped his arms around her shoulders from behind. "For the record, I never meant for you to forget who you raised. I'm sorry if I made it sound that way."

Lorraine clutched his arms and nodded. "We might just make this work, then."

Riley sat back down at the table, and his mom popped the dumplings into a big pot. "Your father should be home any minute. He's looking forward to dinner tonight as well. Don't let his gruffness fool you."

Riley huffed. While his mom had visibly made an effort to welcome Riley back into the home, his dad seemed a bit more reticent. After everything he'd put his parents through, Riley figured his dad deserved some time and space to wrap his head around everything.

"He just doesn't know how to talk to you anymore," Lorraine continued. "I think he always wanted a son, but we couldn't have any more children after you, and he was resigned to only having a daughter. Don't get me wrong. He adored you, but you know how he is, so into hunting and fishing. He wanted to do all of that bonding stuff with a boy."

Riley tore a fry into little pieces and tried not to sulk. "He could've done it with me."

"Oh, he knew that, but you never showed any interest, and they're such manly things in his eyes." Lorraine shrugged. "He has a son now, but it's not what he expected, and like I said before, in so many ways, to us you're still our little girl. Just give him time."

His mom had always rambled when she became nervous, and apparently the subject of his dad had her on edge. Riley couldn't help but be glad for the fact. His dad had never been much of a talker—more of an enforcer than anything else. He worked hard, though, and Riley had never once doubted his dad loved him. Well, not until the end, anyway.

"We'll figure it out somehow." He hoped.

Lorraine smiled over her shoulder. "Tell me about this Kollin. I remember you used to talk about him all the time, but I thought you were just friends."

Riley smiled. "We were. He was my best friend. He was the first person who accepted me like this, even when I looked like a girl. I mean, his dad runs the center I used to sneak away to, and he's great too. But Kollin was the first kid my age."

"You used to sneak away to a center? What kind of center?"

"Oh, boy." Riley sighed. "I guess we have a lot to catch up on. I forget how much I used to hide from you." Riley filled his mom in on HOPE and the time he used to spend there.

Clearly shocked, she shook her head. "Maybe if we'd known how much time you were spending there, we'd have taken your request more seriously." She sighed. "Or maybe we wouldn't have. I remember thinking you were way too young to make a decision like that, but I watched a YouTube video yesterday about a five-year-old boy who was transitioning. Can you believe that? Just five years old."

Riley nodded. "I think I knew around that age that something wasn't right. If I'd had a better grasp on gender, I might've understood. But by the time I really figured it out, I also knew it was shameful to not act like a girl." Riley shrugged. "Everyone's different, I guess."

"I guess," Lorraine echoed and poked at the dumplings in the pot. "You and Kollin started dating just recently, then?"

"Yep. After we ran into each other again, he eventually asked me out."

"He already knew that you're gay? Is that the right word?"

Riley laughed. "Yeah, Mom. Gay is the right word. And yes, he knew. We used to talk about boys together all the time."

"Yes, I remember when you used to talk about different boys you had a crush on. Another reason we assumed you were being foolish about *being* a boy." Lorraine frowned.

Riley again resisted the urge to apologize. "I know it's confusing."

She waved her hand around, seeming to dismiss her own comment, and lightened her tone. "All that time Kollin had a crush on you, then?"

Riley squirmed in his seat. He hadn't told his mom much of what had gone on during his time in Boone, and he wanted to avoid it, if at all possible. Riley firmly believed the knowledge would bring her nothing but turmoil, and there was no reason for her to know. He needed to handle the situation delicately.

"Not really." Riley cleared his throat. "At first I thought he felt bad for me. He knew I wasn't exactly lucky in the love department, given I'm trans. I thought he wanted to prove to me that someone would want me. We had a great first date, though, and it seemed pretty obvious we were into each other. It just grew from there."

"That's lovely. He sounds like a lovely boy. We'll have to have him over again sometime…. I mean, if that's something you would like."

"Sure. I think you'll like him a lot." Riley shifted again. "I know springing the whole gay thing on you on top of the trans thing is a bit of a shock, but if it's any solace, you couldn't put in an order for the perfect woman and have her turn out any better for me than Kollin is. He's been through a lot too and come out of it stronger and more compassionate."

"Hmm…," his mom said as she grabbed some bowls out of the cabinet to set the table. "Sounds like maybe you're in love with him."

"What?" Riley asked. He didn't know why his mom's observation surprised him. Of course he loved Kollin. He always had. Their conversation about having "big feelings" for one another left little to no doubt in his mind that they were tiptoeing around the L word. Hearing his mom say it after they'd spent all of three hours together in the past five years was shocking.

"I'm sorry. I guess I'm jumping ahead of myself. You've only been dating a few months. You just speak so highly of him."

"It's okay. I guess it's probably true," Riley admitted. "I just hadn't thought of it in those terms before."

"It must feel different when you've been friends for so long, especially if you were as close as you say."

"Exactly," Riley said. He wanted to delve into Kollin further with his mom, but the front door opened and interrupted them.

"Oh. There's your father," Lorraine said, somewhat unnecessarily, and then raised her voice. "We're in here. Riley's been having a little snack while the dumplings cook."

"Hey there, Riley," Bob said as he dumped his stuff in the hall closet. "I didn't realize you were here already."

"My boss dropped me off." Riley didn't know how that explained why he'd arrived thirty minutes before he'd said he would, but it was all he could think to say.

Seemed good enough for his dad, who nodded. "I'm going to run upstairs and wash up. I'll be back in just a minute. Dinner smells good, hon," he tacked on as he trudged up the steps.

Riley let out a long sigh. That hadn't gone badly, per se, but the easy camaraderie he had with his mom was noticeably absent once his dad entered the room.

"You're both making this whole thing more difficult than it needs to be," Lorraine said quietly.

Riley scoffed. "You weren't nervous earlier? With all your fluttering and fixing me an appetizer and 'Oh' when I mentioned buying new sheets?"

Lorraine pursed her lips and threw Riley an epic mom glare. "At least my nervous energy diffused the situation. You two make everything worse."

"Well, what am I supposed to do?"

"Talk to him the same way you do me," she urged.

Riley shook his head. "Dad doesn't want to hear that I'm in love with a man or about how I snuck off to hang out with the queer kids at HOPE."

Lorraine tilted her head to the side, as if agreeing with him. "He's trying, Riley. You said yourself that's what's important. Why don't you tell him about your job?"

Footsteps thumped downstairs, and Riley waved his hands around to shush his mom. He didn't necessarily think it was his duty to reach out to his dad first, but he was well aware that life would be easier for all of them the sooner they got past the awkward hump.

Bob came back into the kitchen having changed into a T-shirt and sweats, and the sight made Riley smile. That had always been the first thing his dad did after work. In fact he usually skipped the sweats and just wore a T-shirt and boxers, but Riley supposed he'd donned additional clothes for his benefit. A twinge of regret struck his heart, but at the same time, he was grateful he didn't have to sit around with his father in his underwear.

His dad gave his mom a quick kiss on the cheek and went about fixing the drinks for everyone. Within minutes they were all eating Riley's absolute favorite food in the world.

"The chicken and dumplings are delicious, Mom," Riley said as he fixed himself a second bowl. "I really appreciate you making them for me."

"You're welcome. I'm just glad you still like them."

"It's not like having a sex change makes you like different foods, Lorraine," Bob quipped. Riley nearly spit his mouthful out but caught himself in time and was able to swallow instead.

"No need to be crass." Lorraine ignored his sarcasm as she always had. "I don't know what he's been eating. Maybe his tastes have changed."

Riley smiled. He was warmed by his mom's easy use of male pronouns.

His dad grunted. "So… you're working construction. Do you like it?"

Lorraine's eyes lit up, and she nodded at Riley to encourage him to open up. "I do. I like working with my hands and being outdoors a lot. The physical labor is good for me. Keeps me grounded. After I'd been doing it awhile, I realized I had knack for it. My boss went out on a limb for me to promote me for this job here, so I've been busting my ass trying to prove myself, and it seems to be going well. If nothing else the crew at least pretends to respect me. And we're going to finish a week ahead of schedule, so the uppity-ups are happy."

"At least something good came out of all of this, then."

"Bob," Lorraine admonished.

Riley shrank into his seat as his dad stirred his chicken and dumplings and then threw down his spoon.

"What do you want me to say, Lorraine? Riley let us think shhh— he was dead for years, and then he expects us to be excited and welcome her back, no questions asked. And heaven forbid we have an issue with any of the changes she's made because then we'd just lose her again."

"I don't think now is the time to get into this." Lorraine stood and grabbed her bowl and Bob's, even though neither of them had finished eating.

"Why the hell not?" Bob wasn't shouting exactly, but he certainly wasn't making an effort to keep his voice down either. "When is it going to be a good time? Because the last thing I want to do is get to know Riley again and then express my disappointment in how"—Bob waved his hand toward Riley—"*he* worried us and then lose him again. I have every right to be angry about this."

"Dad—"

But his dad wouldn't let him talk. "I'm *sorry*. Okay, Riley? I wish I was as good of a person as your mother is, but I'm not. I can't forgive you as easily as she has. For years I watched her cry and struggle and worry and wonder where we went wrong. And don't think it was a picnic for me either. I went through everything she did, but I would've taken on ten times the pain I felt if it meant she didn't have to go through that. And now we have to tiptoe around and hope you decide we're worthy of your presence."

Riley thought his heart might rip in two. He hated the thought of causing his parents so much pain over the years.

"Don't you dare blame your anger toward him on me," Lorraine shrieked.

"How can I not?" Bob shouted back.

"I don't understand where this is coming from." Tears fell from Lorraine's eyes, and Riley scooted his chair back and stood. "You said you wanted him back in our lives."

"Don't you dare walk out on us again," Bob said, pointing his finger at Riley as he started to rise from his seat. "You want me to take you seriously, to believe in you? You want to be an adult and show me how far you've come on your own, while you were away? Then you sit here and be a man and deal with the mess you helped create."

Riley obediently sat back down in his seat, and no one spoke for a while. Lorraine remained at the sink with her back toward both of them, presumably to gather herself. Eventually Bob placed his hands on the table and looked at Riley.

"I missed you," he began. "More than I knew possible. When we realized you weren't coming home and then that you were missing... I can't begin to explain the terror that we experienced. I wanted to paste your picture on milk cartons, for God's sake. I hope you never have to live through something like that.

"Your mom—she can let those things go. She doesn't want to make you feel bad. But I am so angry with you for doing that to us. I want to lock you in your room and ground you until you're thirty-five, and I still worry that won't be enough time with you. Do you understand what I'm saying?"

Riley stared at his dad. He thought he might. In a roundabout way, his dad was telling him he loved him. Riley nodded slowly.

"Your mom is right. I do want you back in our lives, but you created a shit storm when you left, and you're going to have to deal with it and prove to me you're not going to run away again. Which means sometimes I'm going to be angry and sarcastic. You laid down your rule the other night, and this one is mine. As long as we're in agreement there, I will accept the new you and try my best to call you all the right names."

Riley nodded again. "Yes, sir," he said, his voice hoarse.

"Good." Bob waved his hand at Lorraine. "Now can I please have my bowl back? I wasn't finished eating."

Riley scooted his chair back to the table and picked up his spoon. His gurgling stomach insisted it didn't want more food, but he didn't know what else to do with himself. His mom returned to the table with both bowls, they finished dinner in silence, and Riley did his best not to break down into tears. Everything his dad had just told him hit hard. Life had sucked after he left college, but he'd spent all of that time thinking his parents didn't want anything to do with him. And the immense relief of finding out that wasn't the case after their reunion had blocked out the possibility of his parents' pain.

Still he couldn't help but welcome his dad's outburst. Similar to when Joe spilled the beans about Kollin, at least Riley knew the truth. He knew how his father felt and what they had to overcome. The five minutes of shouting and ensuing awkward dinner was worth the peace of knowing where he stood.

All that was left to do was to start picking up the pieces. That, Riley thought, was definitely doable.

# CHAPTER 22

THE REST of the week passed before Riley got to see Kollin, since he'd been so busy with school. They barely even spoke for a few minutes each day before Kollin had to beg off the phone to finish his work. Even without seeing Kollin, Riley's week had been pretty awesome. Jenson, the asshole who called him out on site, hadn't shown up to work on Tuesday or any day after.

Riley didn't know if he quit or if Greg fired him, and he had no desire to ask. He was just glad to be rid of him. No one else on the crew brought up Riley's personal life, and everyone treated him the same as they had before. Riley didn't give a damn whether the men truly accepted him or were keeping their opinions to themselves to keep a job. He didn't need their, or anyone else's, acceptance anymore. It was one of the most liberating feelings Riley had ever experienced.

The sun had already set by the time Kollin clomped downstairs and collapsed into bed with Riley. Kollin looked so tired, Riley wondered if he should just turn off the lights and wait until the following morning to finally catch up.

But then Kollin smiled and tucked his arm through Riley's. "Tell me all about dinner with your mom and dad. And no more of that 'it was fine' shit. I want details."

Riley blew out a long breath. "You sure you're up for it? You look pretty beat."

"I am, but I want to know. So spill."

Riley filled Kollin in on how easy things had been between him and his mom, even though they'd both been nervous. That they'd fallen into a relaxed give-and-take conversation, and she seemed genuinely interested in his life. He even told Kollin she'd researched transgender issues. Kollin listened with a huge smile on his face the entire time.

"I knew it." Kollin leaned in and kissed Riley. "I'm so damn happy for you. That's amazing."

Riley smiled softly and nodded. "But then my dad came home."

Kollin's smile faded. "And…?"

"He was okay. Mom said he would make an effort, but he was mostly sarcastic. And then he just lost it. He told me how much I worried them and that I didn't get to just come back like I'd done nothing wrong. And that if they had to accept me like this, I had to accept that he was still pissed off at me for leaving."

Kollin winced. "What'd you say?"

"I said, 'Yes, sir.' I'm not an idiot."

Kollin chuckled, but his eyes looked sad.

Riley untangled his arm from Kollin and rested his hand against Kollin's cheek. "All this time I've been back, I've been so selfish, only thinking about me."

"That's not true." Kollin dragged his thumb up and down the bare skin of Riley's back. "We've come a long way, and that wouldn't have happened if you were being selfish."

Riley took a deep breath. He'd been wondering whether to approach Kollin about everything Joe had told him that day at the park or if he should just pretend the conversation had never happened. Avoidance was the easiest route to take, but Riley knew that doing whatever was easiest rarely meant getting the best of something. "When I had that talk with Joe, he told me some stuff about the time I was gone."

"Oh yeah?" Kollin clutched Riley's wrist and dragged his hand down to his chest. "He wasn't even here most of that time. How does he know?"

"Apparently people talk."

Kollin gasped. "Gossip? At the center? *Never.*"

"Yes. Shocking, I know. Now stop distracting me." Kollin nodded obediently. "He told me how hard you took it when I stopped calling. I know you told me before, but you forgave me so easily. We slipped right back into our old roles so quickly, it didn't sound as bad. Hearing it from someone else…. I dunno. It was different. Made it more real. Harsher. And then, when my dad was going off, all I felt was shame. I'm so sorry I did that to you."

"I wanted you back in my life, Ri. I was just being selfish too." Kollin sighed. "I wish I'd handled things differently, now. If I'd been honest, up front, it would've been easier for me to trust you. But after the way you stood up to your coworkers the other day and hearing how you accepted your dad's anger, I'm there. Like you said, maybe we won't

work out, but if we don't, I trust it's not going to be because you decided
to give up and bail."

"I'm not. I promise. I'm all in."

Kollin grinned. "I know."

Riley pulled Kollin in to kiss him slowly, and Kollin surprised him
by rolling on top of him.

"You know what else I know?" Kollin said against Riley's lips
between kisses.

Riley slid his hands into Kollin's back pockets. "What's that?"

"I'm so fucking tired of waiting to be with you." Kollin jutted his
hips forward, pressed his hard cock against Riley's crotch, and made it
impossible to mistake what he wanted.

Riley's heart fluttered. He'd half hoped Kollin would hurry up and
initiate something between them, just to get it over with, and he half
hoped he'd forgotten their discussion about taking the next step. But the
anxiety was gone. His nerves didn't stem from fear of Kollin's rejecting
him, but rather from excitement to finally move forward, to drop the
baggage he'd been hauling around since Tony and trust Kollin to care
for him.

"I have condoms," Riley blurted out, which made Kollin pull away
and offer his lopsided grin.

"Good to know. I do too."

"I mean, I'm clean. I got tested and everything, and I don't
have a period anymore, but there's been a couple of one-offs where
trans guys got pregnant, and, well...." Riley forced himself to stop
rambling. Why hadn't they had that conversation before *the* moment?
He was nervous.

"Hey. It's no big deal." Kollin's voice, soft with a lilt of amusement,
soothed Riley's suddenly frazzled nerves. "I figured we'd use condoms
for a while, anyway."

Seemingly cool as a cucumber, Kollin leaned in to pick up their
kiss while deftly sliding Riley's shirt up. He dragged his mouth down
to Riley's chest, as always spending time kissing each scar. He'd told
Kollin before that there wasn't much—if any—feeling along his scars,
but Kollin did it anyway. The gesture meant more to Riley than he was
willing to admit.

Riley tugged Kollin's shirt off too, and while he was at it, Kollin
shoved his jeans off and wiggled out of his briefs. Rather than strip

Riley, he returned to lavishing kisses on Riley's stomach. Riley rested his hands in Kollin's hair and savored the feeling of adoration. After all of his one-night stands and everything with Tony, Riley vowed to never take Kollin's affection for granted.

As Kollin moved his mouth lower, he fiddled with the buttons on Riley's pants and shoved them off a little at a time. His nose ghosted over the hairs in Riley's happy trail, and Riley sucked his stomach in and forced himself to remain calm and trust Kollin.

Kollin grazed his thumb over Riley's stiff cock, and his nose nuzzled into the crease of Riley's groin. Without warning, Kollin sucked Riley's dick into his mouth and swirled his tongue around. Riley gripped the sheets beneath him as electricity jolted through his entire body, making him forget to be self-conscious that another man had his mouth on him. After a few passes, Kollin looked up at Riley and grinned.

"Was that okay?"

Riley squeezed his eyes shut and tried to fight off embarrassment. "I don't know if talking is the best idea for me right now."

Kollin kissed up Riley's chest and slid his finger in Riley's slippery vagina. "Holy fuck, that's wet," Kollin mumbled. Cold air washed over Riley as Kollin flopped over the side of the bed and fumbled around. He popped up a moment later holding a condom between two fingers.

"Lookee, lookee." He grinned and ripped it open with his teeth, then fisted his cock a few times and deftly slid the condom on.

Riley reached out for Kollin and tugged him close. "Are you as nervous about this as I am?"

Kollin's smile was lopsided. "Probably more. You've done this before."

Riley clutched him closer. "Not really. Not like this."

"It's gonna be good. I promise." Kollin reached between them and rubbed his tip around Riley's wet opening. "Ready?"

Riley looked into Kollin's eyes. He knew the moment was huge, for both of them. He tugged Kollin's hips forward. His heart raced as Kollin breached him and slid in with ease. Kollin had barely started moving inside him, and already it felt different from being with Tony. Rather than pain, Riley felt a gentle roll of pleasure. In place of shame, Riley felt excitement. Instead of counting down the seconds until it was over, Riley wished Kollin would never stop.

Kollin's body felt heavy pressed on top of his, keeping him anchored to the moment rather than letting his mind wander into dangerous territory. Kollin's quiet panting, dotted with an occasional moan or "oh God" right in Riley's ear, was a constant reminder of how much Kollin wanted him.

Kollin grunted and then rested his forehead on Riley's chest so he could watch himself move in and out of Riley. "You feel amazing, Ri. It's different but... fuck... so good."

Riley couldn't think of a response. Half his brain was mush, and the half that worked could think of nothing but pledging his never-ending love for Kollin. But it didn't seem to be the best time for such declarations.

Kollin sat up and anchored Riley's shoulders to the bed as his thrusts picked up force. "Grab yourself," he said between pants.

Riley obeyed, self-conscious for only a moment before the overwhelming pleasure of being filled and fondled threw his inhibitions out the window. Spasms wracked his body. "Oh fuck," he moaned, speeding up his hand as he chased the flutters that shot up and down his legs. "Oh fuck, fuck, *fuck*."

"That's it," Kollin breathed. He shifted and sped up his thrusts to match Riley's hand. The flutters warped into full out spasms, and Riley curled into himself. Kollin batted his hand away and took over rubbing his cock as he pushed into Riley. "Can you get there? Please."

Riley lost it. He screamed out, his body convulsing as the waves of pleasure surged through him to center on his groin, making him clench around Kollin's cock.

"Oh God," Kollin moaned. His thrusts became jerky and he buried himself into Riley's chest and clutched him close as he rode out his orgasm and finally collapsed on top of him.

They lay in silence for a few minutes as Kollin sucked in great heaps of air, until Riley finally let out a long breath. "That went well."

Kollin laughed. "I'm glad you think so."

"I wasn't even that nervous. Not after the condom thing anyway."

Kollin laughed and nuzzled into Riley's chest. "Liar. But I'm glad it went well. All I want to do is sleep, but I feel like we should talk. That was kind of a big deal. Did I do everything okay? You didn't have to fake anything?"

Riley laughed. "No faking involved." Some of his nerves returned, but he ignored them. "What about you? You weren't... grossed out or anything, were you?"

Kollin rolled off Riley to dispose of his condom, but he snuggled right back up to Riley when he was finished. "I think we can safely assume that no part of you grosses me out. Ever. Not that my opinion should have any influence on your decision whatsoever, but I'm perfectly happy with you just the way you are if you don't want any surgery. And if you do want surgery, I'm good with that too. As long as it's safe." He yawned and looked up at Riley, his lids heavy. "You sure you're okay with everything?"

Riley grinned. He couldn't think of a single moment in his life where he'd felt more content. Between relocating with his job and his rocky relationship with his parents, there were still uncertain parts in his life, but he finally felt at peace.

The Tonys of the world could go to hell.

Riley tightened his arms around Kollin. "I really, really am."

# CHAPTER 23

"I THOUGHT we were going to the beach." Riley pointed out the windshield. "Those are the gates to your community."

"I left the cooler at home." Kollin waved his keycard and waited for the gates to open. "We only have that huge one at the beach house, and I don't want to lug that thing onto the sand for just the two of us."

A moment later they pulled into the driveway, and Kollin got out. Instead of running into the house, he leaned down to peer at Riley. "Aren't you coming in?"

"To get a cooler?"

Kollin sighed. "Fine. You don't have to, but don't expect me to back you when Lizzie rips into you for not coming in to say hi."

Riley rolled his eyes and unbuckled his seatbelt. "We're never going to get to the beach, at this rate."

"Oh, relax. We have all day today and tomorrow *and* the day after that."

Riley couldn't think of a response that didn't make him sound like a horn dog. Six weeks to the day had passed since he had bottom surgery—metoidioplasty and a hysterectomy—and he was finally able to resume normal activity. Which he hoped meant a boatload of sex with Kollin over the weekend.

A couple of weeks after Riley returned to Boone, Greg came to him with the disappointing news that Drummond's had to delay opening a branch in Durham. After extensive conversations with his parents and some cajoling from Kollin, Riley accepted his parents' offer to move back to Cary immediately and live with them. They offered to help with the cost of his surgery, citing that they'd set the money aside for his college tuition, anyway, and Riley couldn't pass up the opportunity.

Riley hardly remembered the first week after his surgery. He refused to take anything stronger than a Tylenol, and he'd been in so much pain he could hardly focus on anything. Eventually the pain subsided, and he'd actually been pain free the past several days. Which he *thought* meant he'd be spending the entire weekend holed up in Kollin's beach house, only coming out of the bedroom to replenish liquids, dammit.

Kollin stopped on the front stoop and kissed Riley on the cheek. "Stop pouting. We'll have plenty of time together. This'll only take a second."

"Yeah, yeah. Just hurry up. Lizzie's gonna keep me here at least an hour. I already know it."

Kollin shoved the door open, and as soon as Riley set foot inside, he was nearly scared right back out.

"Surprise!"

Kollin let go of Riley and joined the group who had squeezed into the foyer. He raised his jazz hands up in the air with a huge smile on his face.

"What's this about?" he asked, staring at Kollin as people started to hug him.

"It's a joint 'happy birthday' and 'congrats on your transition' party," Kollin said, his lopsided grin still firmly in place.

Riley scrunched his face. "My birthday isn't for another month."

"That's the surprise," Lizzie shouted as she bounced up and down.

Everyone laughed, and at Kirsten's urging, the party moved into the kitchen, where some brunch-like appetizers and a cake sat on the island.

"Do you know how hard it is to plan a surprise party for ten in the morning?" Kirsten said as she huddled everyone into the food line. "I hope everyone's hungry, though. I think I went a little overboard."

Kollin threw his arm over her shoulder. "Don't act like you didn't love planning every minute of this shindig."

Kirsten elbowed him. "I did, but only because I love Ri so much."

Riley's mom sidled up to him and wrapped her arms around one of his elbows. "Your boyfriend's family is very… chatty," she whispered in his ear.

Riley laughed. Though she'd met Adam and Elijah on separate occasions, this was the first time they were all together. Add in Adam's sister and both sets of Kollin's grandparents and he could imagine she and his dad had been overwhelmed. The Langley-Lancaster clan wasn't exactly known for holding in its opinions for politeness' sake.

"They haven't traumatized you forever, have they?" Riley asked.

"Not me." She shifted her eyes toward Bob. "Maybe your father."

Riley glanced at his dad, who was waving his hands around while he spoke with Elijah. "Looks like he's managing okay."

They loaded up their plates and joined Kollin at the table. "Thanks for doing this and including us, Kollin," Lorraine said. "It's a comfort to know Riley's chosen someone with such a nurturing and supportive family." She looked at Riley and smiled. "It's all I ever prayed for, when he was little."

Kollin grinned. "Thank you, ma'am. I'm just glad you guys could make it, and I hope my family at least pretended to be normal before we got here."

Lorraine waved him off. "They were fine and had such wonderful things to say about Riley, from recently and back when he was in high school." She turned to Riley. "Elijah in particular praised you for being so responsible and making Kollin so happy. You certainly have a fan in him."

Riley's cheeks warmed, and he stared at his plate. He had made a fool of himself with Elijah the night he almost bailed, so proving to Elijah that he was worthy of Kollin had been Riley's first priority. He had no clue how to do it, of course, but that night remained one of his biggest regrets. He thought, if Elijah approved of him, somehow it would erase that moment of weakness. Turned out all Elijah needed to warm up to Riley was his commitment to Kollin. In fact Riley had come to understand why Kollin called him a big teddy bear. He was almost as affectionate and generous with Riley as he was the rest of his family... *almost*. No one could ever doubt who held the top three spots in Elijah's heart.

"I think he's a fan of anyone who makes Kollin happy," Riley replied.

Lorraine smiled and shrugged. Then she popped a piece of fruit in her mouth. Kollin leaned over and smacked a kiss onto Riley's cheek. "At least you know you'll always be in his good graces."

"Okay, lovebirds," Kirsten said. "Kollin put me on a strict time frame. You got all day to be smoochy-smoochy, once you leave. Get your butts over here for cake and ice cream."

"Kirsten." Kollin gasped and pointed at Lizzie. "Watch your mouth. There are children present."

"I am *not* a child." Lizzie pouted.

"Yes, you are," Adam and Eli both shouted.

Lizzie huffed and folded her arms over her chest. Elijah's mom, Gloria, didn't waste any time pulling her close for a hug. "Ignore those boys, baby. Get your cake, and we'll go plan a shopping trip—just us girls."

Kollin feigned indignation. "What about me? I want to go."

Gloria eyed Kollin over her shoulder. "Should've thought about that before you started picking on your sister."

Kollin laughed. Even Riley knew the threat was empty. Gloria could probably count on one hand the number of times she'd gone shopping without Kollin since he moved in with Elijah. An unlikely pair—elegant and wealthy grandmother walking around with a flamboyant, wild-haired kid—they turned plenty of heads when they went out together. But not much brought Kollin more joy than shopping with Elijah's mom, and Riley had a feeling Gloria felt the same way.

"No one actually believes you, Mom," Eli said drily.

"I don't know," Kirsten said. "Maybe we should plan a girls' day out. Me, Lizzie, Mom, Gloria. You have to come too, Mrs. Meadows. Lizzie probably needs a break from all the testosterone in this house."

Lorraine smiled and looked as if she would accept, but she wasn't fast enough. "I think you underestimate your niece," Adam said. "If you think she doesn't run this house, you're sadly mistaken. And maybe let Mrs. Meadows decide if she wants to be sucked into your day of hell."

"Just because you don't like to shop, doesn't mean we don't," Adam's mom scolded.

"You hate shopping, Mom," Kirsten said, her mouth full of cake.

She shrugged off Kirsten's comment. "Maybe, but I love spending time with my daughter and granddaughter."

The conversation lulled just long enough for Lorraine to jump in and be heard. "I'd love to join you all," she nearly shouted, causing Riley to snicker.

"Ooh, yay," Kirsten squealed, almost cutting Lorraine off. "We should really make a day of it and go to the spa too. Get our nails done."

Eli groaned. "How did Riley's party turn into a planning session for you all?"

Kirsten made a face and pulled her lips down in an exaggerated frown. "Oh. Sorry, Ri. He's right. Let's talk about you. What's on the docket while you wait for Drummond's to open up in Durham?"

Not all that thrilled to be thrust back into the center of attention, Riley cast a glare toward Elijah and then cleared his throat. "Well, Adam said he's got some part-time work I can do at the inn and the center. I'm thinking about taking some classes at the community college too. I like construction work a lot, but if I eventually want to move up, I'll need a degree."

Lorraine placed her hand on Riley's shoulder and squeezed. "I'm so proud of you."

"Thanks, Mom, but you know I wouldn't be here without your help."

Lorraine smiled, but it was Bob who spoke up. "Yes, you would. Might've taken you a bit longer, but you'd have done it."

Riley felt his blush return, and he looked down at his plate. His relationship with his father had been the most tumultuous one over the past few months, but neither of them had given up. They butted heads more times than not, and Riley had spent several nights back in Kollin's basement in an effort to keep from strangling his dad, but they were trying.

The conversation moved on to the expansion of the center—an idea Kollin had come up with to be more inclusive to non-LGBT youth. His theory being that HOPE shouldn't turn down anyone in need, regardless of their orientation, and bringing in a more diverse group of youth would hopefully lead to a greater understanding of the LGBT community and, therefore, more allies. As with any new idea, there were about a billion things that could go wrong, but Riley recognized the gleam in Adam's eye whenever they tossed around ideas of how to make Kollin's vision happen.

Riley listened as he finished his cake. He was happy to simply soak it all in. Kollin pulled him closer, pressed a kiss just beneath his ear, and whispered, "Your dad was right, you know. I'm so proud of you."

Riley looked into Kollin's twinkling eyes, and his heart ached for how much he wanted that adoring look on Kollin's face never to disappear. He shook his head and wondered when he'd become so maudlin. "You know I couldn't have done it without *you* either."

Kollin shrugged. "I dunno about that. You've got some badass scars to prove how strong you are."

"Thank you." Riley waved his hand around the room. "For this and for everything. You've always been my biggest supporter. Even when I didn't deserve it."

"I'd say we both made mistakes along the way. But at least we made it here."

Riley grabbed Kollin's hand. "Yeah. We did. And I'd say here is a pretty good place to be."

Kollin grinned. "Damned skippy, it is."

Riley laughed and leaned in closer. "Seriously, though. When're we leaving? Because as much as I love here, I'm *so* ready to be alone with you."

Kollin popped his mouth open in mock surprise. "Why, Riley, if I didn't know better, I'd say you want to sully my virgin-like reputation."

Riley rolled his eyes. "Virgin-like, my ass. And yes. Yes, I do."

Kollin laughed and kissed him lightly on the lips. "Well, lucky for you, I already told Kirsten we wouldn't be staying long. But don't get too eager, because we still have one more stop to make before we get to the beach house."


"WHEN YOU said we had one more stop to make, I didn't realize it would take the entire day," Riley said as he climbed out of Kollin's car.

"What can I say? I'm full of surprises." Kollin grinned, clearly enjoying the mystery.

"Ooookay. What does this beach, that's two hours south of the beach we're staying at this weekend, have that Emerald Isle doesn't have?"

Kollin held out his hand for Riley and walked toward the public-access ramp that would lead them to the ocean. "Adam, Eli, and I came here the summer after you disappeared. We all had some stuff we wanted to let go of. Adam had been here before and suggested we come."

"That's... nice." Riley zipped up his hoodie as they walked off of the ramp and onto the sand. The strong beach wind cut a chill into him even though the late-winter day was warm. "You throw a bottle in the ocean or something?"

"You'll see."

Riley followed Kollin down the beach. He hadn't been to one in ages, and a stroll through the sand sounded nice. They walked awhile, holding hands and discussing the party, what classes Riley might take, and whatever else popped into Kollin's head.

They walked close to the high wall of sand to their right in a failed attempt to block some of the wind. Occasionally they passed others, but very few people seemed to venture that far out. Nothing on the horizon hinted at anything other than beach ahead. There weren't even any houses on that stretch of beach. When they were no longer passing other groups, Riley couldn't hold in his curiosity.

He sighed loudly. "Is your plan to murder me and toss me in the ocean with no witnesses?"

Kollin laughed. "Nope."

"Are we walking all the way to the point or something?"

Kollin shook his head and looked around. "Nope. But I think we'll be there soon." He tugged Riley closer to the waves and looked around. "Yep. There's the flag pole."

Riley looked toward the land where Kollin pointed and saw the pole, but they were too far away to see what kind of flag blew in the breeze.

"You wanted me to see a flag?"

"No." Kollin rolled his eyes. "It's under the flag. Come on."

Kollin picked up his pace, and several minutes later, Riley could see the red and white stripes protecting the fifty white stars on a blue backdrop. He kept his mouth shut, because he knew Kollin wouldn't tell him why an American flag stood on a beach in the middle of nowhere. They finally reached a break in the sand wall, and Riley saw a long wooden bench next to an old, rickety mailbox, perched on what looked like a hunk of driftwood.

"A mailbox?"

"Come on." Kollin tugged Riley toward the bench.

"Kindred Spirit," spelled out in gold letters, graced the side of the mailbox, and the red flag stood straight up as if someone expected a mailman to come that far out.

"This is the Kindred Spirit mailbox," Kollin said as he opened the box. He tugged out a couple of pens as well as two notebooks that were well worn and had a permanent fold from being in the mailbox. "It's been here for like fifty years or something. A guy put it up one day, because his girlfriend wanted him to. He named it Kindred Spirit because she wanted her name to remain unknown. She wanted anyone who left notes in the journal to spill their secrets to... well, a kindred spirit."

"Wow," Riley said with a mixture of amazement and doubt. Did people really trek all the way out there to write in some old notebooks?

Kollin nodded. "It's amazing, really, when you think about it. The guy still comes out here and changes out the notebooks and makes sure there's pens and somewhere to sit and everything. Supposedly he reads every entry. He says everyone's story is worth knowing." Kollin waved one of the notebooks in the air. "I read a few last time I was here. It's hard not to get caught up in them. Some are sad. Some are full of love or depression. Some people write to someone they've wronged, and others write to people who have passed on."

Riley took the notebook Kollin held out to him. "You don't have to or anything." Kollin scratched the back of his neck. "I feel kind of stupid, dragging you all the way out here, now, without asking you first. But with everything that's happened over the past few months and everything that will happen in the coming months… it feels like we're at a turning point in our lives, and I thought it would be nice."

Dumbfounded, Riley opened the notebook and read the first entry.

*Dear Mom*, it began. The letter was short but filled with pain and grief so raw and real that Riley had tears in his eyes by the time he got to the signature. Nothing but a simple *H*. Below that was a somewhat poor drawing of a cat with *RIP Fluffles* next to it. A few pages later, he smiled as he read, *I asked*, and then in different handwriting was *I said YES!* Those five words took up that entire page, and Riley could feel the excitement pouring off it.

Riley became immersed in the strangers' stories, the secrets they wanted to share with their Kindred Spirit. As Kollin said, they varied from one end of the spectrum to the other. One was from someone just released from prison, another from a grieving widow, another from a scared, pregnant woman, and another from a desperate soul who wondered how to tell his parents he was a drug addict and needed their help to pull himself out of his downward spiral. But they all had one thing in common—every single letter screamed out a message of hope. And why not? Why would anyone drive to a remote beach in North Carolina and then trek who knows how many miles to converse with the Kindred Spirit if they didn't hold hope in their hearts? Those memos of faith and optimism were the most beautiful offerings Riley had ever seen.

Riley peeked over at Kollin. His head was bowed, and he was gnawing on his bottom lip as he wrote. Riley grinned. Kollin had already filled half a page. "Thank you for bringing me here."

Kollin paused his writing to look up. "You're welcome. I'm glad you like it."

Riley nodded and stared down at the first piece of blank paper he got to. He could probably fill up pages of the book, and though he knew that would be fine in the spirit of the mailbox, he didn't feel the need to. He wanted to let the Kindred Spirit, and anyone else who read his words, know that he'd done it. He'd gone through the valley and climbed out the other side, maybe a bit worse for the wear in some areas, but definitely stronger and smarter. He wanted to shout to everyone who came after him that he'd reclaimed his hope, and he never intended to lose it again.

> *To my younger self:*
> *Please know that it will get better. You're going*
> *to make some truly colossal mistakes you wish you*
> *could take back, but you have the best friends in the*
> *entire world. They'll pull you through. Learn from them.*
> *Trust them. Believe them. And never, ever forget to love*
> *yourself.—R*
> *PS—Kollin is a better kisser than you ever dreamed.*

When Riley put the top back on his pen, he looked back at Kollin, who was staring out at the sea. "Do I get to read yours?" he asked.

Kollin raised an eyebrow and glanced down at Riley's notebook. "Do I get to read yours?"

"Not a chance in hell." Riley would never hear the end of it if Kollin read his postscript. He rolled the notebook back up and stuffed it in the mailbox.

Kollin winked and shoved his notebook in on top of Riley's. "Guess I'll just have to drop by on my own one day and see if it's still here, then."

Riley wouldn't put it past Kollin, but he figured if Kollin went to all that trouble, he deserved to know about his phenomenal kissing skills. "What happens to the used up notebooks?" Riley asked.

"Dude keeps some of them." Kollin walked to where the sand formed a step and sat down on the edge. "I think some are in a museum or library or something somewhere in North Carolina."

"This is really amazing. I definitely want to come back sometime."

Kollin rested his head on Riley's shoulder. "I think we can make that happen."

They watched the ocean for a while, on their little perch in the sand, until Kollin squeezed his hand. "You ready?"

Riley laughed and looked at Kollin. The wind blew Kollin's hair straight up, and his smile crinkled his eyes with the depth of its sincerity. He didn't know what Kollin wanted him to be ready for. Ready to leave the beach? Sure. Ready to move forward with him? Definitely. Ready to say good-bye to everything and everyone that had dragged him down for so long? Absolutely.

"For what?" Riley asked, his voice softer than he intended because of the wealth of emotions that suddenly flooded him.

Kollin shrugged, and his eyes twinkled. "For it all, I guess."

Riley squeezed his hand. "More than anything."

THEY'D ONLY taken a few steps when Kollin wiggled his hand free. "Hold on one second. There's something I forgot to write."

He jogged back to the mailbox and grabbed the notebook he'd written in. Kollin found his previous entry and read it again.

> *Dear Kindred Spirit,*
>
> *The last time I wrote to you, I told you about my best friend, Riley. I told you some pretty great things about him, but that he'd disappeared. I told you how angry I was with him, how much he'd hurt me, and how scared I was that he'd disappeared not because he wanted to but because something terrible had happened. It was a pretty bleak entry and not my best moment. But I walked away that day feeling considerably lighter. Something about being in this place gave me the hope to believe that Riley was okay, wherever he happened to be.*
>
> *I brought Riley here today. He's okay. More than okay, really. He's sitting next to me, writing his own entry. I'm tempted to peek at what he's writing, but I fear that would break the magic of this place. Whatever he's writing, I doubt Riley's giving himself enough credit for everything he's accomplished over the past several years, and I felt like you needed to know. He overcame*

*feelings of abandonment, rejection, ridicule, loneliness, and addiction to drugs, and he did it all with little to no help. It's so easy to fail at something, especially life. Disappointing friends, family, even ourselves can be second nature, but it takes a special kind of person, someone with strength and integrity and hope, to admit their faults, to reach out for help, to ask for forgiveness, and to claw a way out of the chaos of his reality. I'm so proud to say Riley kicked his demons' asses. He's whole, and he's beautiful, and he's mine.*

*And just in case, if there's anyone reading this who feels like maybe they don't have the strength to go on, please know there's someone out there rooting for you. If no one else, there's me. If you think you've got nothing else going for you, know that I'm glad you're here and that I believe in you. If you need proof that there is someone, multiple someones even, who want you to succeed, look up the Center for HOPE in Cary, NC. My dad founded it years ago because he wanted to give the next generation hope. There you'll find acceptance and friendship. You can watch people's dreams come true, and you can see lives being saved, and all you have to do is reach out, and the same love and support will be given to you.*

*-Kollin*

Kollin glanced up at Riley, who had wandered down to the water to give Kollin his privacy. Riley stood with his hands in his pockets as he stared out to sea. The wind blew his hair and clothes to the side. He bent down to pick up a shell and then pocketed it. The sight of Riley, so carefree, made Kollin's heart swell, and he knew he didn't need to make the entry after all.

In the spirit of the mailbox, though, Kollin leaned back over the notebook and hastily scribbled.

*Dear Riley,*
*It's been months, and for some reason, neither one of us has found the courage to express our "big feelings" to one another. That's going to change tonight. I don't*

*know why I've been so nervous to tell you how I feel. Maybe because things have been going so well, I didn't want to ruin everything by making it bigger.*

*Sometimes loving someone else as much as I love you hurts and not always in a good way. That can be pretty damn frightening when the rest of your life is laid out before you. Do I? Don't I? What if? It's so difficult to let go and become vulnerable to this type of soul-crushing love. But it's time. After everything we've been through, the ups and the downs and the in-betweens, I wouldn't change a thing if it means I get to say I'm so incredibly head-over-heels in love with you.*

*Yours always,*
*Kollin*

SHELL TAYLOR is a full-time mother of three exuberant and loving kiddos and one fur baby, a tiny but fierce Yorkie-poo named Rocco. As a Christian who practices love and grace and humility rather than hatred and judgment, she tries her best to instill these same virtues in her rowdy kids. She just recently learned how to crochet to start bombarding new mothers with matching hats and booties. She is a huge Marvel fan and, because of the superhero-plastered tees paired with jeans and Chucks, has been told when helping out in her son's classroom that she looks more like the students than a parent. Her favorite way to procrastinate is to binge-watch entire seasons on Netflix. Best of all, she's been married ten years to a man who's turned out to be everything she never knew she needed.

home for hope

REDEEMING HOPE

MOTEL

SHELL TAYLOR

Home for Hope: Book One

Fifteen years ago Elijah Langley's world came to an abrupt halt with the death of his high school boyfriend. He keeps his past—and his sexual orientation—hidden until he attends a fundraiser for The Center for HOPE, an LGBT youth center, where he meets Adam Lancaster, HOPE's infuriatingly stubborn and sexy founder.

A survivor of a turbulent childhood, Adam understands better than most the challenges his youth face. He's drawn to Elijah's baby blues and devilish smile but refuses to compromise his values and climb back into the closet for anyone—not even the man showering time and money on HOPE. Months of constant flirting wear down Adam's resolve until he surrenders to his desires, but Elijah can't shake his demons.

When a youth from the center is brutally assaulted, Elijah must find a way to confront the fears and memories that are starting to ruin his life, so he can stand strong for those he loves.

# www.dreamspinnerpress.com

home for hope

# RESURRECTING HOPE

## SHELL TAYLOR

Sequel to *Redeeming Hope*
Home for Hope: Book Two

Adam Lancaster can't imagine how his life could possibly get any better. He's on the cusp of moving in with his boyfriend, Elijah Langley. Their charge, Kollin Haverty, finally has a loving, stable home environment, and Home for Hope is up and running, keeping over fifteen LGBT youth off the streets at night. But one phone call from his birth mother, Jessica Lancaster, is all it takes to unravel Adam's carefully constructed new life.

Informing Adam his grandfather has died, Jessica expresses remorse for abandoning Adam to the state and begs him for a chance to be part of his life again. Jessica's true colors eventually shine through her façade, and Adam is devastated all over again when he discovers she is only using him to get her hands on the valuable inheritance his grandfather left him. Jessica's betrayal forces Adam so far inside his own hell, not even Elijah or Kollin can keep him from abandoning all of his responsibilities and running away. Adam will have to dig deep to find the strength to confront his birth parents, heal once and for all, and earn back his place with his new family.

# www.dreamspinnerpress.com